Also By Chris Shaw

It's all Relative:
Stories to Shorten Your Travel Time

HMS Warspite
My Memories of World War ll
(pp Wally Shaw)

My New Country:
Loving, Laughing and Learning to Live in Australia

Hey Guys! Here's How You Get More 'Nooky'!
How to build the happiest relationship in your world

Never Let the Truth:
Stories from my imagination

A Trillionaire's Pathway:
My Fantasy Hotel

Chris Shaw

The
Imposter
A Norfolk Romance

IngramSpark/Chris Shaw

Melbourne, Victoria

Chris Shaw/IngramSpark

Publisher's Note: This is a work of fiction. However, some names, characters, places, and incidents are loosely based on the author's family and friends. Others are a figment of his imagination. The author has woven a new tapestry from the real-life tragedy of Cyril Frank Matthews and Gwen Bell, his uncle and aunt, and given them the happy ending they deserved. Apart from these two characters, any other resemblance to actual people, living or dead, or to events, institutions or locales is completely coincidental.

The Imposter: A Norfolk Romance/ Chris Shaw. -- 1st ed.
ISBN 978-0-9805882-5-5

Text editing and book design by Dr Juliette Lachemeier @ The Erudite Pen
www.theeruditepen.com

Cover designed by Christian Hildenbrand

Dedicated to my ever-loving Rebecca, as always.

To Shean and Tanith, my two beautiful children, and their very fine families.

To the Bullens, and all their kith and kin, who have cared for, entertained and educated me in so many ways over the years.

To my sister Vicky, who is lucky enough to live in Norfolk, where the population is riddled with our ancestors.

Contents

Part 1: Love

Prologue

THE LIFE OF A SNIPER

World War One, Somewhere in France, 1916

I was lying in mud – yet again. My helmet, rifle and uniform were camouflaged by it. Only my 'scope sight and my eyes, which were slit against the early spring wind that still harboured winter's chill, were clear.

My gaze constantly roamed the landscape.

And what a landscape it was. Black mud and puddles of grimy, fetid water were endless. Trees stood like dead woody skeletons in a tortured outline against the dark-grey clouds. Those clouds would bring more rain, more mud and more stagnant water. This grim backdrop was everyday life if you added in the constant bombardment of artillery shells, mortars and bullets that assaulted our ears and our bodies; this Devil's Symphony was killing us in so many ways.

Tears filled my eyes as I thought of my beloved Norfolk with its rich land and abundant crops, and its verdant woodland alive with such diverse flora and fauna. I tried not to let my homesickness overwhelm me. If tears blurred my vision, they could mar my best chance of killing Jerries, or worse still, being killed by them.

My arms, neck and shoulders were cramped; I'd lain motionless for a long time, waiting for a German to show himself. About four hundred yards lay between the 'Fritz brothers' and me. Their Maxim machine gun had been busy murdering our young lads all morning.

The Germans would be moving one of those Maxims soon because our mortars had found where those machine guns were positioned late this morning. When they set the gun up again, I'd have them because I was pretty sure I knew where they'd site it. Of course, if they spotted me first, I was gone, and my helmet would be doing double duty as a colander, leaking my brains all over this French field.

My bleak, black humour somehow diminished the horror of the situation I found myself in.

Dawn hadn't yet shown itself when I had reached this spot. I had built a small, irregular mound of clods of dirt and stones as 'natural' cover to hide behind. As long as I moved nothing but my eyes, I would be fine. This God-forsaken land! This bloody hell! It had been shelled to death. Nothing would ever grow here again lest blood worked as a fertiliser.

There was almost no skin on my feet, my crotch itched all the time and the sores on my skin were ulcerated and often infected with yellow pus. My breathing had changed too – the result of a whiff of chlorine gas that Jerry had let loose some time back. My face was lined, and my hair was long and straggly. But all the physical stuff was nothing – that would right itself when I got clean, dry and rested. It was my head that was really messed up.

The months here had changed me. There were some breaks from the fighting, of course, but I'd never been much for the booze, and the ladies didn't stack up against my Gwen. My conversational skills were almost non-existent beyond farming and killing – my only talents, apparently.

I could talk to myself easily, but to other people? That was hard. They said things I couldn't relate to about things I didn't know of. One day, I'd tried to tell another corporal what I do. His eyes had widened, and his lip had quivered, then he fled. Maybe he hadn't understood. Or maybe he had. I hadn't seen a mirror in an age and didn't want to. I could feel the new creases etched onto my face and knew I looked a mess from lying in the mud all the time.

My home had previously been in the peace and quiet of the countryside. I recalled my first visit to London with the cacophony of meaningless chatter of millions of strangers plus the traffic sounds, all of which had assailed my mind at the time. I had tried to make eye contact to see if I recognised anyone from home, until I realised that I meant nothing to any of those strangers. They didn't give a bugger about me. I learned a valuable lesson that day and applied it to my war.

The birdsong and fluting wind of the countryside had been my background sounds at home, which was probably why I was better at this sniping game than most. Country people were natural watchers of birds migrating from our winter, along with the miracle of spring and its vast, almost-instantaneous explosion of new green leaves. The yellow smiles of daffodils and narcissi also welcomed the spring. So if He created all the beauty of nature around us, then what the hell had I done to deserve being here amongst all this blood, terror and human gore?

I had just spotted the Fritz brothers setting up their Maxim behind a mound of earth that would hide them from our trenches, but not from me, nor our poor young soldiers going over the top.

Think it through, I thought. *You need to kill those two, wreck their gun and crawl back to your trench after dark.* My fingers in their cut-off mittens were cold and stiff. There was one bullet 'up the spout' and five in the magazine – more than enough. Safety-catch was off. My rifle needed to traverse slowly east, just about four degrees. The back Jerry of this pair must be hit first so his mate would turn to see what happened. That would give me three-quarters of a second to reload and kill the second murderer. Slight pressure on the trigger. *Don't miss for God's sake or the whole German army will drop on top of you. Be patient. Remember the cat in the wood*, I coached myself.

The conscious brain was far too slow to work out the best shot. By the time the current scenario had been analysed for its feasibility, it would be too late. The calculation must be made with lightning-fast instincts by the subconscious, which was never wrong. The trick was to let my brain know what scenario I needed, and it would do it for me automatically. The rifle would shoot as soon as the right factors were in place. I had no idea how it worked, but it did, every time.

So I waited and lined up the target. Slowly, I squeezed the trigger and took up the first pressure on the trigger-spring, letting my instincts take over and . . .

BANG.

The rifle kicked in my hands, just as all the angles were right.

Bolt back, forward, locked, aim, BANG.

Got them both. Murdering bastards. I had to use just one more round to ruin their Maxim so it couldn't be used to kill any more of our youngsters.

BANG.

Got it. Turned it into scrap.

Only then could I close my eyes against the wind and relax; my head was down behind my lifesaving little earth mound, and I was hoping to Christ they didn't find me. I re-ran the pictures of exactly what had happened in my mind. Yes, got them both.

At nightfall, I crawled backwards to the relative safety of our trench. If I were shot, it would be better to have a quicker and less painful death with a bullet in my head than one up my arse. I wondered who those two Jerries were that I had shot and whether they had girlfriends or wives. They certainly had a mother and a father who would be traumatised for the rest of their lives. Such bad news could kill one or the other, or even both. Their parents' whole reason for living had just been ended by a bullet from my rifle. God. Those poor parents. I kept seeing them in my mind's eye as they received their telegram, their wrinkled faces instantly older and dissolving in tears. I could see their hugs for mutual support, each in their barren loneliness. Their world of hope and pride had gone; their life's huge emotional investment dashed and wasted. Pictures in my head saw them sitting silently in the evenings by the fire, wrapped only in their knitted warmth and their sad, tearful memories. It was all they'd have left.

The sergeant said we mustn't think like that. 'It's "them or us,"' he'd said. I was a killer, but a specialised killer, with the blood of children on my hands and maybe that of all their relations, too.

Old men were sending young men into war, yet again. Perhaps the generals should have sorted out the result on our behalf. Nah. That would never happen. I'd never even seen our colonel but I had to follow orders and kill as many Jerries as I could.

Was it only quantity? Where was the quality? Why not put me in a nice position within a thousand yards of some Jerry bigwig? I'd take him down. That would be worth a hell of a lot more to our side than a dozen or so of their Lee Enfield fodder, surely?

When the hell was this going to end? And what if we didn't win? Would they shoot us, turn us into factory slaves or send us home with a different government? We just had to win or I'd have to learn German, and my brain didn't do that sort of stuff well.

Our vicar, at home, once described hell from the pulpit. A more accurate description would have replaced the heat he'd described with this energy-sapping cold that now enveloped me.

A landscape artist here needed only three colours. Black for the muddy land and stagnant water in the background, foreground and middle distance, and a watered-down black through grey to paper-white for the daylight – that was grey for the cloud, drizzle or rain. And he would use red, the colour of explosions and the colour of blood after the shells, mortars and bullets had done their grisly and terrifying work. Very occasionally this artist may have used blue for the sky – the colour of false peace in our reality. Sunshine seemed so seldom to grace us with its presence that yellow would not be needed.

Lying in the cold, wet mud and waiting for a German sniper to make a mistake freed my imagination, allowing my mind to meander through images, memories and dreams for a little while. Before the bloody slaughter returned. My daydreaming helped me to forget the cold, the mortal danger and my chronic fear. It connected me to a past reality, which was at considerable risk of being lost forever if a German sniper outwitted me.

My mind recalled the memories of first meeting my Gwen. Those memories were still sharp pictures in full colour, locked inside my head. The sounds, smells and tastes of that evening and the glorious months that followed returned vividly to my mind's eye . . .

Chapter 1

First encounter

Norfolk, Saturday 11th April, 1914

The spring evening was cooling quickly now that the sun had gone down. Standing across the road beside a flint and brick building, I watched the young men and women arrive at the dance. The gaslight over the door to the village hall was quite bright and accentuated the different hair and dress colours. The young men looked very smart in their Sunday suits, having been more or less successful in keeping a crease in their trousers and making a straight part in their hair – left, right or centre. The young women had worked harder to make their appearance fashionable by adding lace and ribbons to their dresses, sewn on to soften edges and hide seams.

A rainbow of colours spilled out of the Dereham bus when it arrived near the front door of the hall because the majority of the passengers were young women, giggling and laughing together as a group. This collective and closed intimacy could be quite intimidating for a single eighteen-year-old young man, so I shrank back further into shadow.

As this gaggle of females reached the entrance, one young woman immediately stood out to me. She was stunningly beautiful. Her lovely face was smiling, her eyes animated. My breathing stopped, my heart clenched and sweat popped from my skin. I had to meet her.

I had no memory of walking towards the door of the hall, although I must have remembered to resume breathing. My hat and coat were checked in, but as I walked towards the dance floor, a small, angry-looking young man barred my way. His head was thrust forwards, and his aggressive-looking piggy-blue eyes and tight lips were meant to show me how fierce he was. But his teenage acne spoiled the whole effect. Instead, he looked like an angry apprentice clown with porcine overtones, playing sentry at the Longham Village Easter Dance in my beloved Norfolk. *There must have been some bullying in his background,* I thought. *A dominating father or a bigger, older and meaner brother, maybe.*

'And who are you, then?' he asked brusquely.

'And you are the doorman, I suppose then,' I remarked, smiling while looking down my nose at him.

'Don't you try and play smart with me, farm boy, or it'll go badly for you. People generally remember the name of Mickey Foster.'

'Oh, do they? How strange,' I mused. 'I don't see any accomplices nearby, and you certainly couldn't do anything on your own, junior.'

'I'll see you after!' he threatened loudly. 'What's your name, farm boy?'

'Just so that you'll know who will be landing some very painful blows to your face and body, hurting you so badly that you'll always remember the lesson, it's Frank Matthews,' I told him.

I put my nose about an inch from his, opened my eyes wide and said quietly, 'You need a bath,' and walked away, spinning him around with my shoulder. Behind me, there was a growl, but I didn't turn. *He must be a 'townie,'* I thought. He certainly had nothing in common with we gentle and cooperative farming folk. While I knew all the other families in the district, his face was new. But as I was a very fit eighteen-year-old young man with quick reflexes and a great deal of stamina from working on the family farm, I had nothing to fear from the likes of Mickey Foster. My mind smiled at the speed I was able to bait him. Easy!

Now, the point of going to a village dance was to meet girls. This Foster boy was attacking me before he had anything to defend. What a strange young man. Somewhere in there was a nasty, cruel streak – a weasel, a stoat or a ferret in character, all of which lived by lightning-fast, instinctive violence. But he wasn't my problem.

The band was playing as I went into the hall, and some couples were already dancing. I sat at a table with my back to the wall, facing the door, not letting my guard down in case 'Piggy' decided to have a second go.

She appeared at the entrance as if by magic. By God, she was gorgeous. She looked vivacious and absolutely spectacular. Her hair shone like curls of fresh copper metal in a tumbling cascade, which was well complemented by her emerald green dress. It was in the latest fashion – well, for rural Norfolk in 1914. Her green eyes danced with humour and energy; her full lips curled up in a smile of amusement, of challenge and of so much promise. And as she looked around the hall, her eyes landed on me.

What in the world do I do now? I thought.

Before I could stand up, 'Piggy' had approached her with a practised smile, a little bow and a hand held out for her. She gave him her full attention for two full seconds while time stopped for me. She smiled politely but shook her lovely head, wafting her vibrant curls into vertical waves. She walked past him in a straight line to where I was sitting. My legs felt as wobbly as a newly born foal's as I finally stood up.

This lovely young woman then stood in front of me and treated me to her devastating, intimate smile. I had never felt, seen or experienced anything like the massive emotional impact of a single smile before.

Everything went quiet. Time slowed. There was no one else in the room. I became sublimely lost in those green, all-encompassing eyes as I looked down at her. My chest ached from holding my breath since she had first appeared. I let it out slowly so she didn't realise she'd had such an effect on me.

I slowly extended my hand, palm up. This beautiful young lady put hers on it, and I enclosed it in both of mine.

'Welcome,' I said.

'Thank you, kind sir.'

'Can I get you a drink?'

'No, thank you, but some time with you would be nice,' she replied with mischief dancing all over her face.

'With your lovely smile and your dancing green eyes, I'm afraid all I can offer you is the rest of my life . . .'

I'm blithering, I thought. Where had that come from?

'Well,' she laughed, 'both handsome and charming.' She smiled as I held a chair out for her.

'Shall I call you "Bright Eyes"?' I fumbled.

'My name is Gwen Bell, and yours is Frank Matthews,' she said conspiratorially.

'Yes it is, and how would you know that, Gwen Bell?' I asked, tasting the words of her name as they rolled off my tongue.

'My best friend is your sister, Margaret. She told me about you so I've come to see you for myself, Frank Matthews.'

'I'm going to be extra nice to my sister Margaret from now on, just for having the chance to meet you.'

We talked and danced in our own world, entirely oblivious to everyone else. Physical contact brought an urgent hunger, while our mental connection stimulated, entranced and delighted. Laughter and unspoken messages on so many levels were constantly exchanged. Together, we seemed to have found completeness. There was no other word I could think of to describe that feeling.

When it was time to leave I escorted her to the door, where 'Piggy,' who had fancied his chances, was still standing.

'You got lucky,' he sneered.

I put my face very close to his, letting go of Gwen's hand for a moment, and gave him full eye contact. I said slowly, 'You are so, so right.'

He lifted his chin in challenge. 'We'll have to see about that then, shan't we?'

'Tell me again, who I have to look out for?' I asked, softly.

'Remember the name of Mickey Foster, and also remember I've got a big, strong brother to take care of you if I tell him to. I'll have that girl of yours, in spite of you. You'll see!'

'You remember my name and my warning to you, Mickey Foster. It's Matthews, Frank Matthews. Don't get out of your depth, Mickey Foster, or painful things could happen to you,' I told him in a conversational tone.

His slitted eyes held shadows of revenge and violence in their depths.

'After you've had a bath,' I said as a parting gesture.

Gwen and I walked outside. She commented, 'Well, that was interesting. Thank you, Frank, but I don't think I need protection from such a specimen. There's one of those at every dance hall. Their smile is from the mirror, and their show of manners is very short-lived. Funny, but a girl so rarely finds a gentleman.'

'Gwen,' I murmured, gently holding her upper arms and looking deeply into her enchanting green eyes, 'when can we meet again? I'm going to feel a little strange until then, and we haven't even parted yet. I feel slightly dizzy and unbalanced, as if I've been spinning around on my heels. I don't understand this.'

'Let me know when you find out,' she said with a cheeky grin. 'Now I have to go on the bus back to Dereham. Perhaps I'll see you at Longham Church tomorrow?'

Chris Shaw

Gwen looked steadily into my eyes then dropped them to my lips, raised up on her toes, leaned towards me and said, ever so softly, 'It was very nice to meet you, Frank Matthews. See you in church.'

I stood as still as a graveyard headstone as Gwen walked to her bus. She turned and gave me a smile that melted me like chocolate on a summer's day.

I was hooked.

How had she done that?

How did she feel?

What was I going to do about this situation?

During my confused walk back to our farm, one idea was utterly fixed in my mind. Somehow, I must find a way to be with Gwen, hopefully for the rest of my life. I knew, beyond any doubt in the world that it was our destiny to be together, and I yearned for that in ways I had never experienced and didn't understand.

Chapter 2

A TEST FOR FRANK

Of course, I was in our local St Andrew's and St Peter's Church in Longham village, early and eagerly. With my eyes closed, I could imagine Gwen's body pressed to mine and taste the kiss that could have been from last night, but I mustn't dwell on that. It made me too uncomfortable. Still, her body was so ripe, and her smile, so confident, and yet there was a vulnerability there that appealed to my protective instinct. *Frank, dwell no more.*

I sat in the back row of pews, trying to relax. The organist's fingers wandered around the keyboard, reflecting the early morning mental meanderings of most of the congregation, which filed in slowly on this bright and sunny Sunday morning.

The flower ladies had decorated the church beautifully. This was Easter, that egg-yolk yellow celebration of the year's return to seasonal warmth and fertility, echoed in the flower arrangements around this village church. The many yellows of daffodils, tulips, narcissi and little bunches of primroses were all lifting our spirits after the cold, dark winter months. In the centre of the altar was a small cut-glass vase of pure white snowdrops on fresh green stems – the symbolic herald of spring. Echoes of many ancient Pagan rites reverberated in this Protestant Christian church.

When I looked over at the vestibule, I saw that Gwen had arrived! Waves of pleasure hit my body, followed by their echo mere seconds later. She looked for me, found me and smiled that devastating smile of hers again; the smile that seemed to take my face gently in her hands and softly kiss me. I could never give that up, nor must I ever spoil its innocence, sincerity or warmth.

Gwen came over to join me, ushering an older lady to sit between us. *This must be her mother, so be on your best behaviour, Frank,* I lectured myself.

'Good morning, Mrs Bell,' I said in greeting, leaning sideways to shake her hand – gently in case of rheumatism. 'My name is Frank Matthews, and I had the pleasure of your daughter's company at the dance last night.'

'Yes, so I heard,' she replied. 'I'm pleased to make your acquaintance. Did you enjoy the dance?'

Is this a trick question? There will be some. Parents always do that, but I can't see a problem with this one.

'Yes,' I admitted, 'very much. I really do enjoy Gwen's company. I wonder, would you mind my walking her home from church today? It's such a fine day, and we have a lot to talk about.'

Mrs Bell nailed me with the 'parent look', examining my face, especially my eyes, closely. She waited for a sign of weakness or of duplicity, even my turning away. I knew I could pass this one since there was nothing to hide, except the roaring in my ears and my racing heart whenever Gwen and I touched.

After what seemed like an age, she nodded. I seemed to have passed a significant test.

'Thank you,' I said, just to put the icing on the cake. After all, my parents had taught me manners, and if ever there was a chance to use them, it was now.

'I'll have tea and cakes for you when you arrive,' Mrs Bell added, so unexpectedly that I risked a look at Gwen, who gave me the slightest of nods.

'Well, thank you again,' I said, smiling.

The organist started in earnest, and the service began. We stood, we sat, we sang and we prayed. The vicar had some kind words to say about Easter, both from religious and farming points of view. He knew his congregation well. Then it was over.

As we walked together outside, Mrs Bell revealed, 'Frank, my husband, Gwen's father, died six years ago. He had a heart attack. It was a great shock to me, and I've had to take care of Gwen ever since; although now that she has her job at the post office in Dereham, she has almost taken over that role by caring for me.'

'I'm sorry to hear about your husband,' I said in earnest. 'It can be very hard for a woman on her own, even without children, but more so with a family to raise. I have an aunt over at North Elmham who's in much the same boat. We, as a family, visit her nearly every weekend with a basket of food from the farm, just to help her get by.'

'You obviously come from a good family,' she murmured.

'I think my mum and dad had a rough time when they first bought their farm, and they are just passing on what had been done for them in their time of need. I remember reading somewhere about a character in a story called "Mrs Do-as-you-would-be-done-by". I think the chap who wrote about her had a pretty good idea of how the world should work, and mostly does – in the country anyway.'

That brought some laughter, and the tension melted.

'I'll get my Dereham bus now. It should take you about an hour to walk, so I shall have the kettle on the boil by then. That means you'll have to walk back, Frank,' Gwen's mother said, waiting.

What could I say, except, 'I really don't mind, Mrs Bell, and look forward to a cup of tea with you. Thank you.'

Gwen and I loaded her on to the bus, made sure she was comfortably seated and waved her goodbye. Then Gwen put her hands in mine and faced me.

'Who's my clever man, then?' she asked softly, shaking her beautiful red hair. 'I think you passed her tests with flying colours.'

'I thought we were just having a nice conversation,' I jested with an innocent grin, my eyebrows raised.

'No, you didn't. I sensed you waiting and weighing up the questions to see if there were any traps. You are very shrewd, Frank Matthews. Now, shall we stand here conversing about family politics or walk a few miles for a cup of tea?'

'A cup of tea's got my vote. You are just too clever by half,' I said, smiling.

'Now tell me,' she asked, 'what would Frank Matthews want from a relationship with Gwen Bell?'

'Well, that's not an easy question to answer. Let's start with what I would want to put into a relationship with Gwen Bell, and that may tell you – and me – what I want to get out of it.

'I feel very protective towards you, and feel, in some strange way that I really don't understand, lonely when you are not near. So, I would like to be with you. I enjoy talking with you so I would like to share everything with you as a friend, and learn to please you and love you.'

'Really?'

Maybe, later, we can think about sharing our lives. If that should happen, I think that to watch and help children grow and mature in a happy environment must be one of the best things a family can ever experience. Maybe, together, we could supply that happy home. There now, I didn't really know how to answer your question, but I hope that helps.'

'Yes, it really does.'

'Gwen, I have to say that I've no idea where that came from, but somehow it feels right.'

'That was beautifully said. You really are a romantic man, Frank, and they are quite rare. There are a whole lot of questions that I have for you, but I don't want to frighten you away. So far, I've found you to be a handsome, gentle and a kind man, but there are some priorities to be observed.'

'Go on.'

'One is that I have a terrible fear of ending up as an unwed mother. I couldn't cope with that. Do you understand?'

'I do.'

'Frank, in the minimal time we've had together, maybe as little as five hours, we seem to have developed an excellent understanding between us, and I'm pretty sure I can trust you.'

'Only with your life, Gwen Bell,' I said slowly, looking deeply into her bright green eyes.

'So let's explore this with truth and honesty to see where it takes us. Is that all right with you?' Gwen asked.

'Yes, lead on. I somehow suspect you have more needs than I do.'

'Probably. We women are complicated creatures. To be happy we need certain things in our lives. So I would like to ask you some questions, which I hope you will answer. For every one you get right, I will put a kiss on your cheek. How does that sound?'

'Sounds wonderful; until I worry about what your rules say about my getting the answers wrong.'

Gwen gave one of her tinkling laughs, sounding like a waterfall of little icicles.

'Then you have to put a kiss on to my cheek,' she ventured.

'Oh, I like this game,' I admitted, warming to this game.

'Right. What's the most important thing in life to a woman?'

'A husband,' I said straight away.

'Wrong, and think about it first.'

I thought about my mother.

'Well, there must be more than just one important thing in a woman's life. She needs security and somewhere she is wanted or needed. A husband to provide and watch over her is part of her security, but she needs to be in charge of the house, its contents, its mood and its level of behaviour. She probably doesn't need a husband, as such, but someone to share her day-to-day life, her hopes and dreams. How did I do?'

'Frank Matthews, that deserves a triple-decker kiss. Where did you get that from?'

'Kiss first.'

Now that Gwen had manoeuvred me into our first kiss, I felt a little hesitancy in her body. I put my hand behind her waist, and gently pulled her towards me. I looked deeply into her eyes and saw little gold flecks in the beautiful deep green. Her eyes flickered backwards and forwards over mine, checking my motives and questioning my sincerity.

Her eyes closed and she came to me, her arms around my shoulders. Our lips touched, softly, lingering, then with slightly more pressure. I felt hers slightly part. I followed suit. Then she flowered, holding me so tight, rubbing herself against me, with quick, hot breaths. Her tongue touched mine and wound around and around. We could not be closer. She seemed to suddenly become aware of herself and her surroundings, and that we were by no means in private. In fact, we were standing in the middle of a country road. This is the country, so people usually announce their presence with noise; footsteps, horse hooves or wagon wheels. For us there were only bird calls.

We looked at each other, somewhat dishevelled you might say, both still quivering with emotion. Her eyes were frightened, fearful; no, too strong. Her eyes were waiting for my reaction, knowing it was such a special moment.

'Gwen, in terms of kisses, that was an earthquake for me. It proves that you trust me as I trust you. That was the most extraordinary experience of my life, Gwen Bell.'

I took her face in my hands and kissed her very softly on the lips.

'Frank Matthews, I have wanted to do that since the first moment I met you. Now that I have, what was the answer to my question?'

'Oh, yes. Well, I've watched my mother, who is about as happy and content as I have ever seen any woman. She has a husband, a farmhouse to run and children to organise. She has complete charge of family things.'

'Mum doesn't interfere with what Dad does, but she will listen to any problems he may have, and make suggestions if she thinks he needs them. I believe she would happily replace the horses in front of the plough if she thought it would help him. It seems that although the whole day is given over to work, they are content in the allotment of their duties. Does that make sense?'

'And do you have any wish to follow their example?' asked Gwen, who had stopped walking, waiting for my answer.

'I seriously think I would give my life for a partnership such as that,' I said, meaning every word.

'What sort of curtains would you like in our bedroom?' she asked, totally out of the blue.

'Whoa! That's a big jump, but it's totally up to you. That's your province. I would tell you my opinion if you asked, but the type of spring-weather we are going to have, and therefore what crops we sow and when we sow them, would be much more important to me and, financially, for you too.'

'Probably true.'

'So, you would get the curtains the way you want them, and we would go on from there. I think that, on reflection, if I were a very astute husband, I would tell you that I liked them!'

'You, Frank, go to the top of the class. No man I have ever met, or heard of, understands more about women than you do. You are a real find.'

Somehow, I thought, I must marry this lovely young lady, who had appeared so suddenly and miraculously into my life. I wanted to marry her, protect her and cherish her for the rest of our lives. Nothing less seemed acceptable now. Soon, I would need to introduce her to my family as a first step.

A small thing, but would the tea still be hot when we arrived at Mrs Bell's, or would we be late and make our first social blunder?

Chapter 3

MEETING THE FAMILY

Gwen and I had arranged that next Saturday she would catch the bus from Dereham to Longham village. I would meet the bus and bring her to meet my family on our farm, which was about a quarter of a mile away. Naturally, I was there early, and as the bus arrived, I noted that my heart rate had increased. Several people got off, but not Gwen. My disappointment was crushing. My mind went galloping off in search of answers. She was sick. Her mother was sick. There was a crisis in her family. She'd had an accident in town. She'd been knocked down by a horse on the road, or by a thief in the house. She didn't love me anymore.

More and more outlandish ideas sprang to mind until some part of my brain said, 'Stop! You'll drive yourself mad.' There was another bus in an hour so I would meet that one. But what if she didn't arrive then? My brain interrupted again, 'For goodness sake, stop all this useless speculation!'

I returned home in a bleak mood as if I had been cast adrift, anchorless on a featureless ocean. Gwen must have dominated my conversation because my sisters began to tease me. The fact that Margaret knew Gwen would help break the ice. Our family tends to be a bit overwhelming at times. My two older brothers, Eric and Fred, would behave themselves and might not even bother to come back from ploughing, harrowing, milking or whatever they were involved in at that moment.

'Frank's got a girl. Big deal! We'll see her soon enough – if it lasts.'

My sisters, Margaret and Bobbie, both in their teens, would want to see what Gwen was wearing. Did the colours match? What sort of trimmings did she have? Was she wearing any lace, ribbons or feathers, and if so, where? How long was her hem, and what sort of shoes did she wear?

My mother had been reticent about all this, but I'd caught her looking at me once or twice, probably thinking there was nothing she could do about the situation until Gwen arrived, so she would get on with all the other stuff she had to do.

Naturally, I was at the bus stop long before its arrival time again, but that's what young men do, especially if they fancy themselves in love, as I did. It was a huge relief when the bus ground its way through the village, stopping at the White Horse Inn. Gwen was the first off and looked a real picture. She even treated me to a very surreptitious show of ankle as she descended the bus steps. It was most welcome, and only I spotted it.

As she stepped off the bus, she came straight into my arms, and it felt so right.

'Hello, my Gwen,' I murmured.

'Hello, yourself,' she said, and her eyes were doing their devilish dance on my face. 'I've missed you so much.'

'You have no idea, my sweet lady, how good it is to be together again. How are you?'

'I'm well, thank you, and very glad to be here, even though I have to go through the ordeal of meeting your family. I'm sorry for being late but Mum needed me to massage her stiff shoulders, and I missed the first bus.'

'You'll do very well with my family, and Margaret will be there to ease you in. Mum might try to do a little bit of interrogation but she's a softie really, and I believe she is half-convinced already of our compatibility. I've caught her looking at me with a little half-smile, as much as to say, "I've been there, and I know exactly how you feel". I think Dad's been given instructions to put in an appearance at teatime but he doesn't say very much, ever, and you can't influence his thoughts. So you can relax with him, too. All in all, we'll have a beautiful afternoon.'

We walked along the road, hand-in-hand. I pointed out the fields we owned and the crops we had growing in them: barley, wheat, clover, sugar beet, kale for the cattle, and the meadows where the dairy cows grazed. A small wood nearby sounded full of pigeons, cooing continuously.

'They eat a lot of our grain,' I explained, 'but they also feed us when we need meat,' and pointed up to the sky as if I were shooting one in flight.

'What does pigeon taste like?' she asked.

'Rather like chicken but drier. We have a brace in the cold room, which have been plucked, gutted and hung. I'll pack them up so you can take them to your mother as a peace offering.'

'A peace offering? Why a peace offering?' she asked.

'For all my lustful thoughts.'

'Lustful thoughts? Surely not! Not you!'

'Really? Please keep both thoughts in mind for the future.'

We arrived at the farmhouse. Mum must have seen us coming since she was outside the back door, waiting, with her apron off, which was her concession to formality. She smiled and took both of Gwen's hands in hers as I made the introductions. They looked at each other for a moment then Mum drew Gwen into her body and hugged her.

She had seen Gwen and me approach the farm and had noticed her clothes and our body language. For a farmer's wife who made a thousand decisions a day, noting Gwen's clear skin, good coordination and the lack of 'airs and graces' that were false indicators of status, she was sure that Gwen was a 'good'un' as they say in Norfolk.

'You'll do very nicely, Gwen,' Mum said softly. 'I just love your smile. Come in, and I'll get us a cup of tea. I've just finished baking a tray of scones, so we can have them with some homemade strawberry jam.'

'Thank you, that sounds wonderful,' smiled Gwen.

'In the meantime, you know Margaret, and this is Bobbie. They were longing to see what you were wearing today because they seem to endlessly study the fashions of town people. I can't see why myself. Clothes just cover the body to keep you warm when the weather is cold. They stop young men from going mad when you're young but cover a long list of faults as you get older,' joked Mum. There was laughter, and any lingering tension evaporated.

'Frank, be a pet, and get me a pint of milk from the dairy.'

Ha! I thought. *It's time for the women to talk. I'd better give them time, and not be too quick.*

I took the long route to the dairy and saw Dad in the barn, bent over a machine I hadn't seen before. He beckoned me over.

'Your young lady turn up?' he asked.

'Yes, Dad, but I was sent off to get some milk, so it's obvious that they want to talk. I'm taking my time.'

'Then you've done well and may eventually learn how this man-woman thing all fits together, but I doubt it. I don't know any man who's got that all sorted out. I do know that if you get ninety percent about right, there's a big payoff.' He smiled a knowing smile. I said that Gwen and I had a pretty fair working relationship.

'Maybe you have, and maybe you haven't, but these womenfolk tend to change their minds a whole lot, you know. Be prepared for that one. But how're you going, together?'

'In truth, very well, but it's early days yet.'

'I understand, boy, but now you are eighteen it's about time you took a wife and did some settling. In truth, the sooner the better.'

'Why the sooner the better? What's the hurry?'

'There's some stuff going on outside this country that may influence things soon. I've been reading about it in the *Eastern Daily Press*. There has been a lot of unrest in Eastern Europe for much of 1913, and I have a feeling it may all come to a head soon. Only the good Lord knows where that would place England. If the worst comes to the worst, Gwen will need some security, and marriage will do that for a girl. Go and think about it. It's amazing what men and women can put up with if they have to, but if it's good between you, then you'll live the rest of your life in heaven. I do, even though your mother and I don't see each other but for lunch, an hour in the evening and in bed, and then we're mostly so tired. We don't have the need for very much talking these days, but we know what we know of each other, and take delight in that.'

'I've often wondered about that, and the fact that I've never seen you kiss Mum. I thought she may have objected to your full moustache!'

'Not at all. She's mad for the feel of it,' Dad confided with a rare but lovely smile. 'That's why I always keep it so full. She'll never tell another soul, of course, but if your marriage is as good as ours is, you'll be set up for life.' 'I'll be in for tea in a while and have a look at your lass. What's her name?'

'Gwen,' I answered, 'and I believe that together we can be pretty good too, and that we will last for a long, long time.'

'Good luck then,' he congratulated and turned back to his task.

Having collected the milk, I got back to find the conversation was in full flight. No hope of my competing with that, but just then Dad arrived. He washed his face and hands in the stone sink, pumping the handle to get water from the underground well, and using the yellow soap from the soap dish. There was a freshly laundered hand towel to dry his face and hands. He sat down in the big carver chair at the head of the table.

'Dad,' I said, 'I would like to introduce you to Gwen. Gwen, this is my Dad,' I said, formally. He stood up and shook her hand.

'Hello Gwen,' he said, 'I gather you enjoy Frank's company. He's a good son. You could do a lot worse,' and sat down again. Gwen blushed a little but put her chin up and asked, 'What should I call you, sir?'

'For the moment, Mr Matthews will do,' he offered, with a twinkle in his eye that I had only seen on two or three occasions in my life. Both that twinkle and her smile said that they had reached an unspoken rapport; that my Gwen had now been fully accepted into my family.

After tea had finished and Dad had gone back to doing maintenance on the oat-crusher's engine, Mum suggested that I play something for Gwen on my violin. Everyone applauded his suggestion, so I went through to the front room, got out my violin and bow from the case, tightened the bow, put some resin on the horsehair and tuned the four strings. I put the music for Bruch's 'First Violin Concerto' on the stand and started playing the slow second movement.

After the first few bars, I went 'into' the music; that is, I started to let the music create pictures in my mind. It's a very romantic piece so I thought of Gwen and played it for her. I 'saw' in my mind's eye a green landscape, a cottage with a smoking chimney, lots of flowers in the front garden like hollyhocks, carnations, gladioli and foxgloves – a blaze of colours. Always, there was Gwen with her smile at the front gate of the cottage or in the kitchen garden, attending to bees or looking after a young child. I could hear in the music that the wind came up and blew the trees about. Then the sun came out again, and I finished.

I was given a round of applause and, as I looked at Gwen, something moved in her eyes. It was as if a change had taken place in her thinking, resulting in an acceptance of something she had been trying to understand. I smiled; she nodded and clapped.

We left the others and walked hand-in-hand outside.

'And what other talents is my lovely man hiding?'

'The only thing I do that might impress you is that I'm quite a fair shot. I very rarely miss a target. I've also learned the art of stalking. A few years back a half-wild cat used to visit the house for food. She would follow me into the wood, and by watching her very closely, she taught me patience, sound identification and stealth. Now I can go into any wood and within ten minutes be accepted as part of the woodland community. I used to watch her ears to identify the sounds she heard. If they twitched, and I had missed the sound that made them twitch, I was able to replay those surrounding sounds from memory and then identify what she had heard. It made me super-receptive to everything that was going on around me. I've never heard of anyone else who can do that, but it's not as if I could earn a living from it, Gwen. Come on, I'll show you around.'

'Yes, please. This really is a lovely place, and your family is very loving. Now that I know you a little better, I can see where you get your gentleness and understanding. Your mum is lovely, and your dad and I will be fine. He's just playing hard to get!'

'Yes, he's a softie too, but don't ever cross him. I saw a man do that once and thought Dad would kill him. His rage was incredibly fierce. His family background was Welsh, as the "Matthews" may tell you. The Welsh, in their day were, by all accounts, very fierce warriors. I certainly wouldn't want Dad mad at me! Did you know that the Welsh used to go into battle stark naked, with their bodies painted in intricate patterns with a blue dye called "woad?" Apparently, it scared the Romans half to death, and we're talking about battle-hardened soldiers.'

'That must have taken some doing,' Gwen remarked as we arrived at the stables.

'Now, here are the stables, and this is Duchess, who does a lot of hard work for us, don't you, girl?' I said, patting her on the rump. 'And this is Tiffany, who takes Mother and all her produce into the market in Dereham on Fridays. You may even have seen her from the post office window. Mum named the pony after the famous jeweller. This mare is Picnic, who is the most gentle and loving horse there ever was. We did some terrible things to her when we were children, but she never retaliated. I believe she thinks that we are her foals and she needs to mother us.'

As we were walking out of the stable, there was a huge BANG. Duchess shied in her stall and stepped back. Gwen let out a shriek and fell down. I quickly settled Duchess down with some stroking and soothing words, and then turned my attention to Gwen. She was on the ground, sheet-white and moaning.

'Gwen! Gwen darling, what happened? Where are you hurt?'

I sat down on the floor and lifted her head into my lap. I stroked her cheek and asked her again, 'Where are you hurt?'

She stirred. Her eyelashes fluttered, and she pointed to her foot. I could see that her shoe was mangled, and her foot hung at the wrong angle. I picked her up and carried her to the house. She clung to me and nuzzled my neck, which were good signs and most welcome.

'Mum,' I cried, 'Gwen's been hurt. Can you get some hot water and a bandage?' Margaret and Bobbie came running with their faces full of questions. I gave them a strong look and a sharp 'shush', and they backed off. Mum came running, looked at Gwen's face, then at her damaged shoe and knelt to feel the foot very gently.

'What happened?' she asked, aghast.

'We were in the stables, and there was a loud bang. Duchess shied. I think she stood on Gwen's foot. I really hope nothing is broken, but with Duchess's weight and the sharp edges on her horseshoes, there's a strong chance of a crippling injury,' I blurted, getting quite distraught that my love was hurting.

'Just after an injury like this,' said Mum quietly, 'there is a short time when there's no pain. I'll put on a hot compress and bandage it. Get the trap and take Gwen to Dr Jim Watson's surgery on your way to her house. He can check her foot and maybe give her some Laudanum for the pain. It's ruined her perfectly good pair of shoes, I'm afraid.'

'How do you feel, Gwen?' Mum prompted.

'A bit shaken, to tell the truth, and my foot is starting to hurt quite badly.'

'Margaret, make Gwen a nice cup of tea, please. Frank, this is women's work. Go and get the trap ready. Use Picnic, settle Duchess down, and find out what that bang was.'

Mothers, generally, are excellent in a crisis, and farming mothers seem ready for anything. I found Dad in the barn, still tinkering with that engine.

'Dad, did you hear that loud bang?'

'Hear it? I was on top of it! The timing on this engine is way out, and it backfired. The starting handle came close to breaking my arm. I got this miserable machine second-hand, and it's just a matter of spending some time on it. It'll be right.' He thought for a moment. 'Why?'

'Well, Gwen and I were in the stables, and ...'

'Oh, yes?' he said with a grin.

'I was showing her our horses when there was this loud bang. Duchess shied, and I think she backed up on to Gwen's foot. Gwen's in a great deal of pain, and I'm to take her home in the trap via the Doctor's surgery.'

'Oh my! I am so sorry, Frank, but I didn't know you were there or that this ignorant piece of machinery would play up. I'd better come up and see her.'

'Dad, there's no need. Mum's got everything in hand – as usual.'

'That's all right then. Just tell Gwen I'm very sorry, will you?'

'Of course.'

I checked on Duchess. She seemed well and calm. I gave her some extra hay and patted her while she chewed. I haltered Picnic, backed her between the shafts of the trap, harnessed her and walked her to the house.

Most of the tension seemed to have gone out of the situation. Gwen had a wan little smile and half a cup of warm tea in her hands. Her eyes had lost a bit of their usual sparkle, and the pain had started to show on her face.

'It was the engine that Dad is working on that caused the bang. He says that he's very sorry and hopes you'll be better soon. So drink up, and I'll put you in the trap. Margaret, would you and Bobbie get a spare blanket and some cushions, please? Gwen should be made as warm and comfortable as possible.'

'You're spoiling me, Frank, just like a mother hen!' exclaimed Gwen with a weak smile.

'I feel so helpless and guilty. You come for a nice visit to meet my family, and we almost manage to maim you for life!'

'Frank, I've had a wonderful visit. I love your family, especially your mum, and wild horses couldn't stop me coming again.'

She said her goodbyes from the trap, with a kiss and a little whispered conversation from Mum, and we were off. I was fearful of the damage Duchess had caused. Imagine if Gwen couldn't walk again.

Chapter 4

Sorting out the damage

I gentled Picnic into a walk and kept her there. She wanted to stretch out into a trot or, with a little encouragement, even a canter. Gwen was stoic. She should have been moaning with the pain but wasn't.

'What a mess! I suppose your visit could have been more disastrous, but I don't know how. Generally, we don't have accidents on the farm. We're all careful, but this came right out of the blue. I'm so sorry.'

'Darling Frank, listen to me. I love your family and their gentleness, their unity and how they showed such concern for me. If ever there was a chance to find out what a family was really like, it was today and with my accident. I couldn't have wished for more support, but it was just an accident. So stop fretting. I'll mend.'

We talked about this and that until we arrived at Doctor Jim Watson's house, with his surgery attached. I climbed down and rang the bell. He came to the door.

'Good afternoon, young Frank Matthews. What brings you here?'

'It's my girlfriend, Gwen Bell. One of our horses got a fright and stood on her foot. My mother checked it out and suggested that I consult you and possibly get something to help deaden her pain.'

'Your mother always did have outstanding instincts. She didn't marry me for a start! I will have a look at Miss Bell in the trap. She shouldn't get out. It would only cause unnecessary pain.'

'Good afternoon, Miss Bell,' he said to her, 'please show me your foot.' Very gently, he traced the bones and examined the position of the foot at rest. He felt up her ankle a little way to make sure the tendons were intact, I suppose, and that there was not more extensive damage.

'Miss Bell, you will have a very sore foot for several days, but I don't think there are any bones broken. Your foot should get its orientation back and shouldn't leave you with a limp, but we'll have to wait and see. I prescribe rest, with the foot raised up on a cushion. I will give you a prescription for some Laudanum liquid for the pain.' He then turned to me and said 'She's a lovely young lady, Frank. Look after her.'

'That I shall. Thank you for your help,' I replied, shaking his hand and pocketing the precious piece of paper for the chemist.

'A pleasure,' he assured me as he watched us go down the driveway.

I took the rest of the journey gently, too. We picked up the brown dropper bottle from the Dereham chemist on Church Street, who explained the dosage in detail. He made sure I understood that it should be used sparingly as its opium content made it potentially addictive.

We arrived at Gwen's house, and I lifted her out of the trap, asking her to use the doorknocker. Mrs Bell opened the door and upon seeing Gwen, her eyes flew open and her hand came up to her mouth.

'Explanations later,' I said. 'Right now, I need to put Gwen down and make her comfortable.'

She held the door for us, and I put Gwen down on the sofa with a cushion under her head and another under her feet. I explained to Mrs Bell what had happened, what had been done and about the doctor and his instructions. I told her about the bandage support and said I had to go out but that I would be back in a little while to bandage the ankle after Gwen had taken a dose of Laudanum. They both gave me an enquiring look but didn't question me.

I went out, got in the trap and drove down the street and around the corner to the left. I pulled up, tied Picnic's reins to a fence and walked to the alley leading to the back of the houses that contained Gwen's. My footsteps could not be heard as I approached my target on the path between those houses. Very slowly, with one eye around the edge of a fence, I spotted the smarmy lad from the dance hall. What did I call him? 'Piggy,' otherwise known as Mickey Foster. That's right. He was hiding behind a hydrangea bush in their front garden, trying to look through their front window – to catch a glimpse of Gwen, no doubt.

Two of my talents were 'waiting,' and 'moving silently.' At first, I waited, since he seemed to be in no hurry. Then he leaned forward slightly so that his head was out of my line of sight, behind the brickwork. Silently, I moved forward, stopping about a foot from his head but where he couldn't see me. I could hear him breathing heavily and finally understood what he was doing.

In one lightning movement, my right arm went around his throat, my left hand went to the back of his head and I locked my right hand on to my left forearm. This very effectively cut off his breathing. By pushing forward on my left hand, I could bring pressure onto his throat and spine.

'And what do you think you're doing, you dirty little man? I know who you are, Mickey Foster, and I'm going to put enough pressure on your throat so that you can't breathe. You will pass out for a while. Goodnight!' I hissed in his ear.

He started to struggle, but I bent backwards. His feet came off the ground, and he lost purchase. I counted to forty then let him go. He dropped like a stone and lay there, taking huge breaths. After a while, his eyes flew wide open with shock and fear. He tried to get up, but I dropped a knee on his chest with my full weight and grabbed his little finger.

'Now listen to me very carefully, you nasty little piece of work. Gwen is mine, now and for always. I told you before, but either you are very dim, or you didn't listen. So, again I tell you, forget her and look elsewhere. If I see you, or she sees you, or anyone I know sees you in this town from today on, I will come to where you live, and I will do enormous damage to you. You will never walk again. You will never be able to talk again. You will never be able to work again. That is my solemn promise. Nod if you fully understand.'

I put my face very near to his, looking him in the eye while bending his little finger back. He made an attempt at a nod; his mouth opened, showing me lots of bad teeth, and his eyes were wide with pain. The paleness of his face and the sweat on his skin told me he was in shock.

'You can see that I need no weapons to make good on my threat,' I told him. 'So leave Dereham and never come back. Say after me, "I will go away and never come back."'

He made an attempt at it, but the sounds were raspy and wet.

'Now, make yourself decent and go away for good, you dirty little pervert! I didn't like you when I first saw you, and my opinion hasn't changed.'

He stumbled off along the road and, casting a fearful look back over his shoulder, he ran away. His breathing was still ragged and audible from about a hundred yards. It was a shame that I wasn't naked and painted blue, I thought. That would have scared this peeping Tom to death.

Gwen was reclining on the sofa just as I had left her, but her face was more relaxed as the Laudanum had begun to weave its magic. I made sure that she was comfortable and had everything she needed.

Mrs Bell had a bandage, with which I bound Gwen's ankle and foot. She had changed out of her dress and was in night attire. It was wholly inappropriate for me to see her like this but her mother acted as chaperone and didn't seem to mind.

I kissed Gwen lightly when her mother went to the kitchen. She tried to brighten up. Just the attempt gave her an incredibly vulnerable appeal. The temptation to lie down with her and stroke her to sleep was almost overwhelming, but instead I bade her farewell. Her mother showed me to the door.

'Thank you for all your trouble, Frank. She'll sleep well tonight, and we'll see what tomorrow brings. We tend to be fast healers, we Bells, so I think she will soon become a very annoying patient. But I can cope. You are very gentle and loving with her, Frank. I'm impressed.'

'Thank you, but she is not hard to love. I'll call in tomorrow to make sure she has everything she needs. Goodnight, Mrs Bell.'

She waved me away. I collected Picnic and drove the trap home somewhat faster than I should, but Picnic enjoyed it, and I felt exalted by my win over that nasty-minded little creep.

Chapter 5

DECISIONS

The following morning, after eating breakfast and completing some jobs around the farm, I asked Mum if there was anything she needed in Dereham. She made a small list of things and handed it to me.

'Give Gwen our love. I look forward to your report of how she is,' Mum said.

'I think she'll be much better, but very sore and a bit ratty that she can't be up and doing things, but we'll see. I should be back around four to lend a hand with the milking.'

There was a south-westerly wind blowing the treetops and bringing the threat of rain as Picnic picked up the pace, enjoying the exercise. My thoughts turned to Gwen, and I tried mentally to list the qualities of our relationship.

Was our relationship sound? Yes, I felt so. I had not detected any hiccups.

Was our relationship honest? Yes, we had both spoken our minds.

Could I see our relationship lasting? Yes, and I would welcome that more than anything in the world.

So, what should I do about it? My wish was to ask Gwen to marry me. To find a little cottage where we could settle and start a family, somewhere close enough to be of help to both Mrs Bell and my family would be perfect. I realised that our relationship had developed, in my mind at least, at a very fast pace. I was so sure of our love, our compatibility and our future that I had leaped over any potential problems without considering Gwen's point of view. I needed to be a little less self-centred and accommodate Gwen's wishes for a change.

What would Gwen think of this? I would have no idea until I asked her.

By the time I'd worked my way through this I was outside her house. Mrs Bell let me in.

'How's our patient?'

'At the "wanting to get up and do things" stage, and already becoming fractious, but I told you this would happen,' she whispered with a little smile.

We went inside. Gwen was lying on the couch where I had left her yesterday, but she had done her hair, applied a little lipstick and even put on a touch of rouge. These were encouraging signs for me – subtle, but pointing in the right direction towards our healthy relationship.

'Well, you're looking a tad better than when I left you yesterday,' I commented.

'Yes,' she said smiling, 'it's a wondrous thing, a good night's sleep. Apart from this silly foot of mine, I could certainly do a day's work. It's still a bit painful, and it's developing a set of colours that Van Gogh could get excited about. So tell me, what's happening at the farm?'

'They all send their love and hope you get well soon,' I replied.

'How's Duchess? Not too upset, I hope.'

'Not a bit, but it's just like you to worry about the cause of your considerable pain.'

'She wasn't to blame. No one was.'

I sat beside the couch. We started to talk about the farm, the post office where she worked, relatives we had and where they lived.

Mrs Bell interrupted, 'I've got to go out to do some shopping. I'll go while Frank is here so that I don't leave you alone, Gwen. If I don't go to the shops, we'll have nothing in the house to eat.'

Immediately, my eyes met Gwen's, and we tried not to smile.

'Very well, Mum. We've got a lot to talk about. So don't hurry. I'll be fine with Frank,' she said archly.

Mrs Bell fussed about her overcoat, hat, basket and shopping list.

'I'll be about half an hour, I expect,' she stated as I saw her out. There was just the trace of a twinkle in her eyes as she said good-bye. I closed the front door and walked back to Gwen.

She came so naturally into my arms. We kissed gently, with compassion on my part, and perhaps gratitude for my ministrations on her part. This was time for talk, in spite of what my body was shouting at me, deep talk with some conversation about the future, our hopes and dreams and what we wanted to achieve in our lives.

I learned about Gwen's preferences and tastes in food, in friendship, and the hobbies and pastimes she was interested in. My contribution was that I was using God's energy in growing plants and animals to make a profit from farming. Without his divine spark, there would be no germination of seeds, and no sperm and egg conjoining to produce the calves and foals we so needed. Gwen obviously knew more about differences in people; I just knew about farming, the countryside and the way it worked.

After a little, I made a cup of tea and shared my analysis of our friendship as two people and as two lovers, and we talked about our future together.

'I'm not going to make any decisions until we have discussed it together and both feel happy with what we plan to do,' I said quietly.

'Thank you for that, Frank. If I could have my wish, I would like to stay in your arms forever and explore each other endlessly, but I understand you are looking further. As the woman in this relationship, a lot of decisions are going to be my responsibility, but the main decision is yours to make, and you have to ask me at the right time. The answer will be a resounding yes, shouted from Mount Olympus, but we have to do this right for our families, too. Yes?'

'Yes, my love. I will do the right thing and alert both families so there can be a happy consensus with no nasty surprises for anyone. When I leave today, I'll have a quick word with your mum, but in truth, I think she's ahead of us. Hence the shopping trip.'

'Really? She couldn't be that smart, surely? Could she?'

'If you were in her place, would you suspect?'

'Of course I would, but I'm brighter than she is; but then she does have age and experience on her side. So, maybe —'

'Here she comes now. I've got some shopping to get so I'll take off and see you tomorrow, although, to me, this "apart" thing leaves a lot to be desired,' I maintained with a wicked grin. She threw a pillow at me just as her mother came in.

'I told you she'd get testy, Frank, being in bed and not allowed to go anywhere,' affirmed Mrs Bell.

'You're absolutely right. However, if Gwen behaves herself and stays in bed today, when I come tomorrow she may be fit for a little drive in the trap. I'll have to carry her to and from the trap, but the fresh air may well put some colour in her cheeks. I'll be off now. Goodbye, Gwen. Be good, and we'll have a little excursion tomorrow — if your mother has no objection, of course.'

'Not at all, Frank. As you say, just so long as she behaves herself.'

'You two are ganging up on me. Go away! I'll see you tomorrow,' exclaimed Gwen, a mischievous sparkle in her eye.

With a smile warming her old face, Mrs Bell showed me to the front door. Just before she opened it for me, I confided, 'Mrs Bell, Gwen and I have only been going out together for such a short time, but we have formed a strong relationship. We have discussed everything between us with honesty and friendship. If I were to ask her to marry me, would you have any objection?'

She looked at me for a long time. I could see her thoughts were chasing images elsewhere, so I waited. Then her eyes refocused.

'I can see how happy you two are together and can only find one side to you. I can't find any cruelty or meanness in you. So you have my blessing, Frank. I've been looking at the newspapers, and I think a long courting time may not be in your best interests. It's up to you, of course, but that would be my advice. And Frank, thank you for not leaving it until the last moment. That was very kind.'

'That's only fair to you,' I assured her.

'I'm also unsure as to how I'm going to pay for your wedding and reception. I don't have a lot of money,' she confessed, with the worry lines at the top of her nose deepening.

'First, don't worry about that because we will make it a quiet affair, and second, my family will come to the party, I'm sure. It's strange that my father said much the same thing about not having a long courtship. Anyway, our families need to have their say. I'll talk to my family tonight, and we'll speak again tomorrow.'

'Goodbye, Frank. Gwen's right. You are a good, kind man. You'll do very nicely. And try to call me Janice.'

'Thank you, Mrs – er – ma'am – er – Janice. That may take some getting used to.'

As Picnic took me home, people must have wondered about me, sporting a broad smile on my face and singing a song from *The Pirates of Penzance*.

Chapter 6

Wedding plans

On my way home, my thoughts were jumbled with too much to think about. I was attempting to apply the logic of time and importance to all the items that needed to be done. Picnic went into the stable, and I gave her some hay and patted her for a while to get my thoughts together.

Everyone was sitting at the big table in the kitchen for lunch as I went to the sink to wash my face and hands, drawing out the ritual just to tease them. They had been jabbering away with questions, but I held my counsel.

Now I turned and after a five-second count said, 'Well, my lovely family, Gwen and I wish to wed. Does anyone have any objections?'

What a clamour! The women wanted to know where, when and what the dress was going to look like. The men looked at each other, shook hands, and I had the distinct impression that some money changed hands. Dad looked straight at me, paused and then nodded once.

Mum came into my arms. I'm sure there were tears in her eyes, which she wouldn't want anyone else to see. She whispered softly, 'I don't think you could have done better. She's a lovely girl and will make you a wonderful wife. Well done, my darling boy.'

What I thought was clamour before had become more like a riotous cacophony. I held up my hands, and when I finally had silence said, 'You are my loving family, and I thank you for making my Gwen welcome. She's certainly taken to you, too. So everything should go well, I think. I must have a talk with Mum and Dad first, and then we can start to plan. And yes, girls, Gwen and I would be very grateful for your input, but later.'

After a large plateful of mutton casserole with dumplings for lunch, Mum, Dad and I sat alone at the big table and talked about what needed to be done, when and in what order, who was responsible for which actions and where the wedding would take place. I mentioned to them Mrs Bell's concern about money.

'Tell her not to worry on that score,' Mum offered. 'We will handle the expense of the reception and flowers, but if she can help Gwen with the cost of the dress, that would do, I think. That really shouldn't be up to us, and she will be grateful to have at least some part to play. Frank, I suggest you see the vicar at Longham Church tomorrow to set up the three weeks for the wedding banns and arrange a date that will suit everyone.'

I looked at Dad who held up his hands in mock surrender. He said, 'If you think I've got any part to play in all this, apart from paying for it, you're crazy. You're the only male that has anything to do with this bun fight. Understand, son, that the whole ceremony is focused on the women. Your job is to look clean and handsome, do what you are told and support your bride. Apart from not having too much to drink at the reception, that's your role done – apart from the rest of your life, that is. Frank, we're very pleased for you and Gwen. We've become very fond of her in the short time we've known her. So, we wish you both as happy a life as your mum and I have.'

That's it. That's all my dad said, but I suspected that all the lessons to be learned and all the priorities for the occasion were all there.

It wasn't long before the wedding arrangements took on a life of their own. There were colour schemes, styles and floral arrangements all being planned by the women. Mum tried to remove some of the wilder ideas, and I had to reinforce that it all had to be agreed upon by Gwen, who would always have the final say.

The following day I travelled to Dereham where Janice met me at the front door.

'You'll just have to take her out,' she announced. 'She's driving me crazy!'

'All in good time, Janice. I have talked to my family, and they say, emphatically, that you need not worry about the expenses. They will be covered. If you and Gwen sort out the dress, Mum and Dad will cover the rest. When I take Gwen out now, we will go to a jeweller for her to choose a ring. I mean, we'll need to get one that she likes and that fits.'

I continued, 'The only thing I'm nervous about is choosing the right moment to propose, but that will probably look after itself, or be manipulated by Gwen if she thinks that I've taken too long. We all need to talk about this, but I wanted you to know about the money. That's just between us,' I said with a smile.

'Thank you so much, Frank. That's a big burden off my mind.'

We walked through into the living room. I instinctively ducked because I thought there would be another pillow coming at high speed in my direction.

'What have you two been talking about without me?' Gwen asked hotly.

'Settle down, young lady. All will become abundantly clear in the very near future. Have you been a good girl? Are you ready for a little drive in the open air?' I teased.

At that, Gwen jumped up on her one good leg, holding on to my arm. She was fully dressed, ready to go. She squealed as I gathered her up, went out of the front door and placed her up on the seat of the trap. I covered her knees with a rug, and we waved goodbye to Janice.

Within a few minutes we were in Market Square, parked outside some shops, which included a jeweller.

'Now, my beautiful Gwen, I am going to carry you in for you to choose an engagement ring. It's your choice so that it's to your taste and style, and the size is right. If this were up to me, I would get it all wrong.'

'Oh! You lovely, lovely man. You, Frank Matthews, are all my dreams in one basket. What are you waiting for? Let's go!'

Gwen and the jeweller started a deep conversation. I moved away and got dazzled by all the highlights, which were bread and butter to every jeweller in the world.

Finally, Gwen and the jeweller made noises of agreement, and I refocused.

'Look, my love,' she said, 'this is what I wish for. It's not too expensive, but I love it, and it fits,' she declared, her eyes sparkling. 'That's a diamond in the middle, with a small emerald on each side. With my hair colour, the green sits naturally, and the setting is shaped so that it doesn't catch on things. What do you think?'

'I think I've never seen you look more beautiful. The ring's fine, too. Excuse me a moment.' After paying for it I returned to where Gwen was busily admiring her new ring and then got her comfortable in the trap once more.

'I understand from some sound advice from my dad that this whole thing is women's business and I shouldn't get in the way. So I'm giving this whole project over to you. I am here for anything you might need me to do, and I mean "anything," – but from now on, you take over the reins. Tell me what you think.'

'I think you should pull over so I can kiss you for the beautiful way you went about choosing my ring. If it weren't for this silly foot, I would show my gratitude properly,' teased Gwen, her eyelids heavy. We surfaced from the kiss about half an hour later, or so it seemed, with the beginnings of sore lips.

That was the start of a considerable amount of discussion. Arrangements had to be made with the church, with the florist, with my family and, of course, with Janice and Gwen. It was decided that the wedding would be at St Andrew's and St Peter's Church in Longham, which was within walking distance of our farm. Mum said that, as her present to us, she would do the catering for the reception at the farm. She would have lots of help from Margaret and Bobbie, but could bring in some scullery girls from the village if she needed to.

Finally, Gwen's foot mended, and she went back to work. She had so much to do that she had made lists – and then lists of lists, but was working through them quite well.

I took the trap into town on Friday night with some extra rugs as the nights were drawing in. Perhaps we were not very far from having our first frost. I collected Gwen, and we drove to the best hotel in town where I had arranged for us to have dinner.

The dining room had wall-to-wall deep-pile carpet, a shining chandelier, crisp white damask tablecloths and napkins. The wine glasses sparkled with highlights as we were escorted to our seats. The wine was selected, poured and tasted, and courses were chosen. Only then did the waiters leave us.

I looked into Gwen's lovely dancing eyes, at her full lips and flawless complexion, and at her beautiful hands with their long, slim fingers tipped with exquisitely manicured nails. Her hands spoke a language all of their own, and I was learning to read their subtle movements too, which helped me to understand her thinking.

I lifted my glass.

'Here's to the most beautiful girl in the world and to the luckiest of men. To Gwen and Frank, and our future together.'

I stopped before I became too soppy. Glasses were raised, and Gwen said, 'To you and me and our future together.'

We sipped the wine, gazing at each other. I put my hand in my pocket and brought out the little green velvet-covered box, opened it and offered her its contents.

'Will you marry me, Gwen Bell? Will you be my wife?'

'Frank! How lovely! Oh, how beautifully done, my handsome man. I will marry you and consider myself the luckiest girl in the world.'

She put on the ring, and it looked beautiful.

'Frank,' she said, looking deeply into my eyes, 'I have no idea what will happen in our life together, but know this, and remember it for all time: I will always love you, whatever the situation. You are in my soul, and I love you. As a woman, there is nothing more important that I can give you. Thanks to you, I have attained my most prized gift – the gift of love.'

'As it is with you, so it is with me, my love,' I told her.

The meal was expensive but splendid. The manager had been watching, and presented us with a bottle of French Champagne, saying it was 'with the compliments of the house on this joyous occasion'. I told him we would drink it at the wedding reception and tell everyone where it had come from so that he would more than recoup the cost with some increased business. This brought a laugh, and he complimented me on my business acumen. I complimented him on his food, and honour was satisfied. The evening was a great success, and we strolled out to the trap with the bottle.

'Tonight was the greatest night of my life. I wish I could show you how much I appreciated it, but that will have to wait,' Gwen said, hugging my arm.

I dropped her home, and we kissed until I ran out of breath. The taste and feel of her were intoxicating.

'You're going to be in for a hectic time when we are married,' she chuckled.

'Looking forward to it, ma'am,' I said.

Chapter 7

The Wedding

Norfolk, Saturday 24th October, 1914

From my point of view, all the arrangements I had to make or oversee had been made or overseen. The women were generating a tremendous amount of energy in their enthusiasm. I had brought Gwen and Janice over to the farm for some 'Counsels of War', and there were more lists, more sewing, lots of secrecy and whispers from the girls.

I sought out my brothers for a bit of company, having been banished from the house by the sheer number of women. Taciturn is the word I would choose to describe my brothers' involvement, but maybe it was just a sangfroid male approach to things in stark contrast to the accelerating enthusiasm of the women. Whatever it was, I was ribbed a lot about the wedding night, and given a lot of free advice I didn't need. We laughed together, and my brothers grudgingly said they approved of Gwen and acknowledged she was 'pretty'. I told them she was extraordinarily beautiful and received a grudging degree of agreement.

The wedding morning arrived. I awoke in my bed with the goose-down mattress and eiderdown, thinking about the day. All the women would conspire to turn the beginning of the day into chaos. The further from that I was the better. It was now half-past seven, and the service was at eleven; plenty of time to make myself look smart and make sure that Eric, my youngest brother and Best Man, also looked smart and most importantly, had the ring. Fred, my eldest brother, had told me that he would prefer not to be Best Man, but would willingly usher people to their seats in church. This was quite acceptable because we knew he was quite a shy individual.

There was still some 'lie-in' time yet. Time to consider the wedding and my future. Saturday the 24th October, 1914 would be set in my history, and my family's history, for all time – like births and deaths. I knew, with all my being, that our marriage was right for us. It would have been more efficient and less expensive if the equivalent of a kiss could sign, seal and deliver this marriage, but no, the church had to get in on this social commitment. It would not be right 'in the eyes of God' unless they were part of it.

A handshake had been a person's bond in this part of the world for business dealings and social commitments for a long, long time. But maybe it was the women who were responsible for making weddings such a big affair, in their need to have some pomp and ceremony on the biggest day of their lives. There was also the thought that many more witnesses would put the public stamp of approval on the union, meaning the bride would feel more secure, and the groom was less likely to abscond.

I had arranged, with my forthcoming wife's approval, of course, for us to rent an isolated cottage not far from Gressenhall, just a couple of miles from the farm. She had all sorts of plans for it: new whitewash, maybe in a brownish-pinkish mix, as they do in Suffolk – the well-known 'Suffolk Pink.' She wanted new curtains, and this item fixed, and that item attended to. She needed a kitchen garden, an herb garden, and ... the list went on. I still had to work on the farm for my income too, but sooner or later it would all come together.

I found Eric and, yes, he had the ring safely in his waistcoat pocket. Together with Fred, we put the little bunches of flowers on our lapels, as Margaret and Bobbie had insisted, and set off to walk to church since this maximised the travel seats in the trap for the ladies, and also removed us from the mayhem. We'd never looked so well groomed, we three. We had walked these lanes so many times, usually with our guns for shooting pigeons, rabbits or the odd pheasant or hare. Anyone passing us now would have thought we'd just come from a big city.

We arrived at our welcoming local church, St Andrew's and St Peter's, and I sought out the vicar. He scrutinised me, but I smiled and said, 'It's all right, Vicar. This one's a certainty, with no second thoughts from either party. We're here early, and we have the ring. Gwen and her party have to come from Dereham, and I've told her not to fret if she runs a bit late. We'll understand.'

'My word, you do seem to have things in hand,' the vicar exclaimed, smiling too. 'The ladies of the church have put in an extra effort with the floral displays. Do you like them?'

'Yes,' I approved. 'I saw them when we arrived. Please thank the flower arrangers from both of us. The flowers look beautiful, which I shall mention in my speech.'

When Janice arrived, we smiled and nodded at each other. She took pride of place on the bride's side of the church, thanks to Fred's help. She wore a long green dress and matching coat that I knew would complement Gwen's copper tresses.

Then the organist started with the 'Wedding March' by Wagner, and we were off and flying. I got to my feet and just had to look back. There she was, my Gwen, in the most beautiful white dress and veil, on my Dad's arm. He had readily agreed to give her away in proxy for her own father.

As she came level with me, I stepped out to accompany her. Her smile was dazzling, with no trace of nervousness at all. We approached the vicar.

The ceremony flowed as night follows day and finished with, 'I now pronounce you, Man and Wife'.

It was time for Gwen to take off her veil. She shone with an inner glow – a lady in love. There were no other words for it, and it can never be faked. We kissed – genteelly, in the circumstances – and turned to face the rest of our lives.

We ambled together down the aisle. I noted tears in many of the older ladies' eyes but smiles on their lips. We made it outside to the triumphant tones of Mendelssohn's well-known 'Wedding March', turned to each other and kissed properly.

'Enough of that,' said Fred, my eldest brother, who had done his ushering duties well.

'Never enough, but how would you know?' I shot back. He smiled ruefully.

There was a cameraman from the *Eastern Daily Press*. He got us all lined up for a photograph; we were feeling very self-conscious and wondering if it would hurt since we'd never seen anything like this before. There was a flash of light and a puff of smoke. Then he said, 'Thank you. That was quite satisfactory. You all kept very still.'

He also wanted to ask someone about the bride and groom – who we were and how we fitted into the community. Very cleverly, Dad put Fred in charge of that since he would talk sparingly and not give away any personal details of our family to the press.

We travelled back to the farm in style, in the highly decorated trap with Eric driving. He had already made four trips with family and guests, and now it was our turn.

I smudged Gwen's lipstick even more on the way to the reception. Well, the kissing was mutual really. Gwen was whisked away to change out of her wedding dress, which had looked very special. Margaret and Bobbie had described the wedding dress at length to me. Apparently, it was full-length with long sleeves, a high collar, a full veil and a crossed lace design above the waist. *So what?* I thought. *She looked beautiful in whatever she wore.*

At the reception, I found a seat for Janice. We talked, but were continually interrupted, of course, with all the excitement in the air. She thought the wedding went very well and was so proud of Gwen and the way she looked.

'As far as I'm concerned, she may well be the most beautiful girl in the world, and I'm a fortunate man,' I told my new mother-in-law.

'Yes, you are, and I hope you won't make me a stranger. I'd like to see you both now and again.'

'I'm sure Gwen wouldn't let that happen, and neither will I,' I promised.

The tables filled up in the sunshine. Eric, as Best Man, also did a wonderful job as master of ceremonies. My speech consisted of thanking contributors to our wedding day.

First, to Janice for my beautiful bride, and then to Mum for the delicious fare, to Dad for giving Gwen away, to the bridesmaids for their loveliness and assistance to my bride, to the ladies of the church for their beautiful floral displays, and finally to the manager of the hotel for the bottle of Champagne. I got a laugh by telling everyone where we were going to be living and that visits were welcome – but not yet!

Finally, it was over. Eric loaded with luggage and presents and returned the trap to the farm.

'That went pretty well, I thought,' he said.

'Of course! All down to our arrangements and hard work,' I jested. 'Did that come up to your expectations?' I asked Gwen.

'Oh yes! I thought the service was just lovely, especially the flowers. My one and only wedding day was perfect.'

Our cottage came into sight, and we pulled up outside the brick wall in front. I helped Gwen down, immediately sweeping her into my arms and carrying her through the door. It was a reasonably tight fit as the door was not designed for that sort of activity. Eric kindly brought in the luggage and the presents, kissed Gwen on the cheek and shook my hand.

'Good luck, you two,' he said as he waved and drove away.

Amongst the things I had brought with me were a bottle of celebratory, cold white wine and a box of soft-centred chocolates – her favourites – soon to become our mutual signature of luxury. They helped round off our honeymoon night in high style.

Chapter 8

A NEW LIFE TOGETHER AND ITS GATHERING STORM CLOUDS

At some time, we must have slept because the morning light was strong when I awoke with my darling Gwen beside me, her face soft in sleep. A little smile seemed to hover about her mouth.

I lay there beside her, remembering how she had looked after Eric had left, standing still in the middle of the kitchen in her prim dress and button-up shoes, a look of vulnerability and yet anticipation on her lovely face.

My hands had bracketed her face, and we had kissed gently, then a little harder until she opened her mouth and her tongue met mine. Our bodies pressed together, and our hands started to roam, our breaths coming faster as though we were running.

There were buttons on the back of her dress, which slowly came undone, leaving the smoothest, velvety skin for my fingers to stroke. Soon, our upper bodies were bare and rubbing against each other, the pink nipples on her breasts revealed at last for me to see. My mouth encased one and sucked it gently, and her movements and gasps became more desperate and urgent.

With a pile of clothes in the middle of the kitchen floor, we started to climb the stairs – touching, stroking, feeling, exploring.

Gwen fell backwards onto the bed, and I lifted her feet from the floor. It was obvious that we were both more than ready, and that first gasp was so natural yet so exciting.

The first time was more like a chariot race, just needing to give and take all the dreams and needs we had both felt and built over our courting time. We had both explored that, satisfied that and joined forces in a thunderous shout of exaltation, of satisfaction, of togetherness. Time lost its meaning as we continued to chart new lands, new feelings and responses.

I had reminded Gwen that she had once said she would like to explore each other endlessly, and now was the opportunity.

'Oh! Yes,' she had cried. 'I remember, so let's do that, shall we?'

And we did, for what seemed hours, stroking with fingertips and nails and finding out the secret special places that produced pleasure, until we fell asleep at some time. We awoke only twice during the night, and it was so sweet, new, and gentle.

'Everything I dreamed of,' she had purred after the last time. Then we had slept like spoons.

As my mind returned to the present, I found the tea and sugar in predictable places. I made some tea and put in milk that we had brought from the farm. Gwen responded to my kiss on her cheek upon my return with a stretch.

'Hello, darling. What time is it?'

'By the sun, about nine o'clock. Welcome to a new day, Mrs Matthews. Here's a cup of tea for you. Is there anything else I can do for you?'

'Yes, wait, I'll be back,' and with a distinct hip-sway, Mrs Matthews made her way to the bathroom.

The week's honeymoon saw a prodigious amount of work put into our little cottage. Walls were whitewashed inside and pinkwashed on the outside after the old 'Suffolk Pink' fashion. This had started in Suffolk in Medieval times, but had spread to Norfolk and even Essex. Red clay and even pig's blood, supposedly, were added to the lime whitewash, giving cottages a warm pinkish, brown colour. No two were the same because they were personally made on the spot and the ingredients varied in quantity and type. Other ingredients included elderberries and sloes.

Trees were trimmed, weeds uprooted and composted, and household stuff unpacked and neatly put away. The fence at the back was repaired so that we could keep some chickens for meat and eggs, and a vegetable garden was installed with a small-meshed wire-netting surround to protect it from the chickens, the rabbits and the innumerable other creatures of the area that fancied something tastier than grass.

All this was interspersed with lots of loving, sometimes arriving at the most surprising moments, such as hanging out clothes, bending over the sink and even up a ladder, which had collapsed on us before the 'job was finished,' so to speak. Luckily, we were not injured, and 'all's well that ends well'. However, the word 'ladder' would bring a smile to Gwen's face, and a sensitivity around the eyes as the mental picture was renewed.

Gwen had done some washing in preparation for returning to work, and having her out in the open garden, in total privacy, with her arms up and her hands full of pegs and clothes was irresistible. Her breasts were outlined by the tight material of her temporary blouse, and they cried out for some attention, which was duly given and well reciprocated,

Bending over the sink was equally stimulating, and I got to rejoice in her deep chuckle. Gwen, too, had her moments when she saw an opportunity for fun, called sex. Her eyes sparkled, her lips turned up at the ends, if not kissing, and a thoroughly good time was had by all.

Chris Shaw

It was a memorable week, but in no time we both had to go back to work. On that Monday morning, Gwen caught the bus to Dereham while I walked up the road to the farm.

My brothers said I was looking peaky and should spend more time eating and less time loving. I told them their jealousy was on show. Mum said she could see I was happy, which must mean Gwen was too. I told her about the progress we had made with the cottage, and she seemed genuinely pleased.

Dad had to have his say, but it was about the war, which had begun on 28th July 1914, before our wedding. The current opinion was generally that it would all be over before Christmas, so we should wait and see.

If I was intending to 'join up,' Dad suggested that I help him get in the next harvest first, since Fred and Eric were both considering enlisting too. So it was agreed that we would prepare for the next harvest by ploughing, harrowing and planting the various crops during winter and spring, harvest them in the summer and early autumn and then take stock of the current position of the war, and what Britain needed in the way of any more manpower.

About Christmas time, Gwen whispered her little secret to me that she was pregnant and due in mid-summer, sometime in July 1915, she thought. The family was naturally delighted. She looked, and said she felt, spectacular.

Naturally, Gwen was most unhappy that I was even thinking of leaving her to go away, possibly to get myself killed. I had to do some hard talking to make her see the priorities. There were the family needs of the harvest and the manpower needs of the country.

One argument I used was that I was going to enlist so that I could persuade the Germans not to invade England and carry off all our women. Another argument was that all of us had to help carry part of the burden, and so it went on. We did have most of the year together before we even had to think about making a decision, in spite of Lord Kitchener's posters everywhere, telling us, 'YOUR COUNTRY NEEDS YOU!'

The cottage became smarter and more functional. I bought half a dozen of Mum's best laying hens, built a henhouse with nest boxes and waterproofed the roof with tarpaper. Our vegetable and herb gardens were growing nicely, supplemented with the by-product of the hens. Gwen's meals became tastier and tastier with extensive practice in the use of our fresh ingredients.

The year 1915 saw the farm crops planted, grown and harvested, but news of the war was not good. There was a naval blockade of all German ports, and the Germans had used poison gas for the first time. In April, Allied forces had landed at Gallipoli in Turkey. British, Australian and New Zealand troops were amongst them, and I gather it was very poorly managed. The war was not going well, and considerable pressure was being brought to bear for all able-bodied men to sign up.

Chapter 9

THE BIRTH OF CHRISTOPHER

Norfolk, 13th July, 1915

There was a tremendous amount of activity surrounding the birth of our child. Mum asked me to tell her when Gwen started washing the curtains. Frankly, I couldn't see what that had to do with anything.

One afternoon, I told her that, indeed, Gwen had started washing the kitchen curtains that morning. Mum railed on me for not telling her sooner. I got Tiffany into the trap while Mum put some stew, which had been on the stove for days, into a jug. She brought a heap of other stuff in a large wicker basket, too. I had no idea what was going on.

Margaret had been sent to the cottage earlier to look after Gwen and to fetch the midwife from the village when it became necessary. For me, again, it felt like the run up to our wedding where men were virtually 'surplus to requirements'.

We arrived at the cottage to be told that the midwife had been sent for. It sounded as if Gwen's labour had started!

The stern-faced old midwife arrived and stared at me as though I had committed a crime. I was ordered to produce lots of hot water and clean linen and told to keep well away from what was exclusively 'women's business'. Time went by, the family came and went, and my concern for Gwen and the baby grew. Just when I was about to barge in and demand to know what was going on, there was a little cry. It was just a small sound, but then it was repeated, louder, and again more loudly still. That was the moment! I opened the door and flew inside. Our baby was born on 13th July 1915.

Gwen lay on the bed with an exhausted smile on her lovely face. The stern old midwife had a very soft smile on her well-used face as she held out our newborn, wrapped in clean linen, for me to hold. I took the little bundle very carefully and looked at the midwife, who just said, 'Boy!'

He lay there in my arms. This was beyond words. What do you say at such a momentous time? I had no idea, so I kissed his forehead and bade him welcome to our world. Then I kissed Gwen and told her she was extremely talented to have produced such a beautiful boy.

It wasn't long before the stew came in handy. Then I knew what a canny woman my mother was. She'd seen all this before and knew everything that needed to be done. Fortunately, the birthing had gone through without a hitch.

Janice was brought in the trap from Dereham. She beamed with delight at the little one. Gwen had suggested strongly to me that he should be called 'Christopher', for no other reason than that she liked the name.

There were the feeds, the nappies, more feeds, ever more nappies and just occasionally some sleep. Christopher looked to have the makings of a fine lad, and we all hugged each other a lot.

Caring for Christopher was such a full-time job that if we were not careful, we both stayed indoors concentrating on just one thing, and the days and nights never varied. I saw this happening so made a point of taking over, sending Gwen on little shopping chores and visits to friends, just for an hour or so. At first, she was very fearful of leaving the baby 'in case something happened', but then she became more enthusiastic about these little excursions.

She started to relax about Christopher being in my care, and to look forward to her outings in a guarded sort of way.

At one time, after I had been to Dereham for some groceries and yet more 'baby' things, I returned with a parcel for her. And didn't her eyes light up. When she opened it, there was a little moss-green hat in a box – it was at the same time stylish, cute and somehow humorous, without being in any way comical. It attract-ed attention without being offensive, and it even lifted the mood of the observer. I don't know who had made it, but it was definitely designed by a master milliner.

August, September and October went by, the harvest was in and there was no longer any excuse for me not to go into the army. I had talked myself out to Gwen, trivialising the length of time I would be away and the minimal danger I would be in, referring to the war as a 'brief little skirmish' that we would go and sort out, and soon be home again. She remained unimpressed, withdrawn and even panicky at times.

Our farewell was a lonely, clinging and sad affair. There were lots of tears from both of us but duty called. Patiently, Dad waited in the trap, ready to take me to the station to catch the train from Dereham to Norwich, where the induction would be. After that, we would go to a training camp before shipping out to France or Bel-gium.

'I know you'll do your best, Frank – you always do – but try to come home safe and sound, boy, or there will be a lot of tears,' he said.

'I'll try, Dad, and I thank you and Mum for everything you have done for me, and now for Gwen too. Keep in touch with her, please. She'll be distraught and alone, but she'll make a great mother for Christopher.'

'We'll all do our bit, Frank. Good luck!' He shook my hand, wheeled the trap around and trotted Tiffany away.

PART 2: WAR

Chapter 10

A WAKE-UP CALL

France, September, 1916

A colossal shell screamed overhead, exploding just over the
back of our trench. My ears rang like Westminster Abbey at
a coronation. I was, temporarily, completely deaf. The other soldiers were cowering down and holding their ears too. Some
were covered in earth where part of the trench had collapsed. I
found myself shouting and waving my fist in the air.

'Bloody hell, you kraut bastards! The sun is hardly up, and I was
sound asleep! You rotten sods! There will be payback for this, and
soon. I bloody need my beauty sleep. What about that don't you
bloody understand?'

Then their mortars started, trying to find us, with not even a
cup of tea in the belly yet. Bullets began pinging around us. The
noise of the artillery shells, mortars and sniper fire was constant,
terrifyingly loud and bloody dangerous – and still no breakfast! I
never was at my best in the morning, but I thought my little show
of bravado was quite excellent. I'd given it enough for the moment.
Now, I needed to take stock.

Not knowing where my sergeant was, I started ordering the
new boys to sort things out. I grabbed a periscope and slowly lifted
it over the trench lip to see over the top. The last thing we needed
was to be repairing our damaged nest, like busy little ants, and

have Jerry coming across 'No-man's Land' in force, charging right down our throats.

Good. So far, no Jerries, but with an opening chord like that, the whole orchestra wouldn't be far away. Bloody hell. What a start to the morning. My ears were still ringing.

'Corporal Matthews?'

'Yes, Sergeant.'

'Are you all right, Corporal?'

'Yes, Sergeant.'

'What's been done?'

'Well, I've sorted out a "wounded" detail to see to the injuries and told the squaddies to get stretcher-bearers if they were needed. Another squad is shoring up the trench since we don't want the whole thing to collapse and kill us – doing Jerry's work for them. And I've just had a look up top to make sure Jerry isn't on his way yet. But basically, I've thought of little else than a nice cup of tea, to be honest.'

'Well done, Frank. I suggest you keep an eye out so that Jerry doesn't surprise us. As soon as I can spare the men, someone will organise a brew. It'll give us all a much better outlook on life.'

'Thank you, Sergeant. You know I'm not a morning man, and this little early morning number has given me the shits.'

'Oh, dearie, dearie me! We can't have ugly old Frank losing his much-needed beauty sleep, can we? Corporal, get your act together and up periscope, or we'll all be caught napping!'

'Yes, Sergeant.'

I secured my kit and rifle within easy reach and carefully raised the camouflaged periscope above the lip of our trench again to check on any activity between our trenches and the Germans. Nothing, so far. Hopefully, I'd get my cup of tea before indulging in some wholesale slaughter, yet again. It was a tad different here from home – where I'd have a nice cup of tea and a buttered scone for 'elevenses' on the table with a gingham tablecloth in the bay window with a view out to the lawn, the flowerbeds and the pond circled by horse-chestnut trees.

Arriving in France in early 1916, my nine months over here had been one long killing spree. The fact that I was still alive was a miracle. I have seen more deaths every day than most people would get to see in a dozen lifetimes. I had become a little bit concerned that I was getting used to it.

What did that mean? Probably that I'd started to successfully adapt to this existence, but I had a very nasty feeling, deep down, that there was going to be a downside to that. Death didn't terrify me now because I'd lived with it for so long that it was just part of the background scenery, which was good, but I mustn't get sloppy, or some Jerry would 'top' me for sure.

The 'powers that be' had seen fit to give me a brand new rifle – an S.M.L.E. or Small Magazine Lee Enfield 0·303 fitted with Periscopic Prism telescopic sight. When I had first enlisted and finished my basic training, the army had spotted that I was a good shot and had sent me off for some special training at our sniping school at Acq, in Northern France. Now I did sniper work and forward scouting for HQ. This was good for me because it meant I didn't have to fraternise with a shower of terrified youngsters all the time or indulge in a lot of meaningless chatter. I could be my own man who made my own decisions to keep me alive. Crawling about in the mud is a child's dream of heaven, and I'd learned to embrace that too, although several degrees warmer weather wouldn't go astray.

This bloodbath had gone on far longer than anyone had reckoned, and I recognised at that precise moment with great clarity, that by any means possible I had to survive and return to my family. Gwen and Christopher needed me. That had to be my Number One priority.

A little passing thought triggered the question as to whether my physical or mental survival was going to be the more difficult.

'All right, Frank,' I said to myself, 'you've identified your need. Now monitor yourself and find out just which is the hardest. Be very good at what you do, Frank, and use all your skills because you have to get back to your loved ones!'

Chapter 11

BACON FOR BREAKFAST

I woke slowly, a luxury in itself, rather than being torn from sleep by the sound of artillery shells raining down or machine gun fire trying to rip me to bits, which was the norm. My greatcoat was wrapped around my thin shoulders, allowing me some warmth on this early morning in our trench. My body and mind felt a little rested for the first time in months.

It was nearly dawn. Smoke drifted from the cooking fires behind us, and there was the unmistakable smell of cooking bacon.

Where had that come from?

Were we expecting a visit from a general?

Maybe it wasn't for us after all. Perhaps it was just for some high-ups with their scrambled egg authority spread over their peaked caps, which would go very well with the bacon, I thought. Just my little joke, you understand. I could almost feel a smile coming on, and when was the last time that happened?

I watched the other sleepers in our trench awaken slowly as the bacon smell got up their nostrils and into their heads. Charlie, one of our squaddies who I happened to bunk down next to last night, looked at me, blinked, and asked, 'Is that real or am I still dreaming?' I was so tempted to ask him, 'Is what real, Charlie?' but the Hun had already given us more nightmares than we needed, so it wasn't fair to trouble his little mind with some added insecurity.

'It's real,' I said. 'I just don't know if it's for us.'

'Well, we'd better bloody find out fast before the other buggers swipe the lot!' he said earnestly.

We got to our feet from the bottom of the trench, which was dry for once in living memory, collected our kits, rifles, helmets and webbing, and moved in the direction of the bacon smell that was filling my mouth with saliva. Charlie spat.

'Don't do that,' I said. 'You're going to need all of that to wrap around a big, juicy piece of middle rasher.'

'Shut up, Frank,' he said, and spat again.

We arrived at the end of a queue of soldiers in various states of dress, having also just woken up. The sun peeped at us over the horizon, and just for a moment, I thought it was going to stay there, hiding from my marksmanship. *Almost another little joke there, Frank. Must watch out or we'll have the whole Variety Playhouse cast performing after breakfast*, I thought while laughing silently to myself.

I stretched and heard various 'pops' and 'snaps' from my joints, which were ageing far too quickly. It must come from lying around in wet fields of cold mud for hours on end doing nothing – well, apart from waiting to be killed any second, that is. Always watching, always checking to see if anyone was wearing a Jerry helmet for me to kill. Maybe his name would be Helmut, a very Jerry name. A very jolly Jerry called Helmut in a helmet, sitting in his trench – waiting to kill Frank! I needed food – now!

We were getting closer to the bacon. I pleaded inside my head, *Now, just don't run out before I get there, please*, when I noticed a spot of bother behind me. I turned slowly – never fast because it'll get you killed – and someone had tried to jump the queue. You'd think they'd learn. I mean, we were all in the same boat. We Tommies had to stick together and play fair with each other; especially here and especially now.

Now, what did I have to do today? I'd better clean up my kit. It was terribly mucky from my crawling around in the mud for the last three days. However, my score was seven confirmed, and included a bloody machine gun trio. Old buggers they were. I called them Bach, Beethoven and Brahms before I killed them. Killing seven was good in these conditions. Just ask the sergeant. We went to the same sniper school at Acq, and he knew how much there is to learn. Killing three at a time was far more complicated than just a team of two.

The sergeant was, in truth, not much older than I was, but he already had a touch of grey showing in his hair. I couldn't begin to understand the strain of the responsibility he carried. Then again, he might say the same thing about me. He was a good bloke, fair and strongly opinionated, but, like me, he kept himself very much to himself. We had a good relationship, from an army point of view, but I knew nothing about his 'civvy' life.

My shooting had always been good, but now it was smart too, because the instructors at Acq had taught me how to use the countryside. They had taught me about camouflage and cover, the best use of the terrain and light and shade variations. I could now do all that, given the right kind of environment, like a wood or a beautiful piece of forest. If you gave me a ghillie suit and time to camouflage it properly, I could tie your shoelaces together, and you'd never know I'd been there – until you fell over.

The trouble was, I only had this bloody mud to work with, and while it stuck and camouflaged well enough, it was monochrome, two-dimensional and almost always cold and wet. I couldn't use the ghillie suit because from the air I would look like a golf green that had come adrift from its course. I told myself, 'If that's what you've got to work with, Frank, that's what you have to do. It is what it is. Stillness is your special friend – remember?'

At Acq, they also taught us map reading and range finding. That had helped me out on many occasions. But there was too much to learn in the time they gave us. I thought it was just my being slow, but all the others said so, including the sergeant, who was actually quite bright.

Breakfast was nearly here.

I started to wonder if I should keep a diary. I had thought about this before, but I didn't really think so. What would I say?

'Crawled through the mud again today. Shot seven Jerries and got back safely. Slept in the bottom of the trench, which was dry, and woke to the smell of bacon. Queued for breakfast and cleaned kit.'

I just didn't think that would be of any value to anyone. It was just stuff we did every day. I mean, I wouldn't put in a description about the 'push' over the top yesterday, when seventy-three of our lads lay bleeding, broken or dead in mud that had been bled all over before – and I wouldn't include the fact that it took only half an hour for that to happen. I wouldn't put in the fact that there was the continual thunder of heavy artillery shelling, mortars exploding, lethal rifle and machine gun fire from Jerry, which, together with the screams of the wounded, formed the background lullaby to each and every minute of every hour, day, week, month and bloody year.

This was our war, and it should stay with us. The less the civilians knew about it, the better. Imagine families knowing about all this! They'd never get going again, and there'd be no chance of peace between Jerry and us – ever. It would make for a millennium of anger, fighting and hatred to the point of attempted genocide. There must be hope after this. There wouldn't be much else.

Would a diary help my sanity? I didn't think so. I got a whiff of what it was like outside this madhouse when the new boys came to the front. Their eyes got big, their mouths opened, and I just knew that they wanted to run away. It was only their pride that stopped them. Staying, rather than running, was one of the few significant decisions they would ever have to make in their lives. It would probably kill them, but they would fight harder and be harder to kill because of it.

They looked at me, a fifty-plus-year-old man of twenty, and they didn't believe their eyes. Poor bastards! No one would have told them anything about the real conditions out here. They'd have been acquainted with the Parade Ground, two, three; rifle drill, two, three; and the names of the parts of their rifle, two, three! They'd have been well drilled and nicely turned out in Blanco and Brasso, spit and polish. Then some rude bastard would have come along and torn them away from their mums and sent them over here to this bloody hellhole! I knew, because I remembered it all so well myself.

The real problem was that I had now been on this killing spree for nearly a year, waiting to die literally every second, and have had many of my Tommy mates shot beside me in the trenches. Sometimes, it had been halfway through a conversation, or a fag, that I'd been spattered with their brain matter and blood. Perhaps the real problem was that I understood there was a point – a point beyond which you couldn't go on the battlefield – and then return to Civvy Street and survive. I mean, just imagine this:

'So, you wish to go into business, do you?' the bank manager would say.

'Yes, sir.'

'And what did you do in the war, my good man?'

Now what?

'I murdered my way across most of Europe, sir!' Or, 'I killed as many Germans as I could until I ran out of bullets, sir!' Or, 'I lived in the stinking mud for months and months on end and killed and killed and killed, and I can still hear the screams every minute of every day. So, for God's sake man, give me something to do that will make me work hard and take my mind off all the pictures of death that are in my head! Please, sir!'

I had no idea how I would deal with that situation even now, and I didn't ever want to be in that position.

I was pulled out of my reverie by a sharp, 'Next! Come on Frank, it's not like you to be late for a funeral, except your own maybe.'

'Oh! I'm so sorry, Chef. Does the Maitre d' have a table set aside for the oldest and the best?'

'None of your cheek, Frank, but I do have an extra egg for you on this exceptional day.'

'I'm truly grateful, Chef. May one enquire if this breakfast has been provided because the 'powers that be' have finally realised your hidden talent and made you a general, so you can join all the rest of the insane, authoritarian psychopaths that appear to be in charge? Or is this just because some greedy quartermaster has finally been caught with his fingers in the till, and they've brought in a replacement who hasn't yet learned the "Look after Number One Law For Quartermasters' Survival and Profit"?'

'Frank, sometimes I worry about you. But not often.'

'Yeah, I know, but keep smiling, Chef, and thanks for the egg. I'll remember that when the winter wind is blowing up my Khyber, and I have to lie down in wet mud again for the odd day or three!'

This was as good a breakfast as we've had since I didn't know when. I'd take it!

I decided that I'd been here for too long. How had I survived? I remembered thinking that men are going to die, and if I had made friends with them it would just hurt me that much more. So I didn't. Instead, I took the uncaring lesson of Londoners and made no eye contact. It saved me a heap of heartache. I'd seen bosom buddies, best mates who, when one got killed, the other spent weeks in tears and sadness, sobbing with a broken heart in a dark corner of the night. Not for me! It just meant I had to do a lot of talking to myself, but that was all right, too. No arguments from me.

However, one of the symptoms that told me my mind was not too healthy happened yesterday when we were on a forward 'push' in the early morning. I spotted a lone snowdrop, nodding in the wind. It shone as pure white innocence in this Satanic black mud. When we were pushed back later in the day it had gone, replaced by yet another shell hole. The tears came hot on my cheeks. A small symbol of my current death of innocence, maybe?

Chapter 12

ANOTHER ASSIGNMENT

I heard someone calling me to attention. 'Corporal!'

'Here, Sergeant.'

'Time to kit up, Corporal. We've just lost two new recruits to a Jerry sniper, both of them poking their heads over the top to have a look at No-man's Land. Poor bastards never had a chance, but we've got his number. The best we can figure, he's about three hundred yards due east of here. Can't see him in the periscope but that's your best bet.'

My sergeant continued, 'Now, Frank, you'd better be extra careful with this one because those two lads were shot within a second of each other. So he's experienced, and if he's that experienced, he'll know that you'll be coming for him. Right?'

'Yes. Thanks, Sergeant. Can I get a water bottle; one of those I can put in my pocket that won't rattle about and get me shot?'

'Certainly, I'll see to it. And Frank, I've managed to steal a whole boxful of Kynoch 0.303 ammo. Will that make your little heart beat faster?'

'No, Sergeant, it'll make my little heart beat slower. That stuff is so accurate and dependable that I will feel much safer. Thank you.'

I couldn't allow a Jerry sniper to knock over our new recruits before they've had a chance, but I had some thinking to do as to how I would approach this bastard. Three hundred yards from our east-facing trench was just this side of the smoke from a burning farmhouse, blowing northeast with the prevailing southwest wind. If I went south from here, through the trenches for six hundred yards, I'd be southwest of him, and could follow the other side of the smoke until he was to my north. Then, I could creep up on his position with the smoke hiding me. I could knock him over from about four hundred yards or maybe less, and he'd never see me.

'Here's your water, Frank. Good luck.'

'Yeah! I'll break a leg.'

'Corporal, when you find a suitable spot, stay there and don't come back until after dark. Jerry may be watching for any movement in the field. Hell, what am I doing? Trying to teach my grandmother to suck eggs? You know all this stuff, Frank. Just get back in one piece, or I'll be very cross, right?'

'Well, we mustn't upset the sergeant now, must we? Yes, I'll be careful, but I don't much like the idea of hanging around in case they start up the mortars or artillery in my direction. They might even send up one of their planes. But I'll work it out.'

I was back to the mud, but at least I was used to it by now. I checked all my equipment thoroughly before I left. I didn't want to get there with no ammo. Nice new stuff, that Kynoch. Strange word. Looks and sounds Scottish, and rhymes with Loch. I'd zeroed my rifle to three hundred yards so I could easily adjust for shorter or longer distances.

I knew it sounded bizarre, but they had convinced me, during my training at the sniping school, that I should 'shoot at their teeth,' and that had worked out well. If I was too close, the shot went high, but there was still about seven or so inches of head to make the kill. If the enemy was further than my estimate and my shot went low, I'd still have his neck and chest as big targets with which to kill him.

Check: water bottle with fresh water, knife, ammo—yes, that's enough—webbing, first-aid kit, hard tack, boots, done up tightly with no laces hanging free to get snagged. Map, compass, mittens, and one spade – collapsible. Check. I didn't pack my camouflaged ghillie suit. There was only mud where I was going, no vegetation, so I'd stand out like a cock on a weather vane. Also, I left the puttees behind, or my legs would have cramped up. Trouser cuffs were covered with socks, and the laces were tucked away so they couldn't snag on anything. The ammo clips were wrapped in cloth to avoid the sound of metal clinking. My 'scope sight was clean and clear.

I followed the trenches until I'd passed through the smoke. No one spoke to me on my walkthrough. They knew who I was, where I was going and what I was going to do, so they didn't want to interrupt my thoughts or actions. I reached the place I wanted to be, borrowing a periscope to get the lie of the land. This landscape was so flat there was almost no place to hide – almost.

Jerry had, very kindly, been busy building hiding places just for me to move through the landscape. They were called shell holes, and in some places were so close together that I could dig from one to another with my knife and little spade, travelling unseen from the surface using the Leopard Crawl. All I had to do was to find a line of holes going in my direction, and this angle would do very nicely.

I gave the periscope back with a nod and 'eeled' my way over the top into the first hole. Putting the spade to work, I dug a shallow connecting ditch to the next hole and wriggled through. If an airplane came over, I could play dead and never be seen amongst all the other bodies. Stillness was my friend.

The smoke was hiding me well. This was about the spot I needed to be to get a look at the Jerry sniper's location. I dug a little groove for the rifle's barrel in the dirt with my knife, about an inch and a half deep, leaving the telescopic sight just above ground level. This allowed me to search for him as though he were close by.

This was the tedious part: watch and wait, watch and wait. I'd learned to observe continually for half an hour at a time before resting for one minute and doing that over and over. The trick was to feed the information I needed into my inner mind and tell it what to look for – movement, straight lines or change – and then I could let go. I could remain still with relaxed eye muscles. Any movement or change in the environment would be instantly recognised by the subconscious and reported to the conscious brain, without the arduous work of consciously watching everything all the time.

Half an hour went by and nothing. So I rested below the lip of the hole, doing deep breathing exercises and muscle flexing. Slowly, I raised my head to start watching again.

There! Yes, there!

I spotted a new clod of dirt that wasn't there before. I now knew where he was and would wait for my chance as he didn't know I was here. He had no idea, but I could see his peephole, which was between two clods of dirt. Major breakthrough. Major!

My patience was legendary. I could outwait a spider, so I could undoubtedly outwait this Jerry. As soon as he looked through his little peephole, I'd raise my rifle two inches to clear the dirt and take out his eye, his head and his life, the murdering bastard.

I just noticed movement behind his peephole, but I had to wait until the light reflected on the other side looks as though it had gone out. This would mean not only was he looking through his peephole, but also that he was up close to it.

Slowly. Slowly. There! Now! Light's out. BANG! Got you. I saw the hand arc back and the rifle tumble in the air. No sniper has ever thrown his rifle around, so that was a kill. The sergeant would be pleased.

I thought about getting back the way I came without being seen. His comrades knew his position, and if they thought it was me that got him, rather than vice versa, they would throw everything, including mortars and artillery, in my direction.

So I wiggled my way back through the shell craters to the trench before returning to my unit.

'Christ, Frank, that was quick!' said the sergeant, by way of greeting.

'He took one look too many for his continuing good health,' I advised. 'He won't trouble your peach-fuzzed boys anymore but someone else might, so keep their heads down, will you?'

Chapter 13

AT LAST, SOME TIME OFF

Mid-morning, and it was reasonably quiet for a change. The sergeant was working his way along the trench, quietly talking to each soldier in turn. I noticed that he left a trail of smiling faces in his wake, so it had to be good news. What? We could pack up and go home? Probably not. The sergeant looked at me with a smile hovering around his mouth.

'Well, aren't you a lucky chap, Frank. We've been awarded a three-day pass starting at midday. Take your kit with you. There'll be a lorry here to take you, me and your lucky mates to a village. There'll be a place there where you can store your kit safely. Reinforcements will be here in half an hour. So look lively and leave the place nice and tidy. We don't want them to think we aren't house-proud, do we?'

'Thank you, Sergeant. I'm sure I don't know what I'll do with all that time off. This will be the first break I've had in more than a year at the front, Sergeant. No holiday camp, this, eh? I'll get a detail together to put the final touches to our little palace and try to stop the lads from being too homesick. How many of us are going out?'

'The whole company or what's left of us. Now, get yourselves sorted or they may change their minds.'

He moved along.

'Okay,' I shouted, 'scavenging detail here on the double. I want this place as tidy and serviceable as we would want it if we were just coming in. We don't want any personal stuff left about – no letters, photos, trinkets or other paraphernalia from home.'

I added, 'Square off the firing platforms and straighten the duckboards. We wouldn't want one of the newcomers to sprain an ankle and have them recall one of you, just as you are beginning to enjoy yourselves. When you've done that, go and get yourselves tidied up. You all look as though you've just crawled out from under a rock.'

There was a little titter by way of response as the team got busy. I wondered what I would find to do. The village would probably have a church, and the architecture might be interesting, or what was left of it after all the shelling. I just might scavenge for a sketchbook and pencil to do a bit of drawing. I was no great shakes at art, but seeing any girls would only remind me of Gwen, and that would be worse than seeing no girls at all. Maybe I'd have a drink with the lads after all. There might not be another chance.

The new troops arrived, looking as though they had just come out of a deep mine; definitely disoriented, confused and fearful.

'Don't worry, lads,' I said. 'You'll soon get the hang of it. Basically, it's just aiming and firing, and if you've got enough ammunition and go on for long enough you'll win the war for us, and we'd be eternally grateful to you, wouldn't we, lads? We've left it nice and tidy for you and would like it returned in a similar condition. Pick a spot and get your gear stowed. Your sergeant will be here soon. Good luck.'

Their sergeant arrived just as the other soldiers and I were leaving.

'Got them started for you, Sergeant,' I advised, before making my way to the lorry taking us to the village.

The lorry ground its way through an ocean of mud, swaying like an overloaded mule on a mountain ridge, but our spirits were up. It was quieter here, even just a little way from the front. As the distance increased and the volume of war reduced, I felt the tension fall out of my body. Had I been this tense for all those months? Would I now be able to have a bath and clean my dirty skin?

I was hoping for a chance to check with the local medico about my running sores, the itching, the deafness and my inability to sleep for more than an hour at a time. Then, there were the nightmares. The lads all complained about my waking them with my screaming. All the killing was taking a toll on my psyche.

Chapter 14

SOME TIMELY ADVICE

The lorry struggled into a little Belgian village that was several miles behind the lines. The release valves on the truck's occupants had already begun to open. Heads were swivelling, whistles and suggestive comments were being delivered to the local population, especially to the girls.

The soldiers disembarked with the enthusiasm and single-mindedness of old tourists with full bladders. They fought for the right to the front of the bar first. The sergeant and I looked at each other and grinned.

I asked, 'Old bull, young bull?' He just laughed, knowing the story. We marched in step with great decorum towards the inn, and found a couple of corner seats. Sure enough, in no more than three seconds, one of the lads fronted us with a drink each.

The sergeant looked at me and just said, 'Young bull!' We really laughed – I mean, really out of control, hysterical, couldn't-stop-if-you-paid-me type of laughter. Worse still, the poor young lad didn't know what he had done to cause it. This made it even funnier. Oh, God! That cleared away so much tension from the months of fear in our minds that I was convinced laughter should be required therapy for all soldiers, at regular intervals.

Three officers had come in separate transport to the same inn. They sat together at a table at the far end of the room.

The soldiers from our outfit got together, about thirty of them, and after being a little boisterous for twenty minutes or so at the bar, decided to join us, the NCOs.

The talk started with speculation about the date that the war would be over. The young ones always did that. They wanted to see over the next hill, have a finishing date and time, so they could get on with something else.

'Just like you do with the girls, you mean?' said the sergeant. More laughter.

'Or the boys,' said one wag.

'Oh! Come on. I just want to go home, you fellows.'

'And you think we don't. Is that it?'

'Well, no, but someone must know something that could give us a clue about a finish date to this lousy, bloody war, surely!'

'We're all in this together as a team,' the sergeant said. 'The more experienced soldiers will guide you as to how best to take care of yourselves. They're called orders, but they are always in the best interests of the team, at our level anyway.'

'What about you, Corporal? You're a sniper. How many men have you killed?'

There it was. This was what they'd always wanted to know. So, how in the hell did I sort this out? They were so young, but we were all in this together. I decided to wise them up.

'Yes, I hear your question, but you are treating this as a sixth form school competition, aren't you? It's probably all you know at your age. To you, he who kills the most 'Jerries' wins. Is that what you want to know? All right, put another beer in front of the sergeant and me, and I'll give you the benefit of my understanding of survival, where it counts most – here, in your head.'

The beer came, by which time I had my ideas sorted out.

'A good guess would be that you think I'm a cold-blooded killer, a bounty hunter when there's no bounty. Therefore, I must be a psychopathic murderer in Civvy Street. Am I right? Sniping equals ambushing equals trapping equals unfair advantage? In a word, cheating! Your looks tell me that some of you do believe that.'

I continued, 'Jerry always retaliates, and you think it's my fault that you're the ones who are getting it in the neck, and it's all so unfair, and I'm the one to blame, yes? 'What you are looking for is "truth," and there isn't any.'

All eyes were glued on me. 'What you are looking for are ways to avoid pain and death, and there aren't any.'

'What you're looking for are reasonable answers to sane questions in an insane world, and there aren't any of those, either.

I went on to tell them that their families had survived centuries of warfare, which allowed them to be here. That we ALL felt like they felt, that we were all shit-scared all the time, with headaches, shakes, diarrhoea, loss of appetite and nightmares.

Seeing that I still held their attention, I kept going. The beer must have loosened my tongue. 'To deal with the stress – and please note, gentlemen, THAT WE ALL FEEL – there are three considerations, two of which are wrong and will drive you insane or get you killed.' I counted on my fingers.

'One: if you have some bad stuff in your head that's bloody, raw, and eats at you – and you go over and over it until you can't think of anything else – you'll end up in an insane asylum or more probably dead.' The soldiers just stared at me.

'Two: if you have some bad stuff in your head that's bloody, raw, and eats at you – and you try to forget it and ram it down out of sight where it can't be seen, ever again – you'll end up in an insane asylum or more probably dead.' Now their mouths dropped open in surprise.

'Three: if you are able to treat this insanity, called war, as a temporary reality, as in, "this is how it is just now, but not forever, and I'm not responsible for any of it", then it's as if you are in a play on a stage. Then, and only then, will you have a chance, perhaps, of sanity and survival.'

'Do you mean like climbing on and off a bus?' asked the same small soldier.

'Well done,' I told him, 'that's exactly what I mean. Here you are on a bus, going to where it's going. When you go home, you get off the bus, and it disappears into the distance. That means you can start to reclaim the life you had before you had to get on the bus, and you can let the bus go on its way without you.'

'If you don't kill Jerries, they will most certainly try very hard to kill you. You should not sink the bad things out of sight or focus exclusively on them. They happen to all of us, and you must move on. Do you understand, at least, some of that?'

There were nods of comprehension and some smiles.

'Because if you do, and you practise that then, providing Jerry doesn't put a bullet in you, you can go home to your mums and dads with at least some hope of finding a wife, settling down and having a normal life in Civvy Street. Like most of us, you'll have some nightmares and occasional screaming in the night, and that's normal. It's just the mind settling down after all this shit. Just re-member to warn your wife though, or you may find she's in someone else's bed!'

I looked around at these young men, trying very hard to get a handle on all this.

'You are on a bus, on a stage. When you get off, leave it behind and move forward in the reality you knew before you came to this mad world. Good luck.'

Chapter 15

TEAMWORK

Over many months, we had moved from one wet, muddy, bloody trench to another, another, and yet another. It sometimes seemed as if we had lived in this landscape for years. With the pushes and fall-backs we'd had over the past months, the only change I could see were in the faces of our lads; replacements for those poor bastards who had, incredibly bravely, gone over the top to face those bloody Maxim and Vickers machine guns, but had not returned. Their bodies had to be left out in the elements until they became bloated and stank. It was not a favourite detail to be sent to retrieve them in the night.

At one point, Ken, my new observer, and I had been trucked a few miles south to much more pleasant countryside. Here, there were trees and grass, definitely more my 'cup of tea'. The whole ambience was more restful than those terrible trenches. The effect on my mood was uplifting, almost to the point where I could smile – almost.

But the nightmares were still with me, and getting worse, probably because there were more dreadful things to dream about. My brain would never be able to clear out all those terrible sights of bursting bodies from artillery fire, complete facial disintegration from sniper fire and fatal damage to men from mortars, leaving them as carcasses. At least there were no tears, no sadness now. I just had flat emotions. *A definite plus*, I thought.

The change of countryside meant that I could start using all that knowledge I'd been given at sniper training school. I could also start using my ghillie suit, which was basically a string suit with bits of brown and green camouflage material attached. Its main aim was to break up any lines that were anywhere near straight since straight lines do not occur in nature.

We were taught to attach local plant material into the netting as well, and also to incorporate stuff to break up the outline of my rifle and 'scope sight – an obvious ploy when I thought about it.

During training, we'd had a demonstration from the sergeant there, and I took to it immediately. I just knew that, with my previous experience of stalking and field-craft, and enough time to prepare the suit correctly, I could get very close to another sniper without being spotted.

By this time, Ken, my observer, and I had had a couple of random assignments but nothing regular. He had very sharp eyes, aided by a pair of binoculars with a small tripod, and he was now assigned to me permanently. Sometimes, a signaller also accompanied us with a telephone and a spool of wire so we could communicate directly with HQ.

As a small squad, we would move forward to a place of concealment to observe enemy troop movements and artillery emplacements. The signaller would arrange it so I could report these positions back to HQ, and they would order our artillery to shell a particular area. We would report on the coordinates of the 'sighter' shells, to get the best possible accuracy to their shots in the shortest possible time. It worked pretty well until Jerry worked out where we were and sent out their snipers to kill us.

However, I'd worked out a system of my own to optimise that situation. The three of us would get to where we were needed, report what we saw, help the artillery with range finding, then the signaller would retreat, leaving Ken and me in our ghillie suits. Ken's job was to cover my back as I set up my position to wait for the Jerry snipers to appear, and then leave. I'd kill them from my concealed position before returning to report to my sergeant.

A dangerous game, yes, but since I was in the area first, I could choose my ground and my cover. We had to be a bit careful that Jerry hadn't put someone out there first, of course, but Ken's eyes could spot stuff that even I couldn't see. Thanks to his observational skills that had been honed by his hobby of bird watching, we had avoided being 'trumped' every time – so far.

We were sent out one morning at about 7 a.m. What day or month it was, I had no idea, but the sun was shining, and it was warm. I'd guess maybe April, 1917. The three of us went out into the sparse woodland to establish an observation post where we could see Jerry's movements to the north of us. There was a rumour that a Jerry 'push' was coming from an unexpected quarter, and the brass didn't want to be caught napping.

There was a small hill in precisely the right place for an observation post to the north of our lines with a slightly elevated view of Jerry's positions. In truth, a hill in these so-called 'Low Countries' was little more than a molehill in my native Norfolk.

I told Ken and our signaller, Paul, that the hill was too prominent and would be an excellent position for a Jerry sniper to be in place already. If so, he would think that we would approach from the southwest, where our lines were, and he would be waiting, covering precisely that quadrant. So I would need to come at him from the east, from behind him. In this position, while the Jerry lines would be hidden, I would be able to see the sniper and take him out. Then we would have a choice of position – provided there was only one sniper.

When we arrived at the bottom of the hill, I told them to hunker down and wait for my signal to join me.

'How long will you be?' asked my signaller Paul, apparently not having done much of this type of work.

'Why? Have you got somewhere special to be?'

'No! Of course not! I just wondered how long it would take you to signal us to join you.'

'Well,' I said, 'maybe two, maybe three days.'

I watched him try to assimilate this and fail. I winked, told them to take it in turns to keep a lookout and then wriggled forwards. About ten yards out, I looked back and was pleased not to be able to see them. I did another ten yards and turned, very, very slowly, and still couldn't spot them. I continued on to the north-east.

At some point, I turned, focused on where they should be, and saw Ken's stationery finger, just visible in the grass. It was pointing to a spot directly in front of him, to my left.

The next time I looked, the finger had two fingers from the other hand forming scissors about halfway up. I waited, and slowly three fingers were raised. Ken had spotted something about halfway up the slope, about three hundred yards from his position. I continued my way north-east and upwards, watching and waiting, before very slowly moving to the west at the same level on the hill and towards the spot Ken had pointed to.

'Slowly, Frank, always slowly. Quick movements will get you killed,' I muttered to myself.

Suddenly, I smelled something. It was alien to the environment. No flower or blossom I'd ever smelt came anywhere close to it. It was ... meat! Meat, with a sort of herby smell. Bloody sausage! Jerry was eating a sausage while he waited to kill me. Thank you, prevailing southwest wind. Now I knew where he was, within a few yards.

Yes! There was his front sight, quite still, but the straight line of a piece of his rifle barrel had given him away. I followed the straight line back and saw his camouflaged 'scope sight with just a hint of the edge of his helmet.

The front sight dropped slowly. The German sniper had been having a look through his 'scope but had not seen anything. He relaxed by putting the rifle down and leaned forwards, maybe to get some more sausage.

BANG! My rifle fired, under instructions from my subconscious, and I saw the fluids from his head form a curve in the air before falling to earth. A definite kill, but would it alert any others?

I waited for another half-hour before I signalled for Ken and Paul to join me. I thought about Jerry's sausage but really didn't fancy it in its probable current state.

The three of us went around the hill more to the south-west, where there was a view of both our lines and the German lines. I would be able to brief our artillery as to distance and direction to Jerry's primary targets of artillery and mortars and then to the secondary targets of their forward HQ and its officers. Should Jerry take it in mind to come after us, we had all our forces in range on this side of the hill to persuade them otherwise.

Two boulders were ideal for spotting cover. The smaller one held less risk since the large boulder would be the obvious choice for anyone who had not been through our training.

I contacted our Field HQ with the wired telephone that Paul had brought, where officers were standing by to hear from us.

'Poppa, this is Sherry. Poppa, this is Sherry. Do you read? Over.'

'Sherry, this is Poppa. Sherry, this is Poppa. Read you loud and clear. Over.'

'Poppa, we have artillery emplacements, mortars and rear trenches as their possible forward HQ. Our position is 800 yards due north of your current position. Jerry's artillery is 2000 yards from us at an angle of 120 degrees to that. The mortars are 1600 yards from us at 150 degrees. The possible forward HQ is equidistant between those two but a further 800 yards to the rear of a line joining the previous two targets. Work that out, and I will give you readings on a couple of sighters. Over.'

'Thank you, Sherry. Let us know how well my boys do their sums. Over.'

'Keep a lookout, Ken. They'll be in play very soon.'

'Right!'

The scream of the first shell came overhead almost immediately. After a brief moment, it exploded about one hundred yards behind their artillery.

'Sherry to Poppa. You are one hundred yards long, Poppa, but your boys do quick maths! Over.'

'Thanks, Sherry. Next one. Over.'

This one took out their forward gun. It was hard not to cheer.

'Bull's-eye, Poppa. You have the other readings. Over and out.' I turned to the others.

'Right, you two. It's time for you to get out of here before the whole of Jerry's available troops come charging over that hill. Run south-east, behind the hill, so Jerry can't see you, and go round the back of our lines before reporting in.'

'What about you, Frank? Where will you be?' demanded Ken.

'I'll be just fine, covering your little backsides on your way out. Don't worry about me. I'll be back after dark with any luck, but we don't want a return match with Jerry. Let's leave it at one to nil. Now get out of here!'

Chapter 16

A LONE ASSIGNMENT

They scuttled away out of sight, and I found a nice little depression that would hide me, keep me out of the wind and, with my camouflaged suit and rifle, allow me to be invisible except possibly from the air. I thought about the care I'd taken with the suit, and maybe I would even be invisible from above.

There was a large angle of the hill to watch because if they did come for me, they could conceivably come over the top or from the left. However, it was much more likely they would come from the right, or east, where they would be in the shadow of the hill and safe from our troops.

Now I needed to watch and wait.

I thought about my family. My death, for them, would be pretty bad – especially for Gwen. We had such a special thing between us. We needed each other, but bubbling away in my head recently had been the question of how she would deal with me. How would she, and more especially Christopher, cope with this psychotic night screamer who couldn't hold a conversation or an idea for any length of time, even if his life depended on it? Well, apart from my garrulous talk to the troops, which had come out of nowhere.

Why was that? Maybe it was a throwaway gesture of hope that I could keep some of this lot alive for just a little longer. But I still couldn't relate to anyone else, with the possible exception of the sergeant.

'Trained to kill; trained to plough.' That would pretty well sum me up. Wording for my headstone, perhaps? 'Beloved' too; surely? I just wanted to survive and go back to live with Gwen and Christopher.

'It'll never happen,' said my head. 'You're too messed up to live with her ever again, or at least, not without messing her up too. What about Christopher, growing up but not able to sleep because he doesn't know when this strange man, supposedly his father, who has suddenly come into his life, is going to start screaming again? It would be like living with an old man who has Tourette's syndrome.'

There would be continual apologies from Gwen to other people: relatives, friends and strangers. Some I would insult, some I would belittle, and the rest I would ignore by giving them my silent treatment. Kill, embarrass or ignore: those three responses were the sum total of my social skills after all this crap. Not much to recommend me in Civvy Street.

I speculated about where my skills went that I once had. I used to be relaxed when talking to farmers, blacksmiths, vets and their wives, anyone really. It didn't matter whether it was at the markets or at a social tea. No man did well with beautiful young ladies, except perhaps the sort that had once met Gwen at the doorway to the dance, and if I ever came across him again, I might just teach him another lesson: not to be so proud of the notches on his gun. I knew I had to sort out some way of mending myself before going back to my family.

I was pulled out of my confusing thoughts by someone sneaking around without the benefit of a ghillie suit. It was a German, leopard-crawling through the grass and making a great hash of it. I could hear him from fifty yards away. The grass was waving all over the place. Maybe the Jerries were running out of experienced scouts and snipers at last. That would make my life a whole lot easier, but if I became in any way sloppy, it would be 'curtains' for me.

Of course, if they were really, really bright, they would use this soldier as a decoy and send an experienced sniper to find me and kill me, when, or hopefully for the noisy young man, before I killed him.

Again, wait and watch, wait and watch. The noisy 'lad' had long gone down the hill and would no doubt circle back to the east, then north, to avoid being seen by anyone on our side.

I needed to swivel to see behind me, and uphill, but as usual, slowly, very slowly. Even with all my camouflage, it took ten minutes to turn my head. With the mesh over my face, no one could see the shine from the whites of my eyes. The slight breeze was moving the local plant material that I had attached to my suit, in a natural way. It would be doing its job.

I waited.

There! A glint. He was just above me, about one hundred yards away. A 'piece of cake', Marie Antoinette. The shot would be at a slightly awkward angle for my body, but I'd found that relaxing the muscles would extend them with less tension, and I could maintain an extreme position for longer, and my aim would be steadier.

I was becoming an unfeeling killer. Well yes, of course I was. It was the easiest way to survive psychologically here. It was the way that I'd found least hurtful. There could be no hurt when there was no feeling.

BANG! His head exploded. Too bad, my aged enemy, this was war, and we will win.

I'd have to stay here for another couple of hours until it got dark, then I should be able to get out of here safely.

Chapter 17

Contact with the enemy

Another chilling winter in the trenches was over, and I was still in one piece. The last few months had seen me lose even more weight and age well beyond my years. My conversation and social interactions were virtually non-existent – my manners brutish. My body was falling apart, and my mind was following suit. My concentration was fading, and I relied on that to get my kills and get me back to the trenches again after my successful skirmishes, but if my deterioration continued, it would be curtains for me, for sure.

One of the company officers, Captain Stone, came to see Ken, my observer, and me. The captain was not very tall and looked as though the war had stripped some weight from him, too. He was a pipe smoker and had a comfortable, good-natured way about him.

'Good morning, Corporal Matthews. We've got a bit of action coming just a few miles from here. I've been asked to supply a scout and an observer for duty there. Your assignment will be a few miles north of Armentiéres. We need a couple of competent men to look out for any enemy in a small valley near some woodland. Take a few hours to get yourself cleaned up. There will be a lorry waiting for you at sixteen hundred hours. You're to report to Captain Youngman. He'll show you the ropes. Understood?'

'Yes, sir,' we said together and saluted. 'How long will we be away?' I asked.

'No idea,' the captain said and added with a smile. 'Of course, they'll feed you if you get hungry!' A captain's idea of humour. Not funny. Nothing was. Well, it was back to the trench for a quick wash and brush-up.

Something was trying to get through my muddle-headed fog. Finally, it came to me. There were so many songs at the front that conjured up images of 'home'. There were: 'Pack up your troubles in your old kitbag, and smile, smile, smile'; 'It's a long way to Tipperary'; and the unofficial version of 'Mademoiselle from Armentiéres', which went something like:

> Mademoiselle from Armentires, parlez-vous?
> Mademoiselle from Armentiéres, parlez-vous?
> Mademoiselle from Armentiéres,
> With lily white tits and golden hair,
> Hinky-dinky, parlez-vous?

Of course, the Brits, without exception, had no flair for French, no Belgian and certainly no Flemish, so 'Armentiéres' became 'Almond-tears'. Still, singing about 'lily white tits and golden hair' at the top of our voices was a great tension releaser.

Ken and I put our kit into the lorry, which was on time, and the driver took us to Armentiéres. He was from Portsmouth, so he and Ken, who came from the village of Hook, shared Hampshire as a county. Listening to their conversation, I learned more about Ken, which was that basically there wasn't a lot to know. He lived alone in a little cottage near Hook, did some bird watching, but had no living family. If two people were exploring Hampshire, there was not a lot you could add to the conversation about Norfolk, so I shut up.

When we arrived, the driver introduced us to Captain Youngman, a tall, fair-haired Norfolk man from Norwich. The last thing I wanted to do was to get friendly just because of our close territorial ties, and frankly, the difference in rank came to my rescue.

We reported for duty. Captain Youngman sat us down in a tent that had a blackboard and chalk and told us about some stuff that was going on a bit north of there. He said that the Australians, New Zealanders and Canadians were involved in some scheme where they needed their backs covered.

Then he said, 'Now, you chaps, you need to be up here in Plug Street Wood. Silly bloody name, I know. Trust the Frogs! It's about halfway between here and the next town of Mesen. The wood extends from both sides of the road. I want you two to go to the west, which is called "Bois de l'hutte".'

Showing off our little French or Belgian, Mon Capitaine?

'When you get in there, work your way north until you come to the boundary where you will be on a slight rise. I want nothing to go past you wearing a Jerry helmet. If you see any Jerry helmets, kill the owners. We don't expect any enemy to be in the wood already, but I suggest you take all necessary precautions. The Jerry lines aren't far from there, so don't take anything for granted. Any questions?'

'How long do you want us there, sir?'

'Thank you for the reminder, Corporal, that's a crucial question. Well, this is the third of June. It's vitally important that you are out of there before the sixth. So at dusk, on the fifth of June, leave the wood and make your way back here. It's only a short distance, so you should be back here in time for a cup of hot cocoa, a wash-up, and some sleep. Any more questions? Oh! I forgot one thing. I will send the lorry driver to take you there with enough supplies. You two have worked together before?'

'Yes, sir.'

'Good show! All the best, chaps.'

Chris Shaw

We saluted, got our kit organised again and found our driver. He already had rations, ammo, water bottles and some sundry stuff in the back. We added our equipment and climbed aboard.

Captain Youngman had been right; it wasn't far. The driver let us off on the side of the road just at the beginning of the woods, which looked quite dense. We unloaded all the kit, waved him farewell and watched him reverse into a gateway, turn and drive out of sight. We distributed the weight and bulk evenly between us and crept just inside the wood.

'Ken, you stay here. Watch all the kit. I'm going in for a "look-see". Trust me – this is what I was born to do. I'll be an hour or more. We don't want any little Jerry surprises, do we?' I whispered.

'Not at all, Frank. I'll wait here. Take your time. It's quiet and peaceful. I may even have a little sleep.'

'Don't you bloody dare, Ken! I want you alive and alert when I come back, not with a slit throat and an ambush for me. Do you understand me?'

'Yes, Corporal, I understand you,' he said, sheepishly.

'Camouflage the kit – and that goes for you, too.'

My rifle and knife would be all I needed on this trip. My footsteps could not be heard over the soughing of the wind in the treetops as I worked my way slowly and very carefully, about fifty yards in. Then I waited behind a large tree, listening and watching, finding the patterns of sounds: wind in the trees, some faint bird calls, just an occasional rustle. Motionless and silent, I waited with only my eyes and ears working overtime. Gradually, there was an increase in the volume and variety of birdcalls as the local residents got over the noisy interruption of our lorry.

An occasional vehicle went past on the road, but it caused only a minor and temporary softening of the natural volume. Still, I waited. The half-wild cat's patience at our farm came to mind, nearly making me smile. I was listening for whether the sounds came from all parts of the wood or whether there was an area of silence where there should have been sound.

When I was satisfied that the bird songs were evenly spread, I began to use my eyes because if, by the slimmest of slim chances there was someone else in the world who could do my trick of 'woodland integration', I didn't want to die at his hand.

There was no artificial movement. Trees and bushes, blowing in the breeze, were regular and predictable, all curved like waves in the sea, but a person had to go in a straight line over the ground. As the path of their movement was straight, it stood out.

I reminded myself, *Watch and wait, Frank. Watch and wait. Your life, as well as Ken's, depends on it.* I had already programmed my mind as to what to look for. It was essential to check for 'bits', like boot-heels or a rifle muzzle or even loose, flapping uniform protruding from near the bottoms of tree trunks. I scanned the treetops too, just in case someone thought an aerial approach could outfox me.

My heart skipped a beat. There was something alien to the wood, about twenty-five yards from me, and it had just moved. It was part of a rifle because it had a straight line. Straight lines meant death to snipers.

The tree I had selected to hide behind had a large diameter, and I was standing up. I thought to myself, *Frank, this may be your most significant test yet. Do not be found wanting!*

A plan – I needed a plan.

Would he move towards me or also wait? We could be here until the end of the war if he had my patience. He must have seen me come in. Maybe he couldn't be sure of getting in a killing shot because of the trees between us, plus the fact that there were two of us.

Right. I had my plan. I'd drop down behind the right-hand side of my tree and lie on the ground. My rifle would just protrude through the dead leaves, around the base of the trunk. If I tilted it over to the left, the 'scope would be hidden. There would be only the end of the rifle barrel, which would be in amongst the dead leaves and virtually invisible. This meant that I could wait comfortably and be ready for a shot if he made a move. I wondered how patient my brother-in-arms was.

We had this stalemate for half an hour; an hour; an hour and a half, when something alerted me. What was it? I went back over the sounds, just like I used to do when following the movement of the cat's ears when they reacted to something I hadn't identified. I watched and listened with high concentration and worked out what the sound had been. The enemy had scraped his back down the tree trunk to sit down. The slight, abrasive noise followed by the rustle of leaves was the only interpretation I could put on that particular combination of sounds. He was now sitting with his back to the trunk and would look around occasionally to see if I was doing something silly. I thought, *This man is good!*

The ground between us was reasonably flat, with tufts of fine-leafed grass and a few dead leaves. The volume of sound made by the wind would cover my approach, but it would have to be done quickly. He had been standing and waiting. Now he was sitting, and would not look round his tree for some time.

I knew what I had to do, quickly, quietly and now. Only my knife was needed. I aimed for the left side of the tree because the odds were that he would be right-handed and would look round to the right. He might just miss me if I was close.

I rose with my knife in my left hand, and ran so softly and silently that even I couldn't hear myself. Twenty, fifteen, ten yards, five, nearly there, my heart was hammering in my ears. My knife was in my left hand, and the fingers of my right hand gripped his helmet at the forehead, pulled his head back and slit him from ear to ear. I used pressure to get the two carotids and four jugulars. Severed his windpipe too. Messy, very messy.

He looked at me in surprise; a slight smile passed across his face. It seemed to say, 'Finally, peace.' I dodged back behind the tree just in case he had some backup. My process of searching began all over again, but there was no other threat. I retrieved my rifle and set off very carefully back to Ken.

Chapter 18

A BIG SURPRISE

Ken pointed his finger at me from his camouflaged hiding place as I returned to pick up the kit. I was trying to catch him napping, in both senses of the word, and was stalking him carefully, but he spotted me long before I reached him, which pleased me.

We made it safely to the northern edge of the wood with all the kit. On the way, we found a small stream. Having washed the German's blood off me, I suggested we have a rest and something to eat. There was a slight depression between two large trees at the northern edge of the wood, making a good observation post. The field of fire was about one hundred and fifty degrees, which was quite acceptable, and we had some sparse cover in front of us to break up our outlines. We had donned our ghillie suits to make entirely sure that we couldn't be spotted from the front.

The surrounding countryside was delightful, quite reminiscent of Norfolk. There was a slight dip in the land in the middle distance with minimal cover. If a Jerry sniper had worn a well-camouflaged suit with local herbage and spent twenty-four hours getting to us, then just maybe we wouldn't spot him, but I wouldn't want to be the one to try against our accumulated experience.

This area was blissfully peaceful after those bloody trenches with the continual bombardment bringing imminent death. The tranquillity of this woodland was almost as good for me, and my troubled mind, as going home. Here, however, death could still be just around the corner. Large Oaks, Sycamore and Mountain Ash were the principal inhabitants, with Holly, Elm and Lime trees dotted sporadically. Blackbirds, thrushes and pigeons were the main bird species.

The night was warm with just the rumble of artillery in the distance, not unlike a summer storm. I put Ken on the first watch and got some shut-eye, with strict instructions not to let me scream – a rather important order. Apparently, I had a silent night, feeling well rested in the morning when he finally woke me.

Breakfast was bully beef and water from the little stream. It tasted like a banquet. Ken told me the night had been quiet. There had been some owls searching for prey over the field in front of us. They had been utterly silent in flight, but he had seen them outlined against the light of the artillery flashes on the horizon.

This was day two, so it must be the 4th June, 1917, and we had today and tomorrow to go before we were to leave. This looked like a pretty comfortable job, which I thought we deserved after some of the previous stuff we'd been through.

It was about eleven o'clock that I started to think of getting a bite to eat and a drink for 'elevenses', when my heart stopped beating. A dusty, brown, soft leather boot landed silently beside my left ear. I noticed a right foot as I threw myself over with my knife in hand, prepared to kill instantly.

'Not bad,' said a voice with a strange twang to it. 'Whoa, it's all right, mate. Trust me. Relax, mate. I'm on your side!'

I looked up into a long face with twinkling blue eyes, a lopsided smile, a big, thin nose to go with his big, lanky frame and his raised, empty hands. He was wearing a khaki uniform with a large hat with one side of the brim pinned up. Slowly – very slowly, I relaxed.

'And who the hell are you?'

'Murray, mate. Australian tunneller. Or don't you know what's going on around here?'

'Frank Matthews and this is Ken Bullen, my observer.' We shook hands.

'You're a sniping team?' he asked.

'Yes, and we've been sent to take care of any stray Germans in this area, I suppose to help protect your backs. And no, we know nothing of what is "going on around here". How the hell did you creep up on us like that? Christ Almighty, I thought I'd have a heart attack! I pride myself on hearing and understanding all the noises around me. How did you do that?'

'You ever hear of a black-tracker, mate? No? Well, we have these Aboriginal trackers in Australia who are able to track a bird in the sky or a thought passing through your mind. I spent some time on a station in the outback where we employed one. I'd better translate that for you. A "station" in Australia is a bloody great big farm, and the "outback" is the middle of nowhere, right? Anyway, I got friendly with him and asked him to show me what he did. It took him months because I'm a slow learner and a "white man", but I can now do what very few, if any, white men can do.'

'I agree! You can,' I told him. 'I really thought I was excellent, but obviously not the best. What are you doing in this wood?'

'I just came to make sure that no krauts were hiding in here to give any of my boys a nasty surprise.'

'Well, you bloody well gave me one!' I said with feeling.

'Sorry about that,' Murray grinned, but with no obvious signs of sorrow. 'Was it you who outsmarted the Jerry back there?'

'Yes, he tried to ambush us as we arrived. He was very patient, but not careful enough.'

'Fair enough. Well done, mate. Now, just to fill you in,' Murray continued, squatting down on one knee, 'we're building a bloody big bomb to explode under that hill in the distance. Just as a matter of interest, when do you have to be out of here?'

'At dusk, on the fifth. Why?'

'The "why" is that you would probably not survive, in one piece anyway, if you're around here after that; and that's dead serious, mate. So be very sure you're out of here no later than the fifth. I'd better get a wriggle on. Can't be standing around yakking to you folks all day, but it's been a pleasure. Keep your eyes open, keep us safe, and I'll say thank you on behalf of our lads. See you,' he said, and just faded away as silently as he'd arrived.

God, what a start he'd given me! How the hell had he done that? I would probably never know, but he was very, very good. Just as he left, I noticed a major's insignia on his tunic. A major? Why the hell would a major stop to talk with us, as friendly as you like? What's with the Australians, anyway? A bomb? A hill in the distance? What sort of bomb? Sounded to me like an enormous one. We'd make a beeline out of here a bit before dusk so that we were at the road by nightfall. It probably wouldn't hurt to do a sweep before we moved, too. We wouldn't want to be ambushed just when we were getting back to freedom.

It was my turn for the night watch. I did a thorough scrutiny of the area in front of us, and a careful one behind us, too, so as not to put any more strain on my poor old over-burdened heart.

I wondered what sort of owls were here and whether I'd see any tonight. They were probably Barn Owls. What the hell were they still doing here with all the artillery flashes and the noise of bombardment? You'd think they'd go somewhere else.

My night was spent watching and thinking. I tried to entertain my mind, which was so confused that it had started to disintegrate and fail to function correctly. It was probably best to allow it to freewheel and go about its own business. I hoped it would rationalise some things that I was not yet able to process, forget some memories associated with the chronic stress and wander into the realms of the comfortable just to bring me a bit of peace and quiet. A doctor would probably have a fit if he could see what went on in my head from day to day, but I was not responsible for any of it.

Apart from volunteering for King and country, the only thing I'd done was my duty, and the task I'd been given was mainly in the mud, one-on-one with the enemy's best snipers. All of that in an environment that included a constant barrage of high explosive artillery, mortar shells raining down and machine gun and rifle fire trying to cut us to pieces. The good Lord didn't build us to able to deal with all this stuff long-term; it was all so terrifying and depressing.

Before the war, we would have met our German counterparts as accountants, scientists, bankers and grocers. Now, we were at each other's throats, but in one or ten years' time, we shall, no doubt, once more meet them as accountants, scientists, bankers and grocers. Stupid! And as bad as it was for we men who had been pulled into this terrible loss of valuable life, it would be our women and children whose lives would be affected forever.

Gwen and I could have had a wonderful life together; laughing, loving and bringing up Christopher. We had all the ingredients for a 'happy marriage' – a state envied by the majority of the population who didn't have one.

Although my ultimate fate was unknown, I saw death as being the most likely outcome; an arm flung out and a spreading stain as the last of my heart pumped away my leaking blood. The fields of Flanders would claim some more human body parts and, depending on where it happened and who found my body, maybe there would be a grave, or maybe there wouldn't. The whole thing was so unfair.

I snapped my mind back to the present and tried to think of something more uplifting, like what would happen when I returned home. There would be our little rented cottage, which would be quiet and productive with chickens and eggs, fruit, vegetables and herbs. I could get pork and beef from our farm, cheaply, but must pay my way for the farm to profit.

Sooner or later, Janice would not be with us, and the house in Dereham would revert to Gwen. Then, if we duplicated what we had done at the cottage, we could live about as cheaply as possible for three people.

My mind kept asking, 'And then what?' but I didn't know. I couldn't predict what would happen. We would have to wait and see how the great scheme of life unfolded. 'How would Gwen cope with me?' was a recurring question in my mind, to which, at the moment, I had no answer.

My eyes had continued to do their duty as my mind roamed. I searched all around us but came up empty. The faint breeze moved the plants and trees, but there was nothing sinister there. The artillery flashes on the horizon were continual, and I finally saw the owls that Ken had been talking about. They looked like Barn Owls with their pale feathers, but I couldn't be sure.

The stars wheeled overhead, and the thin sliver of a nearly new moon sank in the west. It was a clear night with some starlight, and it all seemed safe and clear. I let my mind wander again, but kept alert to the job in hand. The night was safe. When the sun came up, Ken awoke, well rested and in need of some breakfast.

The next day passed in much the same fashion and was very restful. There were no more visits from friendly, silent Australian ghosts. Ken told me the owls were Barn Owls — two pairs — and a single Tawny Owl, which was probably a young male hunting for food and looking for a mate.

On this last day, we kept a particular lookout in light of what the Australian had told us, but there was no activity, either in the wood or the field in front of us. At about sixteen hundred hours we started to pack up all our kit, taking everything with us and leaving no sign that we'd been there.

I left Ken to finish off and reconnoitred the wood, but it was all clear. The flies had found the Jerry sniper's corpse, but I couldn't do anything about that. I returned and carried my share of kit back to the road just on dusk. The road was clear of traffic, but bearing in mind the proximity of the Jerry lines, the sound of any vehicle would have had us in the ditch or over the hedge.

We made good time and reported to Captain Youngman at about eighteen hundred hours. I gave him my report, including our contact with the Australian major.

'Must have given you a bit of a start, Corporal, eh?'

'Yes, sir,' I said, not wanting to add anything that may have given me a black mark for incompetence. 'What happens now, sir?' I asked.

'I think you'd better stay with us for a few days, Corporal. We've got a bit of a push coming and may need your skills. So, bed down, get a good night's sleep and report to me at ten hundred hours tomorrow.'

'Yes, sir. Thank you, sir,' I responded with a salute.

Chapter 19

THE BIG BANG

Both Ken and I had a good night's sleep in our allotted camp beds. What a change from the mud beds in the trenches! I could get used to this, and that thought, more than anything else, told me how far down that road I had come.

Our breakfast was delicious, much better than at the front. There were bacon and eggs, fried bread and beans and lashings of tea. A man could really go to war – and mean it – with that lot in his stomach. It reminded me of the 'bacon for breakfast' morning in the trenches, with Charlie, and my extra egg.

Afterwards, I went to the toilet and ablutions block and had the luxury of a toilet and toilet paper – a bit raspy, but dedicated toilet paper nonetheless. There was an opportunity for a wash and a shave, and I was able to look at myself in a mirror for the first time in ages. Who was this man? Who was this old man? Who was this old, worried, stressed, fifty-plus-looking old man who walked with a stoop and had bags and wrinkles around his eyes? I couldn't believe it, and again the tears came, hot and depressing.

Oh, you bastards. How could you do this to a human being? Ageing a man by thirty-five years or more, in just two years! What would my lovely Gwen think? How in God's name was she meant to love a young man who looked like this, especially if he was crazy, too? It was too much. She couldn't possibly see me like this, or have to deal with my addled mind, either one of which could be the final straw that could break our marriage apart. Hot tears ran down the furrows in my cheeks.

What else had gone to pot? How was my manhood? Could I perform? Could I get an erection? When did I last think of sex and get hard, apart from the mornings with a full bladder? This war had sucked me dry. I had nothing left but my killing skills.

So, I would take those skills, use them as best I could and try to work out some sort of solution to this problem. I had no idea of what to do, where to go or how to survive. Everything had turned inwards, and it was sometimes difficult to process the army stuff, but I had to if I were to survive.

My shave was less than satisfactory in that it showed even more wrinkles. It was like seeing a clown after he took off his make-up. Christ! How would I survive? But it was so good to be clean again. How long had it been? Don't ask; you really don't want to know.

Ken and I reported to Captain Youngman, who just required us to stay in the vicinity, get our kit clean and prepare to be used if the situation called for it. That would be easy. Catch up on sleep for me. It was back to the camp bed.

Someone woke me with a sharp shake of the shoulder and a loud, 'AYE! Stop blitherin' ya heed, oold man!'

'Sorry,' I said instinctively to the soldier wearing the kilt. 'Happens a bit,' I said, by way of explanation.

'Ay. Ma'be a' does, but yer'd be'er tack a be'er grip on ya'sel,' laddie, or y'll lose a' altogetha.' Probably sound advice, but he looked raw. *Your time will come*, I thought.

There was no action that day, the sixth of June, but I noticed an increased artillery barrage throughout the day. I rested, had lunch and managed to have a quiet afternoon nap with no interruption from my Scottish pal.

At some time in the evening, there was an increase in activity. People started dashing about with a sense of urgency. I stopped one lad and asked him what was going on.

'Just don't go to sleep. That's all I'll say.'

Cryptic, I thought. There had been more than enough hints given, but I couldn't seem to put them all together. Ken was no help, either. So we watched and waited, until a little before 0300 hours when there was a sudden silence. What had happened? Why had the noise stopped? We waited, expectantly. Everyone around us was anticipating something. But what? Should we protect ourselves against it? But against what? Others didn't seem to be doing anything special.

Suddenly, there was a flash that lit the whole sky, followed a few seconds later by a massive blast of wind. There was a feeling that the earth was turning into mud because of severe shaking. *An earthquake,* I thought. But what did I know? The night sky suddenly bloomed with white, red and orange, and the noise came across the landscape like a fist. It knocked me over, and just as well, as it burned and blistered those who managed to stay upright in its path. The trench we were in started to collapse its walls together. I dodged around a corner, tugging Ken by his collar, and we were temporarily safe. After what seemed an age, but was probably no more than five minutes, things around me started to slow down and get back to normal.

'What the hell was that?' I asked the bloke next to me.

'That's Hill 60,' he said with a winning smile. 'Bloody Messine Ridge. Blown all to hell. Thanks to the Aussies, the Kiwis and Canucks, we've torn the guts out of Jerry's control of that area. Can you bloody imagine sitting on top of that lot?'

'Good God! Those poor bastards. There'll be nothing left of them. How many would there have been?'

'Dunno. Certainly thousands though.'

This was slaughter on such a massive scale that what was left of my basic humanity couldn't cope with it. I had to let it go. I wasn't responsible for it, and I could do nothing about it. I had to leave it alone or I'd really go mad. This was all good advice from my little inner voice, but it left me feeling very fragile and, for some reason I couldn't explain, sad, teary and depressed.

This war was becoming apocalyptic in its proportions, to the point that I thought God might intervene. Something, or someone, had to. This slaughter could not go on, or there would be no one left, not a man in Europe. Imagine that! And my poor Gwen would be alone for the rest of her life, and she was so alive. That shouldn't be allowed to happen. Maybe some prayer was in order here. It surely couldn't hurt.

The following day Ken and I were sent back to our previous platoon. We were given travel in a truck and deposited back to 'my' sergeant, in yet another trench.

Chapter 20

ENDGAME

The war ground on and I was still alive – crazy, mind you, but alive. My nightmares and screaming had become worse, so I had to sleep as far as possible from the other troops. My ability to communicate with others had deteriorated even further, with silences and aggressiveness in about equal quantities. My sergeant was able to get through to me with conversation that was nearly normal, although I could tell that even he was wary of me. I could take directions from him, but as for the rest, I didn't want to know.

'Corporal, are you all right?'

'With you, Sergeant, I'm just fine, and with my observer, Ken, too. Nothing that anybody else says seems to make much sense.'

'Fair enough. Have you had a good breakfast, well, a breakfast anyway? I have a little job for you and Private Bullen. Some soldiers about a mile east of here are having some attention from a sniper, and we've lost three this morning. Young lads, too – never had a chance. I'd like you two to go and kill him.'

'Sergeant, it seems as if I've already been here. Didn't the same thing happen before to a couple of your peach-fuzzed lads from our area not that long ago?'

'Yes, Frank, it did, and you dealt very nicely with that situation, although I have to tell you that it was well over a year ago. Unfortunately, these boys arrived and were killed before I could give them the ground rules. I was overseeing a detail for a couple of our boys to go to the hospital when these three popped their heads up before I could tell them otherwise.' He pulled a map from his pouch and placed it on a small table.

'Now, we're here, facing nor-nor-east and about fifteen hundred yards from their trench, which is here, facing due east. Their captain has suggested that the shots came from about there,' he indicated. 'Therefore, this Jerry sniper would have to be northeast of their position. Distance would be somewhere between four hundred and six hundred yards, they think. So, if I draw a line from their trench along that northeast angle and, if the captain is correct, he should be about that far along that line. If you go due north along from their trench to a point northwest of his position, then approach him to the southeast, you could just blind-side him.'

'Sounds about right,' I said, 'provided the captain knows what he's talking about. Give me information from a long-term sergeant at any time. You know what those chinless wonders straight out of the local Manor House are like – all public school accent, knowledge of horseflesh and horny as hell, but with no bloody idea about warfare or much of anything else if it comes to that!'

'Nice little description there, Frank. Just between you and me, I also checked with their sergeant. He confirms the general direction. You should know me better than that, Frank.'

'Thanks, Sergeant. That leaves me with the problem of the approach. I'll get together with Ken and see what can be done. The distance would be about a mile and a half from here, but there's a bit of woodland around there. We'll both get suited up and camouflaged, but the angle could be a bit tricky. I'll work on it. At least it's nice June weather, and we've got the bastards on the run in most places. Could be over soon. What do you think?'

'Sergeants aren't allowed to think, Corporal. You know that! But between you and me, I think three or four months could see us shut this whole bloody mess down, and then we can all go home!'

'Right. I'll find Ken, and we'll get out of your hair.'

'See you, Frank. Good luck!'

I found Ken playing cards with three other soldiers and called him over.

'Time to go, Private,' I said. 'Kit up with your suit. We've got a sniper down the road that desperately needs our attention. This may be a long one. You will need to pick up some food and water, too. Meet me back here in twenty minutes.'

'Yes, Corporal.'

We kitted up and meandered along the duckboards in the trenches to where the youngsters had been killed. I grabbed a camouflaged periscope to examine the countryside: cover, light, shade and elevation.

Then I put myself in their sniper's position, working out where I would hide if I were in his boots. Then I reversed it to see how I could come at him using my knowledge of where he was. Then I changed again, to see how I would protect against this happening.

'What do you think?' I asked, handing the periscope to Ken. He spent quite a lot of time with it and then sat down. I recognised this as his thinking position. I left him to take another look from a different location.

When I returned, Ken said, 'I don't think he's four to six hundred yards. I think he's more like seven hundred and fifty yards, which would put him smack bang in the middle of that pile of rubble. It would mean that our sniper has an almost all-round view, with a sniper plate in front of him for his protection, too. Also, he's a bloody good shot from that range. Their company didn't mention anything about wasted rounds. So he got three out of three at about seven hundred yards, and that's very, very good shooting. This is going to be a hard one, Corporal.'

'You're quite right. That's where I think our sniper is, too, and I think he has all this ground covered. The only way to get to him is from his back, which is between him and the Jerry trenches. If they spot us, we'll end up as mincemeat. If they tell him, he will move, and we'll be caught from an unexpected angle. I'll have a word with the captain to see if we can move him with some mortars in his near vicinity.'

I found their captain and explained our dilemma. He smiled very broadly.

'Well done, chaps. That's a tremendous idea. I'll get on to HQ and get their cooperation. Now, tell me where is he again so I can get the coordinates?'

About a quarter of an hour later the three-inch mortars started up. I relayed the position of the 'sighter' shells to my captain, who spoke to the officer in charge of the mortars, advising them to adjust their aim.

I was minutely observing this piece of ground when I saw the Jerry sniper move away from the approaching mortar shells. There was just a flash of helmet and rifle barrel as he scrabbled backwards. Then I saw him settle to the right but below his previous position. This gave us an area of dead ground that we didn't have before.

'Lovely,' I said to myself, 'just what I wanted. Now I can get to you without you seeing me, and I will kill you. You must not destroy our young ones before they've had a chance to kill you.'

'Come on, Ken. He's moved about ten yards to our right and about the same distance down the back slope. If we creep up on him from our left, his right, he won't see us. It'll probably pay us to go further north and take off from a trench in such a position that we approach him to the southeast, but we'll need great caution.'

We had now come nearly two miles from our trench position, and that should have given us an angle of approach that will hide us from him until we are quite close, say two or three hundred yards.

We donned our ghillie suits and gathered some local vegetation to attach, further helping to camouflage them to fit into the local countryside. We checked each other until we were finally satisfied.

It took us four hours to move three hundred yards towards our objective, climbing a slight slope at the same time, with Ken on my left and a little behind me.

As far as I could tell, our arrival had gone unnoticed. We settled down to watch and wait, yet again. I wanted to be high and to the sniper's right so that I could look down on this sniper to make the kill. I was looking through the 'scope sight when I saw him stand up and shoot at me. My rifle fired. I saw him fall backwards. The shock of the suddenness hit me, and I took a moment to get my breath back.

I turned to Ken and asked, 'You all right?' No answer. 'Ken! Are you all right?'

I looked closer and saw that the force of the bullet had blown off his face. He would be unrecognisable, even to his mother. I knew I had killed the other sniper, so there was, at last, no urgency – then everything went dark.

Chapter 21

THE IMPOSTER

Belgium, 21st August, 1917

The silence was the first thing I noticed. How could that be? Had we stopped shelling and shooting each other? Had the war finished? Where was I?

I looked around to see rows of beds with men in various 'costumes' made from bandages and slings. Moaning, crying and the occasional scream of pain pierced the air.

Again, where was I? A hospital tent? I lifted the blanket and saw bulk bandages. I must have been out for quite a while. How typical that I was catching up on my sleep at every opportunity.

A tired-looking man in a white coat approached. He had a stethoscope around his neck, a clipboard in his left hand and captain's pips.

'Hello. I'm Doctor Rankin. How are you feeling, old chap?' he asked.

'A bit sore,' I admitted. 'What happened?'

'As near as we can work out, you were part of a sniper team who managed to kill the opposition, only to be right next to a German High Explosive shell when it went off. It killed your partner, I'm afraid.'

'Can you tell me about my injuries, Doctor?'

'You sustained a broken left clavicle – collar bone to you – a broken left ulna and a couple of ribs on your left side, numbers five and six. You had many abrasions and a couple of missing toes from your left foot when your boot was blown off. We've put you back together as best we can, but I think you came off rather well, given the circumstances. Are you in any pain?'

'Not really. Just a bit sore and slightly woozy.'

'That will be the morphine I gave you earlier. We'll keep that up for a couple of days and see how you go. Now, I've got some paperwork to complete. Give me your name, rank and serial number.'

In spite of the morphine, or maybe because of the morphine, it all came together in a split second.

'Bullen, Ken,' and I gave him Ken's number.

'And where do you live, Private Bullen?'

'I was living in Hook, in Hampshire for a short time, but I was born in, and grew up in, Norfolk,' I replied, to cover my accent yet still comply with Ken's history.

'Are you married?'

'No, Doctor.'

'Date of birth?'

'October 19th, 1895.'

'Which unit were you with?'

' Originally the 1st Portsmouth, but I was seconded to the Royal Norfolk Regiment to act as sniper observer, Doctor.'

'Good. Now, just to set your mind at ease, we'll look after you until you can travel, at which time we will send you to a convalescent home, broadly in the area of your choice, and when you are better, you can be released, collect your invalid war pension and go about your business. I trust that's satisfactory?'

'Yes, Doctor.'

'Right. Well, I'll leave you in peace to get on with your healing. I'm sorry about your sniper, but there was nothing we could do for him. He bore the brunt of the explosion, I'm afraid. Just relax now.

Get some sleep, and eat and drink all that you can because you are quite emaciated and dehydrated. I understand that you are also much younger than you look. Rest, Private, and I'll see how you are tomorrow. Is there anything you particularly wish for, bearing in mind we're in a hospital tent near the front, in wartime?' he asked with a slight grin. His humour did nothing for me. I shook my head, and he left.

The kindly doctor looked in on me daily, checked my blood pressure, my eyes, ears and mouth. The nurses looked after my sores, and they were improving every day.

Three days after my operations, Doctor Rankin came to my bed, pulling the screen curtains around.

'How are you, Private Bullen?'

'Feeling better than when I arrived,' I answered honestly.

'The nurses have reported that you have woken the whole ward several times each night with your screaming. What can you tell me about that?'

The tears came, and I told him, 'I can see bodies, and sometimes only half bodies being thrown into the sky by the exploding shells. Snipers crawl up to me when I'm asleep and put the barrel of their rifle into my ear and pull the trigger. The blood and brains of young soldiers splatter me in the trenches, and I see thousands of young boys getting mown down by machine gun fire, their guts and blood all over No-man's Land, with their mothers weeping for them. Their fathers suffer in the silence of a big, booming voice, screaming inside about their loss with a straight face. I see feet blown off by landmines, arms and legs blown off by mortar shells, and HE shells killing trenches-full of young boys, fresh from school. They never had a chance at life. I see a man trying to hold in his guts, which were spilling out like warm, pink sausages faster than he could tuck them back in. He's screaming for help when there was no one around!'

Chris Shaw

'It's all right, Private Bullen,' the doctor said, hugging me to his body. I wept and wept. I just couldn't stop because of all the pain and ugliness out there.

'I wake up surrounded by blood and guts, the smell of cordite in my head and the honed edges of bayonets about to stab me to death, and I can't do anything to help them or myself. What can I do? What the hell can I do, to get rid of this guilt, this fear and my failure to help my fellow comrades?'

'Steady now, soldier. Steady. It's not your fault. Listen to me, because this is very important for your future. You are not alone. Much of this is called "survivor's guilt", and it's very real. That you feel an overwhelming need to help is who you are, really deep down. You shouldn't be here. None of us should. But when you accept that you are not alone, you will have nearly halved your problems. There is no guilt in dying, being wounded or surviving. It's just the way things are.'

The doctor continued, 'When you get home, get off this bus, let it go and go to wherever you want to go. The bus will take the reasons for all this guilt and fear away with it. Do you understand some of that?'

'Nearly all of it. I told our youngsters about the bus too,' I admitted with a near-smile.

'I'll give you something to help you sleep deeply, without nightmares. Please believe me when I tell you that these sights, real or imaginary, will slowly fade as you get back to a real life, which will, at least, have some relative peace and quiet in it.'

The doctor continued, 'Trust me when I tell you this will be as bad as it ever gets for you, and when you get home, these nightmares will gradually fade away. You may, however, have episodes when bad memories superimpose themselves onto your reality – onto experiences you are having, especially if there are stress factors involved. This is perfectly normal, and "no", you are not going mad, but your life may be a little weird for a while. So, mixing with civilians should be kept to a minimum until you feel up to it.'

Doctor Rankin recommended that when I got home, I should get as much rest as I was able.

'Do little, rest a lot and sleep a lot,' was the way he put it, and this would help my mind heal. He re-enforced that my mind would heal, as would my body, but I needed patience. He also suggested that since I had hit rock bottom, the only way from here was up.

'Now, the nurse will bring you a draught, so drink it down and get some rest. Eventually, those demons will leave you. Trust me on this. Now sleep.'

'Thank you, Doctor. Sorry I let off like that, but thank you for your kindness.'

'Don't be sorry. It's most necessary for that to happen. Sleep now, and I'll see you tomorrow.'

After about a week, Doctor Rankin revisited me with a wad of forms on his clipboard.

'Right, Private Bullen, here's what is going to happen to you. You have been here for a week now, and your physical condition has improved amazingly. I can also see great improvement in your mental condition. Well done!'

The doctor went on, 'The nurses will help you to the shower from now on, and you can do your own ablutions. We have a waterproof wheelchair you can use for that purpose.'

Doctor Rankin also revealed that I had apparently been on the battlefield for about twelve hours in full sunshine, having had my uniform mostly blown off by the shell. Both those factors had contributed to my losing large areas of skin. I had been sleeping for two full days after having been brought to the hospital tent. Typical Frank!

He told me that in about a week, I would be taken from here and transported by ship to a place for convalescence in the area of my choice. At some time in the future, when I was up to it, the doctor said I would have to get myself to an Army Recruiting Office to receive my honourable discharge and my back pay. I would need either a bank account or one at a post office. He would give me a letter to that effect, and I would be free to go about my business.

'In the meantime, get as much rest as you can, eat and drink as much as you can because you are still considerably underweight. I gather that you have survived for the best part of two years at the front, which is quite extraordinary in itself, and as a sniper's observer too, which is almost unique in my experience. On behalf of the army, I offer my thanks for your contribution, and my congratulations on your survival. I wish you a happy life from now on.'

'Thank you, Doctor,' I acknowledged, trying to take in the details of my unknown future. What my mind had done in that instant lie of being Ken Bullen was to have constructed a new present and a new future that allowed me to live apart from Gwen and Christopher until I got well.

This meant that, given the time and the right conditions, I hoped to be able to integrate into society, converse and work at something to earn some money, and not shout the house down all night, every night. If I could get myself and my life back on track, and if I ceased to look like a sixty-year-old pensioner, I would gently see if Gwen was ready for me to make a re-appearance. I knew that she wouldn't comprehend this gap in time, but I'd have to do it, for all of us. Still, she'd be cross with me; there was no doubt about that.

I just hoped she would want to see me again after believing that I, Frank Matthews, was dead, only to be resurrected as a stranger to her – the imposter, Ken Bullen.

Chapter 22

HOME TO NORFOLK

Over the next few days, in early September, 1917, I felt myself getting better and better. The physical pain went away for the most part, although I was still somewhat unsteady on my feet. The loss of two toes didn't help but I was quite optimistic about the future although there was still no actual plan in my head.

I seemed to go from pillar to post as arrangements were made as only the army could make them. Sometimes it was one step forward and two steps back, and at other times it seemed as though miracles were accomplished.

Eventually, on a drizzly, early September day in 1917, I was stretchered onto a rusty old steamer in some Belgian port that was carrying the wounded across the North Sea to the docks at Great Yarmouth, along with war supplies on the return trip. The voyage across was quite calm – a bit of a rarity for the North Sea. The screams and moans of wounded soldiers should have been enough to tear at my 'heart-strings' – if I'd had any, but they'd all dried up. Another phase in my recovery, I suspected.

On arrival at the Great Yarmouth dock, there was a small bus to transport a few of us. Plenty of willing hands were available to carry patients on stretchers, and the people around me were charming and supportive. After about half an hour we ground up a gravel driveway to a beautiful house – well, a stately home would be more accurate, where we were offloaded near a vast green lawn,

Chris Shaw

surrounded by flowerbeds full of colour. I felt the tears scald my cheeks. After months and months in the cold, wet, black and tainted mud, this was heaven on earth. Its beauty just dissolved me in tears.

The nurses and volunteers clucked and fussed around me like well-meaning hens, helping me to a bed, getting me comfortable and presenting me with a cup of tea and two shortbread biscuits. That completed my conviction that I had died and indeed had arrived in heaven.

I must have slept for ages. When I finally woke, there was a nourishing chicken broth, some beef stew with dumplings and apple pie and custard for dessert. My, what a feast!

Over the next six weeks, I learned that the 'convalescent home' was a real home called Hoveton Hall in the east of Norfolk, not far from Potter Heigham. It had been converted to a Voluntary Aid Detachment to help wounded soldiers. The volunteers' kindness and care were akin to angelic, and the food was some of the best that Norfolk had to offer.

However, the most healing aspect of this place was its calmness, relative silence and the beauty of the grounds. I soon got the hang of crutches, taking little walks with one of the staff, delighting in identifying the birds and the flowers and interpreting what was taking place in the countryside. The word 'Home' was an idea, an identity and a soul-deep foundation for me that brought the tears again.

I loved the 'identity safety' of this place too; no one asked questions. They would listen avidly if I wanted to talk, but questions were considered 'rude'. With all this pampering, I knew there would have to be a price to pay. Things in life just go like that, so I started to plan. I was still waking the household some nights with my screaming, but they gentled me back to sleep, and it never happened more than once per night.

'Where to go and how to support myself?' were the questions uppermost in my mind. Ideally, I needed an isolated cottage near the Norfolk coast where there would be a beach to fish from, and some marshes, fields and woodland so that I could go shooting for rabbits and pigeons, ducks and geese, and room enough in the cottage garden to grow fruit, vegetables and herbs.

There should be a village shop, wherever I settled, to get sugar, tea, milk and an occasional newspaper. A pub, to have an occasional drink and to catch up on current affairs, would be ideal, as would a post office – a safe place for my pension to be sent.

Well, that was my idea of a little piece of paradise. First, I would have to report to the Army HQ in Norwich, which seemed to be the most central place in the area, to give them my current details with a promise to supply my account details later on. Then I would get a train from Norwich to Sheringham and find the best place to live-from there.

I would buy a bike as it would be cheaper and more convenient than keeping a horse or a pony. It would also help me to get fit, along with walking on the beach and around the marshes. I would also buy a good pair of binoculars for bird watching and maybe a pad and pencils to do some drawings.

That was a pretty good plan. It meant that I would eventually be paying a minimum for food and shelter, could cook for myself, make jams and preserves for the winter, and preserve eggs and smoke hams. Then all I would need would be a chicken run for eggs and meat. I recognised an echo in these plans and had a little smile.

Chapter 23

ESTABLISHING MYSELF

Norfolk, 24th October, 1917

When it came time to end my stay at the Hall to make room for some other wounded soul, one of the maintenance men gave me a lift in his van to Wroxham Railway Station nearby, where I caught a train to Norwich. He said he had enjoyed my company at the Hall, and wished me future success, which very nearly brought on the tears again.

It was a short journey to Norwich. I noticed that my mind had started thinking and planning ahead, and that was excellent news.

As I stepped out of the carriage, an old porter walked past wheeling a trolley. He had a brown, weathered face and a pair of twinkling blue eyes that seemed to reflect his optimism and amusement of life around him. I asked him if he knew where the Army Recruiting Office was.

'Yes, I know where that is, sir. We get a lot of you blokes through here. If you walk straight out of the station, you'll be on Prince of Wales Road. Turn right when you come to King Street, keep straight on and you will come to Magdalen Street. The Army HQ is there. Good luck, and get well soon,' he said with an encouraging smile.

My walk, which began at the station, signified the beginning of the rest of my life through, arguably, the most beautiful city in the

British Isles. What lay ahead, I had no idea, but I had to survive, incognito, and get myself well. When, and if, my head and my body started to function again at anything approaching normality, I would think about revealing myself to Gwen and Christopher.

For now, I gloried in this quiet and beautiful city. The elegant and slender towering steeple of Norwich Cathedral, the market square with its bustle and colour and history from medieval times, which still showed in the city's architecture. Lovely old timbered houses, a hospital and the 'Adam and Eve' pub, all dated from the mid-1200s. The Castle and Keep and remains of the city wall were also testament to the age and history of Norwich. For those who preferred to live in a city, Norwich would be hard to beat.

My limping stroll had led me to Magdalen Street where I found the Army HQ. The sergeant inside the door gave me an intense look. He noted all my paraphernalia, my appearance and my body language much as a policeman would.

'And what can I do for you?' he asked, following the policeman's trick of asking questions and staying in control of the conversation.

'Good afternoon, Sergeant,' I said. 'I've been told to report to you. Here are my papers.' *Keep it simple, Ken, and take it slowly.*

'Over here, and sit down while I have a look at these. Then there will be some questions.'

I sat and waited. There was a smell of tea, boiling water, furniture polish and dust. Recruiting posters adorned the walls, with Lord Kitchener's forceful one positioned quite near the Union Jack flag and the portrait of King George the Fifth.

The sergeant returned with a clipboard.

'Right,' he said. 'Name?'

'Ken Bullen.'

'Rank?'

'Private.'

'Duties?'

'Observer for scouts and snipers.'

'Address?'

'Non-existent at this time, Sergeant. I'm heading for North Norfolk and will let you know as soon as I have a permanent address and a post office account number.'

'Mind you do, or there'll be no pension for you, my lad.'

'Yes, Sergeant.'

This pompous little stay-at-home NCO was beginning to get to me, but I had to keep it down. He was probably feeling inferior because he wasn't able to go to war and resented those of us who did.

'Very well, Private Bullen. Sign and date here, and here.'

This could have been the end of me if I hadn't seen Ken's signature in his army pay book when we'd been queuing together on occasion. As it was, I made the best likeness I could on the Confirmation of Discharge Form and dated it Thursday, 24th October 1917.

'Right, Private, here's the back pay I've calculated is owed to you. Got a bit of a limp, I see.'

'Yes, Sergeant. I got too close to a Jerry HE shell. Lost two toes when my boots were blown off and then got sunburned lying unconscious for twelve hours in No-man's Land, with most of the bones on my left side broken and no clothes left on from the blast. But, truly, there was nothing much to it,' I told him with conviction, since I was talking by way of comparison to the damage to my head.

'Have you everything you need?' asked the sergeant, with a gentler voice, skipping over my wounds, trying to make me believe he didn't think they were severe. But I'd watched his eyes. He had been appalled. His assessment of me now had changed around, shown by just a hint of awe and compassion in his voice.

'Could you tell me where I catch the train to Sheringham, Sergeant?'

'Yes, Private. Retrace your steps to Norwich Thorpe Station. The Sheringham train goes from there. If you put your skates on, you will just catch the last one at four o'clock.'

'Thank you, Sergeant. You have been most helpful. I'll send you all my details by post as soon as I've settled.' I limped out, making him feel like a waiter, I hoped.

I did hurry and caught the train with just five minutes to spare. After travelling through yet more relaxing countryside, I arrived in Sheringham about half an hour later. There was a tired-looking boarding house not far from the station that provided evening meals. The landlady cooked a highly nutritious stew – rabbit at a guess, and it was much like the food we were used to at home. It seemed like years ago that I'd eaten a home-cooked meal. Gwen's cooking was good, but nothing could beat my mum's culinary skills – and here came the tears again.

Damn! When would this annoying sensitivity end? The probable answer was: when I settled into my own place and stopped missing my family.

Of course, I was depressed. On the one hand, I had very narrowly escaped death and all the dangers of all-out war for two whole bloody years at the cutting edge of the Front. On the other hand, I had lied about my name, which meant that I had absolutely no one to share anything with, including my loving family. The story I was following, although it was logical, had me cut off from the rest of the world in my need for secrecy. That was a relatively full definition of 'loneliness' in my book, and I would just have to grit my teeth and bear it. Hopefully, it would become less raw as my own things accumulated around me.

The morning brought a better mood and a great breakfast at the beginning of another beautiful autumn day. As I sat and digested my meal, I made a list of some things I would need.

First, I needed to find a sturdy bike that would last a long time and have some sort of carrier as well as a basket. I would need some hardwearing clothes to complete my immediate wardrobe. With these basics I could travel all over Norfolk, even riding to Norwich if necessary. Then I needed to find an isolated spot with a small cottage.

The landlady told me of a second-hand shop around the corner. The sun was truly shining on me today! They had precisely the sort of bike I had in mind. It had two removable panniers at the back, a carrier on both front and back, and a pump. The tyres were in good condition, but I bought two extra inner tubes just in case, and there was a repair kit in a small leather pouch attached by two straps to the back of the seat. It was a Sunbeam Military bicycle, so it was built sturdily to last in wartime conditions. It had no gears but would otherwise suit me well.

My luck held as the shop next door was a second-hand clothing store where the focus was more on substance than style. The boots, socks, trousers, underwear and shirts that I bought were all good quality, my size and serviceable. There were many waterproof coats, which, while being good quality, clean and cheap, reflected a service colour, navy blue or khaki. I chose another one, a mottled green colour, which gave me cause for a little smile inside as I realised I was still camouflaging myself. Finally, I bought a map of the area, a pair of binoculars and a flat cap, which was very common in that part of the world. It was a camouflaging mottled brown. Surprise!

Back at the boarding house, I bathed and changed my clothes, packed everything away, thanking the landlady for all her help. She wished me luck, telling me I was welcome to stay whenever I was in Sheringham. This came as a surprise as my social skills had become generally very rough. Perhaps I was gentler with the ladies? I was pioneering new country here, both physically on the bike, and mentally in my head, which had started to taste freedom once more.

The bike took me along the coast road heading west out of Sheringham, and it ran well, even with my load. The day was clear, and I found myself whistling as I peddled. Now that was good news. It was as though I were two people: one doing stuff, and the other observing, monitoring and interpreting my progress.

Imagine doing this in winter with frost and snow, slippery roads and freezing cold wind. Well, November was just around the corner, so I needed to get settled soon. The last thing I wanted was to die of starvation in a cottage somewhere where food was unavailable because of the snow.

My map told me that I was approaching Weybourne, and I cycled as far as possible down Beach Lane to the sea. The beach was pebbly, and had a few small fishing boats, which smelled of the dried seaweed and long-dead fish that had been pulled up the shingle slope to above the high tide mark. The village had not a lot of character or variety. It was pretty but didn't really interest me. I had a cup of tea and a bun at a tearoom and then set off once more, leaving behind the beautiful Weybourne windmill.

A little further on was Kelling, which again was pretty enough but much too small. Within twenty-four hours, everyone would know everything about me, or try to.

Next thing I knew, I was cowering in the ditch beside the road. How? Why? What caused the crash from my bicycle? I lay still, feeling my body, waiting for pain or blood leakage to tell me where I had been shot. Nothing. There was pain in my ribs and left arm, but that was just because I'd fallen on the still-healing bits of me. There seemed to be no more broken bones, and I saw my transport lying down near the centre of the road. I thought back but there was no clue as to what I was doing in the ditch. My trusty bicycle was not damaged, and the tyres were still hard, so I started again on my journey.

There was a whistling sound above me. Looking up, I saw a hawk of some sort – a Marsh Harrier maybe – which sounded exactly like an incoming shell. Now I knew what had caused my problem. I would have to desensitise that reaction so as not to be dropping off my bike or hiding under a pew in church, should there be a repeat of such calls in the future.

The sooner I got settled in my own place, the sooner I could start work on eliminating these wartime tics.

Next came Salthouse, which beckoned me in a way I couldn't explain. I cycled around until I found the post office incorporated with the 'little general store that sells everything'. There was a notice board in the window, which I studied minutely. About halfway down was a handwritten note reading, 'Cottage to rent. Long-term preferred. Apply within'.

When I went in, the doorbell rang, nodding on its spring above me, and I was assailed by the smells of ham, cheese and fresh bread. How wonderful! An elderly man in an apron greeted me from behind the counter.

'Mornin',' he said.

'Good morning. I was wondering about the cottage for rent. What can you tell me about it, please?'

'Saw you looking at the notice. Are you walking or riding?'

'Cycling.'

'Well, go back the way you came, turn right in about a hundred yards, go about half a mile and you'll see it on your left. There hasn't been anyone in it for a while so the garden's a bit out of control, but the building is snug and sound. Here's the key. Take your time.'

I thanked him, mounted up and followed his directions. Part of a thatched roof came into view. Trees and overgrown shrubbery obscured the rest of the cottage.

The cottage itself was beautiful in a romantic rural sort of way, and had been recently whitewashed. The thatched roof looked in good condition. There was even a rose trellis over the door.

Wouldn't Gwen have loved this? As soon as the thought entered my mind, I cried more tears. I needed this to stop, and soon.

To break the mood, I opened the front door and was confronted with a set of stairs past a tiny hallway. The room to the right was empty but could act as a storage area, I thought, beginning to plan ahead. There was a room to the left, which had been the dining room. It led into the kitchen and scullery. In the scullery, there was a sink with taps, not a pump handle, a kerosene stove to cook on and a slow-burning wood stove in the kitchen. The sink was clean, and there were a solid kitchen table, an oak dresser and some counter space. A separate walk-in larder at the other side of the cottage was cold. Since this was a surprisingly warm October day, that was good news for the meat, eggs and milk of the future.

Opening the back door, I was almost overwhelmed by the perfumes of roses, sweet peas, honeysuckle and lavender. These had grown in profusion and needed some tidying. There was an herb garden that someone, who knew and cared about food and cooking, had planted. The rabbits had taken their toll, as had the insects, but I could fix that with some fine netting.

It was a more spacious block of land than I had expected. Looking down the slope beyond the hedge at the bottom of the garden, I saw some beautiful Norfolk scenery – deciduous woodlands and low, rolling, lush meadows with a small beck or stream meandering through a water meadow at the bottom of the slope. There were fields upon fields of stubble within view – barley and wheat mostly. In the background, there was dense woodland with the square Norman tower of the local church pushing through. It was a pastoral scene of tranquillity and beauty, which satisfied some inner need in me, buried deep down in my soul, perhaps borne of countless generations of life in this countryside.

I went back indoors and upstairs. The little bathroom was adequate for my needs. There was one massive bed with a goose-down mattress and eiderdown that smelled a bit musty. It needed an airing but looked clean enough. There were three other bedrooms.

I looked out of one of the tiny windows at the rustic view and knew straight away that this was for me. I was sold. It was, as the man had said, 'snug and sound'. It was also isolated and without neighbours – a considerable advantage to me just now.

My return bike ride to the shop was quick. The rent was negotiated after telling the owner that I would take it for the foreseeable future. Some rent was paid, and some tea, sugar, milk, bread, jam, butter and ham were bought. The key, I was told, fitted both front and back doors, so I kept the original one.

'My name is Paul, Paul Bolton, and there is no need to lock your doors in the country, you understand?' he said.

'Ken Bullen,' I said, shaking his hand. 'Yes, I understand, but I will.'

My dealings, with the same Paul, but in the post office portion of the shop, were equally successful. I opened an account and was issued a passbook with the amount I had deposited in it, details of my address and an account number. I wrote and posted a note to the Army HQ in Norwich with all these details so they could forward any back pay and pension. Hopefully, that would happen soon as my money was down to very little. With all that done, I was now free to pursue my new life.

Chapter 24

GWEN'S TRANSITION

Norfolk, 31ˢᵗ August 1917

T he instant Gwen's fingers touched the brown envelope from the postman, she knew, with a tearing, sickening shock, what it was. The pre-printed official form, (B. 104_82.) coldly confirmed that her Frank, her husband, her lover and her friend, was dead.

'Sir/Madam, It is my painful duty to inform you that a report has this day been received...' etc. 'Killed in action.'

The hairs on her arms and the back of her neck stood up, and her face blanched as her blood pressure dropped like a stone down a well. She managed to close the front door before her knees gave way. She sat heavily on the mat just inside, her back against the door, with her head dropped between her knees. Her home surroundings came back into focus after some deep breathing.

Oh, no, she thought, *this can't be true. Frank's so strong and brave – this just can't be true. What to do? What to do? Christopher! I must take him to the farm to give me some time alone to deal with this. I need that. What will I do? How will I manage? Oh, Frank, no! Please, not you.*

Christopher went to his grandparents while Gwen went home to her bed to grieve, long and loudly. For three days she bemoaned her loss, the loss of her friend, her lover and her rock. The pillows absorbed her tears and her frenzied fists, and the sheets consumed more tears while she thrashed and keened and wept.

She re-lived their meeting, their courting and their loving. She brought back the smell of Frank's body, his smooth brown skin where it had seen the sun, his muscles and his beautiful, expressive brown eyes that talked to her, telling her his thoughts without words, but always with overtones of optimism and humour. She remembered how he had looked asleep with her head on his shoulder, and his tender caresses of softness and urgency. His consideration, caring and his tricky sense of humour were all parts of him she loved and, together with his strength, both as a man and a husband, completed her total intoxication and commitment to him. Now, he was gone – forever.

By the third day, her body and mind were exhausted; sleep was a compassionate release. On waking, she realised that her attitude had started to accommodate her loss. A positive change had replaced her desolation. The time for tears was over. She had work to do; she had to re-focus her energies on Christopher and make him as happy and as well adjusted as possible.

Her work, his schooling and their time together had to be planned – for learning and laughter, for music and stories, and exploring his talents, whatever they may be.

There was just one other time that her tears had broken through. That was at the inauguration of the wet and glistening knapped-flint War Memorial in Longham village, which she attended with the extended Matthews family. Their words of love and mutual support only helped to lower her resolve against tears. Christopher, now nearly four, stood beside his mother, his hand stretched up to hold hers, his weight leaned against her leg in his gesture of love and support – quite advanced for his age.

The speeches had words about the hardships that these now-deceased servicemen and women had undergone, their bravery in going to war and the courage they had shown against daunting odds. Their eventual loss had left a great depth of sadness in families and friends, which had affected most people in the area, either directly or indirectly.

The War Memorial was but a small gesture of gratitude to those who would not return, by those who had been made safer by their actions. These ideas, along with her own personal devastation, beat down her defences.

After everyone else had moved away, Gwen and Christopher stood alone in the fine drizzle. With tiny droplets of sadness beading their hair and clothing, Gwen felt her hot tears mingling with the cold rain streaming down her face as she let go for one last time. After a little while, she closed the door on Frank and squatted, facing her little boy in his grey cap and suit, long socks and black lace-up shoes.

'Do you see your father's name, Frank Cyril Matthews, there, on the memorial? That's a reminder to everyone to say "thank you" to him, and the others, for going away to fight for our country. Some came back, and some didn't. He didn't. If you ever want to talk to him, darling, about anything at all, at any time in your life, just come here. He will listen.

'Now, let's get dry, have a hot cup of tea and maybe some shortcakes with strawberry jam. Then I've got a book to show you, which we can read together, and I want to take you to see ...'

Part 3: New Beginnings

Chapter 25

GETTING TO KNOW THE VILLAGERS

Norfolk, 1918

The winter months had been spent cleaning and changing the inside of the cottage to get it comfortable and practical.

Each week, it was obvious that I woke up less often from the nightmares. Also, after a couple of false starts, I didn't keep looking for cover when the screech of hawks or other predatory birds came at me from the sky.

I was getting better. It was the feeling I had had when we'd been granted some leave, and left the 'front' in a lorry, away from all the sounds of war. Back then, I had felt my body slowly relaxing as the noise quietened, and now that was happening again. The only sounds around me were the wind and the birdcalls of black-birds, thrushes, robins, rooks, crows and pheasants. It came to me that I was living the life of a hermit.

When the spring arrived, I went out of doors to review the garden, starting to make short- and long-term plans. My physical exercises for speed, endurance and strength were quite pleasing in their progress. The physical ill effects of being 'blown up' seemed to have gone and, although I thought my mind was in good shape, it hadn't been tested on anyone but myself. When the social isolation finally became apparent to me, I walked to the local pub, the Dun Cow, meaning The Brown Cow, for a bit of company.

The public bar was a warm, smoky room with a large welcoming fireplace harbouring a big log fire. I took a quick look around at the other drinkers as I limped through the door. Conversation stopped as I went to the bar to order a small beer. Soon, it started up again, with me being the subject of the discussion, no doubt. Well, there wasn't much else to talk about except weather, crops and the progress of the war.

I spotted a man sitting on his own, nursing his drink. He had the right sleeve of his jacket pinned up, showing me that he was probably married because the pin was straight, and that he had been wounded, presumably in the war. I walked over and asked him whether he would mind if I joined him.

'Please do,' he said straightaway. 'I'm Peter,' he continued, waving me to the seat opposite.

We looked at each other. Peter had noticed my slight limp and my otherwise good health, except for the shadows behind my eyes. Apart from his arm, I also saw some nightmares in his soul.

'Did a bit, did you?' I asked, pointing to the arm.

'Yes. You?'

'Yes. Just a bit.'

'You're new,' he said. It was a statement, not a question.

'If you mean that my family and I haven't been here for ten generations, then, yes, you're right, I'm new. My name's Ken,' I informed, putting out my left hand to shake his.

'Welcome,' Peter said warmly.

'Thank you. In truth, I've been so busy getting my little cottage into shape and my larder stocked up for winter that I sort of forgot to mix with people. Most of what I need to do has been done, so I have a bit of time to socialise. The pub seems nice enough?'

'It's fine, mostly, although people don't know how to treat us – we who've come back from the war. For all we did, we seem to be outcasts. There's a lot of sorrow everywhere because of so many lost lads. Whole families are grieving. You will understand that.'

'Of course I can. Where do you live?'

'Three doors down from here at number thirty-nine.'

'I'll get us another beer,' I offered, 'and please don't argue. It'll work itself out over the years.' His smile was more payment than the gesture deserved.

I had my back to him when there was a blast of cold air as the front door was opened. Slowly, I turned my head to see three big, burly farm boys come in, sporting the sort of smile that bullies all over the world have in common.

The leader, a huge, muscled man like a Viking warrior who was dressed in a mud-spattered blue shirt, brown corduroy trousers and big, black leather boots, looked around to find someone weak to pick on. His cold piggy-blue eyes fell on Peter.

'Who's this armless old man, then?' he jeered, laughing loudly at his own joke. 'Let's hear you play the fiddle then! Oh, dearie me, but you can't do that, can you, with only one arm? How sad. What can you do? Sod all, I expect. You should be put down, old man!'

I walked over and tapped the Viking on the shoulder. He turned and looked down his nose at me with an arrogance I'd experienced before. I put a smile on my face and took a step towards him, opening my eyes wide and staring very intensely into his.

'Who are you, then?' he asked, not quite sure why I had moved towards him. I shouldn't have done that, according to him.

'I'm someone who's going to ask you, politely, to leave.'

'No way! I'm just beginning to enjoy myself.'

'Well, let me put it another way. That man over there who you seem to think is in some way humorous, lost his arm being braver, and having more inner courage, than you and your thugs will ever have in the whole of your pathetic little lives. Tell me, how many arms have you got?'

'Well, two, of course,' he said uncertainly.

Smirking into his face, I said, 'Then, my question to you is, "Which one would you like to keep, idiot?"'

There was a long moment during which he tried to work out the question. He finally understood and came at me with a big right-hander. I slowed everything down to a snail's pace, concentrating very hard. *Just lovely*, I thought. I waited, since he seemed to be working in syrup, then swayed back out of the line of his speeding fist, grabbed his wrist as it came level with my face, pushed it down and round, taking his arm up his back. Using his own momentum and a bit of a push, I ran him into a spare slab of wall. He was almost parallel to the ground, doing a fair speed when he struck it. He hit the floor hard too, and was out cold.

I turned to the other two and, with a hand around each shoulder, said in a light conversational tone, 'I'm delighted he brought you two boys along tonight. You're strong enough to carry him home.'

I manoeuvred their heads together and said, very slowly, making sure my audience heard too, 'Now, this is going to be very important to your sleeping friend, and for you two, maybe. If, and when, any of you three, who I will refer to as "Faith", "Hope" and "Charity", come back to this bar when either Peter, over there, or I, am here, you will ask our permission to come in. If we both say, "Yes", you will then ask the publican's permission, and if he says, "Yes", then you may come in. If any of us say, "No", then you don't come in. Do you understand that? Oh, and one more thing. When your friend "Faith" here wakes up, and if he wants to try to have another piece of me, please do tell him he'd be very welcome. But do also tell him that I do this sort of stuff for a living, and I eat little boys like him, raw. Now get him out of here.'

I stood still for a moment to let the world to return to normal speed, picked up our beers and sat down opposite Peter.

'If I had two hands, I'd clap,' he said, with a huge smile lighting up his old face as we watched the trio form a capital 'H' and leave.

After the door closed, there was a round of enthusiastic applause, backslapping and offers of free drinks in the future. The publican, Owen, came over to thank me.

'That was as nice a piece of work as I've seen in many a year. You're welcome here any time, Ken, and I'm not one to ask questions. Just ask Peter, if that's his real name.'

Well, that had revealed more to the villagers about who I was than anything I would do in the next twenty years, probably. The tongues would be really wagging – for a week or two at least.

Chapter 26

A trip to Dereham

Norfolk, November, 1918

A fter several months of hard but satisfying work, my garden was flourishing. I had dug, fertilised, raked and weeded, then planted with considerable forward planning. I loved gardening because, put simply, I'm a farmer, so growing things and enjoying the very organic nature of the soil is deeply embedded in my soul. It's up there with love and music, revealing itself as a passion.

There was a dresser in the kitchen, probably left by the previous tenants. Every farmhouse seemed to have one, with crockery displayed on the shelves and bulky items stored in the cupboards underneath. As I was putting away my meagre cooking equipment, I had discovered that the previous owner had left behind his or her recipe book. It was written in beautiful copperplate handwriting on pages that had been splashed with any number of soups, sauces and gravies, showing it had been much used and loved.

The message came through strongly that the person who had compiled it was a great preserver of nature's bounty. They had taken whatever they had and in some smart way made it available in the winter months. That resonated with me because of the stories I had heard my family tell about the fierce winters of the late 1800s in Norfolk and Suffolk where people had actually died from the cold and the lack of food or the money to buy food from lack of available work. There was a considerable amount of possibly life-saving material in this book. I decided to use it wisely.

Soon, I had begun to harvest my vegetables – onions, radishes, runner beans, broad beans and peas. Next, I bought a five-gallon drum of malt vinegar, several pounds of sugar and salt, together with some selected spices, and started to preserve my vegetables, and any fruit I could get on the cheap. I scrounged around for apples, plums, greengages, gooseberries and as many other berries as were available; even collecting wild blackberries from the hedgerows.

One of the local farmers was slaughtering a small number of cows and pigs, so I cycled over to see him. He was very amenable to receiving cash in hand for a quantity of beef and some cuts of pork, which, to my delight, he delivered. I salted and smoked them to see me through the winter. A large saucepan, a wire rack made from fencing wire, together with some dried hardwood sawdust sprinkled on the bottom, served me as a smoker, which I also used for some of the fish I caught from the beach. I had an excess of potatoes, onions and apples, which I bedded down in the cold outhouse, over and under straw, to stop the frost from getting to them.

Finally, with the nights drawing in, and a chill that lasted during the day, I realised that November 1918 had arrived. Before the frosts and snow set in, I had to make a visit to Gwen and Christopher, to make sure they were safe and prospering. *But they might not still be in our original cottage*, I speculated.

Whether or not Janice Bell had died, they might have moved to Dereham anyway. Janice had owned her house and would have passed it on to Gwen. Living in Dereham would have been cheaper and more convenient for both of them. It was just around the corner from Gwen's work at the post office, and Christopher could be sent to a family during Gwen's working day. He would now be three years old. Fancy that! I found myself longing for a look at him to see how he was growing. What would Gwen look like? Ravaged by sadness? Doubtful. She had more personal resources than that, but she must have suffered at the news of my death.

I had improved out of sight but still awoke some mornings to the smell of cordite – all in my head. Stress seemed to precipitate strange states of mind, where my blood pressure would drop and I would see modified scenes in tones of grey that may or may not be there. English people became Germans, and woodland looked like advancing tanks. I kept scrutinising the scenery over the back fence wondering whether or not a sniper was getting me in his sights. I knew it was rubbish, but paranoia can actually save your life. It would all pass eventually, and I had come such a long way.

I decided to get on my bike and go and see Gwen and Christopher.

The following early morning, with water and sandwiches in the panniers, I set off for Dereham, which was over twenty miles away – no distance on a bike. I took the road to Holt and then to Dereham, passing through Guist.

My cycling allowed me to appreciate that an autumn morning in Norfolk could be a fairyland. On this particular morning, there was a ground mist so I could see only the tops of the trees. In the middle distance, from the top of a small hill, those trees looked like the grey backs of a herd of elephants. Total silence added to the 'other world' experience – the sounds dampened by water droplets in the air. Soon as the sun started to come up, those grey 'elephants' slowly turned pink, looking as though the sun was breathing life into them. All too soon the pink turned to orange, then yellow, destroying the myths in the mists, which burned off, turning fantasy into reality, leaving me vaguely disappointed.

I took a detour to have a look at the cottage, our little love-nest for such a short time. Our work with the brush still showed, but the curtains had gone, and the weeds had started to take over. It was apparent that Gwen and Christopher were no longer in residence.

My walking stick, flat cap and a full beard for camouflage, together with my coat collar turned up in the cold weather, made a very competent disguise, I hoped. The proximity of our farm and people I knew in the area around Longham village made this very dangerous ground. I had to protect my new identity.

Once in Dereham, I leaned the bike against a wall, well away from the bustle of the town centre, detached the leather panniers and threw them over my shoulder. Then I walked into town towards Commercial Road where Janice had lived.

There was an optimistic buzz in people's conversation, an excitement almost. What was it? What had happened?

I stood still, supposedly looking in a big shop window, but watching reflections and listening to fragments of speech as people walked past. Finally, the penny dropped. The war was over! Heaven be praised! Those poor lads could now come home out of the mud, the blood and the guts, and get back to being ordinary citizens living an everyday existence. Whoever would have thought that the greatest gift on earth, for our service men and women, would be to have a mundane life?

What did this mean to me? Nothing, I realised after some thought. My life pattern had been set. There would be much rejoicing in my village, too, but it would make no difference to me.

'Frank!' said a voice behind me. I froze. My blood turned icy, and I felt the beginning of shock dropping the blood pressure in my head. Slowly, as in the old days, I turned to see two old men behind me embrace, then start a heated conversation about old times. The sweat of relief broke out on my body. I moved on quickly to get rid of the adrenaline. For just a moment I thought my disguise had been penetrated and my worst fears realised. Suddenly, I had become reacquainted with fear and sweating.

Janice Bell's house on Commercial Road hadn't changed much, I noticed, shambling slowly past. There were new curtains to go with fresh paint on the window frames. The small front garden was tidy, containing the remains of a large variety of flowers that had bloomed in the summer months. It must have looked a picture in the summer sunshine.

Further along the road was an entrance to a field, a portion of which was used for sport or a recreation ground. It had football goal posts at both ends and looked as though there had been a cricket pitch in the middle during the summer months. My walk across it took me to the cover of some trees on the boundary, with a view into the back of Gwen's mother's house.

Here I set up my observation post, continuing my bird watching and using the binoculars I'd bought in Sheringham. They allowed me to see into the house. This was a Saturday, and she should return from the post office with Christopher at about twelve o'clock, I thought.

To use up the time, I identified the birds around me. Country people, in the main, knew the names and habits of the wild creatures around them. 'Townies' tended to either ignore them or saw them as an intrusion. The mass of messy pigeons I'd seen in some cities most certainly came under the heading of 'intrusive.'

There was movement in the back garden. A small boy was playing with a stick with a wooden horse's head on top. He was pretending to ride around on a real horse. So that was my Christopher, my son, my boy. My heart swelled, and the tears came again. He was beautiful, coordinated and thoroughly enjoying himself. How wonderful!

Just then, there was another movement as Gwen came out through the back door on to their small piece of lawn. She smiled at him, said something, and they both laughed.

Suddenly, I was seeing the same scene, but in black and white. But the woman was not Gwen. I was back with a French woman hanging out her washing, who I watched from my sniper's nest. She seemed happy in her chore until she suddenly folded elegantly to the ground. Her hair changed from blonde to blood red. I realised she had been shot, whether intentionally or by sheer chance, I didn't know. It took me ten minutes to locate and eliminate the Jerry sniper responsible.

The colour came back to the scene as my blood pressure rose, and I was looking at Gwen and Christopher once more. I wasn't ready for this yet! There were still mornings when I woke to the smell of cordite in my head.

My family were safe and happy though. I must be content with that.

I'd seen enough. Hot tears coursed down my cheeks as I left. A man, walking in the opposite direction, stopped in front of me.

'What were you looking at?' he asked aggressively.

'A pair of blue tits and a male robin on the fence,' I said with a smile. 'Bird watching's a hobby of mine. I've just spent the last six months looking for a Waxwing, with no luck I'm afraid, but I did find a pair of nuthatches in a churchyard just north of here. Are you interested at all?'

'Not at all!'

'Oh well, good day to you then,' I countered, walking off.

'What about the war?' he shouted after me.

'Great news,' I said, not slowing.

My walk to escape him took me to a strange area of Dereham, but I continued on until there was a recognisable street sign, and then found my bike.

If I were to take advantage of all the wild food around me in the countryside, it was probably time to buy a gun. I could supplement my winter meals with some fresh rabbit or pigeon, perhaps. There was a second-hand shop in one of the side streets off the market square, which had a doorbell on a spring that clanged as the door opened. There was a vast assortment of things that people didn't seem to want, or perhaps they needed the money more. There was no dust anywhere. This was a shopkeeper who looked after his stock.

'Good morning, sir. How may I help you?' he asked. He was a tall, thin, cadaverous man with a deep bass voice. His black hair was slicked down and parted in the middle. He was relaxed, with a slight smile, and very focused. I smiled inwardly at the 'sir.'

'Yes. Good morning. I'm after a gun, a twelve bore, for rabbits and pigeons.'

'Certainly, sir. I have three for you to choose from.'

He brought out the first one. It had seen a lot of use and, in spite of some care, from the shopkeeper I suspected, was not up to much. I broke it and saw that the barrel was pitted, the workmanship was average and there was some looseness in the left hammer. The second gun was much better, with some inlay in the stock, a tight mechanism and clean barrels. Some bluing remained, and it had quite a delicate balance.

The third, however, was an absolute masterpiece. I looked at the shopkeeper. He showed interest only in gauging my reaction. I guessed that he didn't know what he had. It had 'Holland & Holland' on the inlayed stock, which was made from walnut. The inlay was intricate. It was a beautifully crafted wildfowl scene on gold and silver plates on each side of the stock. The balance was better than fine, and the barrels were clean and hammerless. The mechanism was tight but smooth. It was a pleasure just to break it, so perfect was the craftsmanship. I knew it would be beyond my pitiful budget.

'Can you give me prices on all three, please?'

'Certainly, sir. The first is twelve pounds, the second is twenty-five pounds and the third is forty-five pounds. It's quite a good-looking gun, that third one,' he said, sweetening the pot for the better sale, but confirming his ignorance of 'Holland & Holland' as master-craftsmen.

'I don't suppose you could tell me where that particular gun came from?' I asked, holding my breath.

'It came from the estate of the late Sir William Sheringham, sir. My esteemed employer suggested that that would be a fair price.'

Could I afford it? Should I afford it? How could I afford it? Well, it would be an asset, from which I could recoup my money at any time I needed to. It was actually worth much, much more than his price. I would say it was worth in the region of five hundred pounds. Now that was quite an investment. I could use it to get and share the meat it brought me, and if I looked after it well, it would only increase in value.

'Does it come with a case?' I asked with a straight face.

'Yes, sir. It's quite a handsome embossed leather case, sir. I shall fetch it for you,' he said, and scurried off.

Forty-five pounds was most of my money, but it would help me survive the winter. If I shot enough rabbits and pigeons, I could perhaps build up some credit around the village.

The shopkeeper returned with the case that, again, was beautifully crafted. It had been oiled and looked to be of the same quality as the gun.

'And what about cartridges?'

'I'm so sorry, sir, but this is a second-hand shop, and we are not allowed to sell explosives of any sort. However, there is a gunsmith just past the market square. Just one thing I forgot to mention; the right barrel of that gun is choked, sir, a modified choke.'

'Thank you.' Better yet, for the longer-distance targets.

I paid in cash and took my prize out to my bike, attaching it firmly along the crossbar where it wouldn't interfere with the steering. *About time I got out of here*, I thought. It would be nearly dark when I reached home. I drank some water, ate the last sandwich and then I was on my way, via the gunsmith's shop.

My thoughts drifted to my busy day, but the primary consideration was that Gwen and Christopher were safe and happy. As I peddled the miles home, I watched the sun start to go down, producing some spectacular reds and golds, with silvers and deep purples mingled in the approaching sunset. Who in the world would prefer to live amongst tall buildings and miss all this? Only people who didn't know, or appreciate, that nature's beauty was out here.

My little cottage seemed to greet me as I peddled the last few hundred yards. It had been a long day, but very satisfying, especially so since my legs were not at all tired.

I cut some bread and ham, spread on some of my own pickle, and washed it all down with some crystal-clear, cold water from the tap. The silence and the candlelight turned it into a right royal feast. There was just one thing missing – well, two really.

Chapter 27

Village life

The cold winds off the North Sea during those winter months of 1918–19 were very stimulating. My walks along the beach and through the marshes, with binoculars and sometimes my gun, were full of bird sightings. I had a great appreciation for the sea, with its crashing waves and their crushing, pebbly sounds washing up on the beach. This was accompanied by the muted whistle of the wind through the tough sedges and grasses of the marshland, which were mixed with the calls of a myriad of water birds escaping the rough, stormy weather, by seeking shelter here. Herring gulls and terns, curlews, redshanks and greenshanks, and many species of ducks and geese all contributed to this cacophony. The winter landscape around the village, with St Nicholas Parish Church as its dominant feature, was a rural classic.

Sometimes, as a result of a walk with my gun, I had fresh red meat. Or I caught a fish or two on the tackle I'd bought locally. Anything I had in excess, or when I needed money, I could take to Owen at the pub, and he would give me cash.

One evening, feeling like company, I peddled over to the Dun Cow and sat with Peter over a small beer.

'I shot a couple of nice rabbits today, and thought you and your wife, if you have one, might be able to use a nice fresh rabbit.'

His eyes lit up, and a smile started. Then there was a quiver of his lip, and tears came. He turned away and used his handkerchief.

'So sorry,' he said.

'Don't worry about it, Peter. It still happens to me sometimes, too.'

'Nobody treats me with kindness, except Pat, my wife, of course. They think I'm a bit of a monster; a killing machine.'

'Are you?' I asked with a smile.

'Soft as butter, me,' he said, with a flash of humour.

The money in my bank account kept rising because I was living about as cheaply as anyone could and was being paid for my excess fish and game. Apart from the occasional visit to the pub, which mostly cost me very little, I grew, shot and cooked my own food. I even baked my own bread. There was nearly always more acquired food than I could eat, which left some over to sell or barter.

My plans for the cottage garden were all sorted out, so I knew what needed to be planted next year. Last year had provided me with precious experience as to what and how much to plant. Some crops I had got right, but others were either in excess or in such short supply that I had made a list of next year's priorities. Filing records of yields and the number and contents of sales I had made allowed me to modify next year's planting for even better results.

I also had some plans to modify the cottage. On my next visit to the shop in the village, I had a word with the man who owned the cottage, who also just happened to be the shopkeeper, Paul. He happily agreed to the modifications I suggested. I also asked him about the possibility of purchasing the cottage. He thought about that, but, not being one of nature's born decision-makers, told me he'd think about it.

As I was cycling home, I took out that piece of conversation and examined it. Why did I want to buy? Could I ever afford to buy? What would I do with a cottage and a debt around my neck?

It was the same as trusting my instincts. There had to be a reason why my mind had stimulated those words to come out of my mouth when, in truth, I had never considered buying the cottage.

This echoed back to the 'two people' experience soon after I arrived in Sheringham – one was acting, and one was watching.

It was the 'why' that continued to bother me. Something was going on in my subconscious mind that was being cryptic. Whenever this happened, I found the best plan was to sleep on it and not to fuss with it. The answer would arrive when it was ready.

At the beginning of April 1919, the days were drawing out, as they say in these parts. Outside the back of the cottage, I was putting the finishing touches to a sawhorse that would make sawing logs for my woodshed so much easier. It was very sturdy and would last a long time. The design I had come up with enabled it to be folded before being put away, thus taking up less space in the shed.

There was a sudden awareness of being watched, and I slowly turned my head to see a little girl in a floral dress and a pink cardigan, which had evidently been knitted by her mother.

'Hello,' I said, with a smile. 'What's your name?'

'Paula,' she replied shyly. She was holding something small and furry in her arms and looked as if she were protecting it. I had to take this slowly. She was very shy, looking as though she might run away.

'Hello, Paula. I'm Ken. Would you like a glass of milk?' I asked. 'It's nice and cold.'

I knew she wanted something but didn't know how to begin. She nodded. I went indoors, returning with two glasses. I handed her one.

'Come and sit on the seat with me, Paula. Now, is there something I can help you with?'

'Would you look after my dog? She's the runt of the litter, and my Dad wants to drownded her!'

It all came out in one breath as though she had been saving it all up. Tears welled in the corner of each big, blue eye. She would be about six years old and quite beautiful with her long, blonde hair blowing in the wind, framing her rosy cheeks and sapphire blue eyes. I recognised, intuitively, that she was the quintessential Saxon girl. Give her ten years, and she would be devastatingly beautiful. The pathos of our little scene touched me quite deeply.

'Bring her here, Paula. Let me see what she looks like. Do you have a name for her?'

'I call her "Jo",' she said, gaining in confidence.

'Well, Jo, welcome to my little cottage,' I said to the puppy, and Paula grinned, thinking it silly that a grown-up man would talk to an animal. That was children's stuff.

'Paula, why did you bring her to me?'

'I ran away with her before my Dad could drownded her, and I took her to Mister and Missus Norton, and they both said to bring her to you.'

'Who are Mister and Missus Norton, Paula?'

'You know, they live near the pub, and Mister Norton has only got one arm,' she said, folding one arm in parody.

'Oh yes, Peter. Why did they think I would need a dog?'

'They said you might be lonely.'

How simple. How beautiful. How fitting.

'Well, we mustn't let Mister and Missus Norton down, must we? Let me have a look at her.'

Tentatively, Paula passed over this bitch, this runt of the litter that was going to be 'drownded'! The pup was part Labrador, and part something else, with the softest golden fur I'd ever felt. There were dark brown patches on her haunches, presumably inherited from the 'something else'. She lay on her back with the trusting eyes of the very young, but sensing my presence as being new she sniffed my smell, licked her lips, blinked her eyes, and I swear she smiled. Her body seemed in order, with the right number of legs and toes, but what does a man know? Women look at a new born baby for hours, studying it. Men look at the one head and two arms that they can see, and then mutter something like, 'Good. That'll do,' as though there was an option. Gwen would be able to tell me if she was sound.

I caught my breath! There it was! That was what my subconscious had been trying to tell me. I wanted Gwen and Christopher to share the cottage with me. All my plantings, all my modifications and furnishings were for her, not for me.

'Are you all right, Ken?'

'Yes, Paula, I'm just daydreaming a bit. I think Jo is beautiful and would really like to keep her. Right now, we have to discuss a couple of things, you and I. First, what do you want for her?'

'I don't want anything, 'cept she's safe, and you care for her.'

'Well, let's go and see your mum and dad to make sure that it sits well with them, shall we? I don't want to do anything behind their back. I would prefer that everyone is happy with the situation, but she'll be very safe with me, and you can visit her any time you like. Are you happy with that?'

'Yes, but I don't want to get into trouble.'

'You won't. I promise. The other thing is that I'd like to change the pup's name from "Jo" to "Nan". How would you feel about that?'

'Yes,' she said, 'I like that. "Nan,"' she said, tasting it and finally approving it.

'Would you like to leave Nan with me now?' I asked her.

'Yes, that'll be good.' Her favourite phrase for a positive outcome.

'When would be the best time to see your dad?'

'Probably best you come back now. He's not doing much at the moment.'

'How far is your farm, Paula?'

'About four miles, I think.'

'And you walked all the way into the village to see Mister and Missus Norton, and then out here to me?'

'Yes.'

'I think you have earned yourself a ride on my trusty bike.'

Her eyes shone with excitement.

'Could I?'

'Of course,' I exclaimed, feeling very pleased that I could make her day at least a little more exciting. 'We'll bring Nan with us so that I can do a proper handing over from your parents if they approve.'

I locked the back door, got Paula and the puppy settled on the crossbar and peddled merrily down the lane, past the fields of maturing crops in this warm growing time.

Just before we reached her farm, I asked Paula what her father's name was.

'Harold,' she said, with a hint of distaste and rebellion.

Leaning my bike against the farmhouse wall, I helped Paula get down with Nan and followed her to the back door. It was good manners to stay outside while she went to fetch her father.

This large brick and flint building and its surrounds were tidy and well maintained. The thatch was in good shape, and the curtains and windows were clean and tidy. There was a small, trimmed lawn with rose beds around it that would have looked beautiful in the summertime. The whole area had a 'cared-for' feel to it.

A man in a tweed jacket, jodhpurs, leather gaiters and boots came towards me with his hand outstretched. He was big and buff, with a red face but a lot of intelligence in his eyes. This was going to be easier than I thought. I held my hand out, and we shook.

'Ken,' I said.

'Harold. Thank you for bringing Paula home. I'm afraid she got quite emotional about that runt. Tell me what happened.'

'Well, she came to my cottage and asked if I would look after the puppy. That would be up to you, I told her. I brought both of them home so that I could ask you if you wouldn't mind. What do you think?'

'I think a cup of tea would be nice about now. Come inside. This is my wife, Esme. Esme, meet Ken, who wants to adopt the runt of the litter.'

'Hello, Esme,' I said. She was a sizeable lass, who'd give as good as she got, I thought.

'Hello, Ken,' she said. 'How do you like your tea?'

'Milk and two sugars, please. I've got a bit of a sweet tooth.'

It was a comfortable farmhouse that I guessed saw a lot of activity during the harvest. My mind suddenly focused. I seemed to have picked up a vibration of his thinking. He would want to know about me, so I had to be prepared.

'Just out of interest, was that you at the pub who sorted out the bully picking on Peter the other night?'

'That's me, and it was a pleasure.'

'You did yourself, and Peter, a bit of good there, because everyone loves Peter. He doesn't think so, but we do. Had a bit of war experience, I expect?' he asked me.

'With respect,' I said, giving him a direct look, 'I never talk about my past life. Some of that stuff is too painful, so I tend to leave it where it is. All right?'

'Oh, yes! Sorry! I didn't mean to pry. A man's life is his own, of course, but you did well against that bully. A big man, too, by all accounts.'

'Only in his head,' I said with a grin.

'Now,' Harold said as the tea arrived, 'about this runt. I don't want anything for her. If you think she'll suit you, take her by all means, with our blessing. Do you have a gun?'

'Yes I do, but I have no intention of shooting her!'

That broke the ice.

'I was actually thinking more about us going shooting sometime, you and me. The pigeons and the rabbits are getting out of control, and a bit of fresh meat never goes astray. What do you think?'

'I'd like that, and if it's not convenient for you and you say there is a problem, how about I come alone to take their numbers down? Would that suit you? I'd check with you first each time, of course.'

'Certainly, it would, and I'd be delighted,' claimed Harold. 'Of course, if you go on your own and you have a spare bird or two left over, it wouldn't go astray in our pot,' he said with a grin.

'Done. Now, just one last thing; Paula is quite attached to that puppy. I offered her to be able to visit whenever she likes, but I'd like your blessing for that to happen.'

Surprisingly, he turned to Esme and asked her opinion. She said she thought an occasional visit would be good for Paula. There was no question of trust or not. I guess my reputation as protector had started to spread its ripples in village life, and this was an unexpected bonus.

After saying goodbye to Paula and promising to care for Nan, I left, with a wave from the whole family and a promise to return the following Wednesday for some shooting. Nan was in my side pocket so that she could look out. It all felt very satisfactory; even the wet pocket when I got home, strangely.

Chapter 28

More trips to Dereham

D uring that April of 1919, I watched the vast but delicate spring miracle happen. Trees opened their umbrellas, and the bushes and hedges sprouted their skirts. The creatures of the countryside were in a frenzy of mating, nesting and reproducing while food would be available for their growing offspring. The migratory birds – the swallows, ducks and geese – returned in high numbers, all seeming to be calling their pleasure to be back.

My head felt much more in control now; my mind was much quieter, and everything looked to have greater clarity. The ambience around the cottage endowed me with calmness and quietness of spirit.

The nearest explanation would be like a piece of music that started with a jumbled, jangled, discordant dissonance that slowly calmed to a solo violin rejoicing in a single pure note that gradually gained in quality as the vibrato gentled in, before setting the melody with the leitmotif. Steadily, other instruments were joining in, adding new levels of emotional appreciation, concordance and depth. One day soon, I hoped, the whole orchestra would play perfectly together, which would signal that my sanity and equanimity were finally fully restored. The improvement, from the jumbled noise in my mind when I had returned from the war, was the result of my simple lifestyle and the quiet, unstressed life of the countryside.

One morning after breakfast, I went outside with my second cup of tea to be greeted by one of those miracles that country people appreciate as a unique personal bonus. There was a spider's web suspended in a bend of my honeysuckle's stem, where the dew on it caught the sun. One particular drop sent out shimmering rainbow colours, sparkling better than the best diamond ever found in any jeweller's shop in the world. Its brilliance was breathtaking, and I stood for several minutes in wonder and gratitude for this free gift. It reminded me of the little snowdrop on the battlefield, so far away and so long ago, but this time – no tears.

Diamonds. Rings. Gwen. It was time for another visit to see Gwen and Christopher in Dereham. I would aim for Friday market day, where the crowds would help hide me. I made preparations with my 'camouflage' of a stick, cap, beard and overcoat collar. I left Nan to look after the cottage. She was coming along very nicely with her training and was growing well and filling out. Of course, she had an almost bottomless appetite to match.

The roads I cycled along on that spring Friday were full of information if you could read it. The dock plants and nettles had resumed their growth beside the drainage ditches, many of which still had water in them from the melted snow, sleet and rain of the winter and early spring. Some areas here were heavy clay country from the moraines of Ice Age glaciers. They took a long time to shed excess water. Hedgerows were greening and had signs of buds, which would burst into white flowers around May and be a glorious sight; just like a fall of snow all over again. The grassy banks had bunches of yellow primroses in the sunshine. The winter wheat was showing as a green tinge to the brown earth, and the grass in the meadows was so lush that the cows were having trouble keeping up.

The sky and the trees seemed full of birds, all chattering and busy. The chestnuts and oaks, the limes, sycamores and elms all gave shelter and nesting places for them now that the growing leaves gave a degree of privacy and protection. Occasionally, a flight of geese would arrow across the sky, silhouetted against the backdrop of soaring white clouds like magnificent glacial cliffs, or the huge, billowing sails of a tea-clipper. These geese would probably be making their way towards the wetlands near the coast at Minsmere in Suffolk or somewhere in the Norfolk Broads. It was a great day to be alive.

My fitness was good. My sight and sense of smell were as good as I ever remembered, and my legs were strong enough not to be tired, however fast or far I pedalled.

Leaning my bicycle against a church railing, I removed the panniers, had a drink and a sandwich, and decided to approach the field at the back of Gwen's mother's house by a different route. Once there, my binoculars showed me an abundant bird life in this little stand of trees and that no one else was around. So I focused for a short time on their back garden. Nothing seemed to move in the house, suggesting that Gwen was at work in the post office and Christopher was staying with someone. Rather than hang around, I decided to come back in the afternoon when Gwen finished work, and I made my way into town to do my shopping.

As I was approaching the grocer's shop on the corner, H. S. Kingston, the throng of people on this market day was funnelled into a single line on the narrow pavement. Just in front of me, separated by one old man, was a back that I instantly recognised. It was her walk that had given her away – my mother! She, too, must have been going to the grocer's shop, and I watched her slightly bustling walk with sadness and guilt that very nearly overwhelmed me.

I had caused this lovely, kind and very gentle woman, who had given birth and nurtured me, a tremendous amount of heartache, which she neither needed nor deserved. She had cared for me in full measure, with no hint of favouritism to any of her children. My mother had been the hardest-working person I had ever known, and probably that's where she now hid from her sorrow.

The memory of the Fritz brothers and their machine gun, setting up in a position that allowed me to kill them, returned unbidden. I recalled thinking afterward about their loss to their parents, girlfriends and family, and now it had come back to haunt me. My own parents would have felt this profound sorrow at the loss of one of their children. For this, I was genuinely sorry, but for the sake of Gwen's and Christopher's future, my plan was sadly still for the best; it was the only course open to me.

It pleased me that I had retained some compassion after it had been entirely stripped away on the battlefield. Mentally, I said a prayer of love and warmth for my mum and dad, and to all the family who had suffered from my decision. Luckily, my mother didn't turn round, and I took another route to the grocer's shop, via the churchyard of St Nicholas to complete my prayer without a mass of humanity surrounding me and diluting my concentration.

I had been shocked at being so close to my mother. The enormous temptation to sweep her up in my arms, hug her and explain that, although I was alive and happy, I couldn't see her again, but that she should know I loved her but had to lead a separate life. It underscored the different pattern of my life now, from the one that had seemed almost inevitable, before meeting Gwen.

Eventually, my mind cleared, and I returned to the Mid-Norfolk Supplier, H. S. Kingston, who packed up my purchases in a box, which I would collect before they closed. My next call was to the gardening shop for a selection of vegetable seeds, raspberry canes and strawberry plants as well as a damson and a Victoria plum tree. I recognised the long-term commitment inherent in these choices. How interesting! My mind was still working independently in its cryptic little core, apparently needing to build food security for the long term.

When this had been sorted out, it was time to go back to my small stand of trees. Two mothers were caring for their children, who had a ball that held their attention. Once they had discounted me as a threat, identifying me as just another old bird-watcher, they wandered off to the far end of the field, and I turned the binoculars towards Gwen's place.

I could tell that she was home because the light was on indoors, but neither she nor Christopher made an appearance, and I had to return empty-handed. Well, except for the groceries, the plants in boxes attached with rope to the bracket behind the seat and a full set of panniers. It felt a long way home, but I got there just on dark. Nan went wild on my return. She ate her meal and had a cuddle. We did a little training then both of us slept soundly.

It soon became apparent that I would need more supplies. Lists were composed, my account was tapped and Friday, June 13th, 1919 was to be the day of my visit – a Black Friday! Maybe I'd get a flat tyre?

I had been 'home' for two years and reflected on my mental status, then and now, and gave myself a tick for improvement. There was now no screaming and no nightmares. I knew this because Nan would have woken me with confusion in her eyes, wanting to know what danger I was in and how to protect me. My mood was equable, and I could feel all the previous 'stuff' in my head was slowly disappearing. Battlefield scenes that I knew to be true could still be visualised, but the emotion had gone away, as though I was viewing them through someone else's eyes. But, best of all – no tears.

The daily noises at the cottage were those typical of rural England: bird calls, the wind rustling through the trees, the clucking of chickens, the gobbling of turkeys and an occasional bark from Nan when she wanted my attention. The sound of rain falling on broad leaves and the roofs of the henhouses was soothing too, and very good for my garden. Just occasionally, when the wind was in the right direction, I could hear the blacksmith's hammer ringing on his anvil in the village at the bottom of the hill. These were time-honoured sounds that hadn't changed in centuries; sounds that I had so sorely missed in the middle of the madness of war. No wonder my head had become so discombobulated.

I ate well-balanced meals like my family used to have and drank cups of tea or the clear well water from my tap. Nowadays, my sleep patterns were regular – going to bed as the sun went down and getting up with the sunrise. There was constant exercise with planting and picking, weeding and mulching, cooking and bottling. I had built some henhouses and free-range enclosures with wire netting for both chickens and turkeys, which I raised from day-old chicks, just like my mum used to do. See? No tears now. That had to confirm my improvement. It felt as though the bubbling cauldron of raw survival emotions that used to boil every minute of every day had lost its fire, and all the terrors of the battlefield had cooled down and lost their energy.

Chapter 29

AN OLD NEMESIS

It was now June again, Friday the 18th, 1920, and for me, this was the most significant shopping trip of the year. Almost all the crops came to maturity in August and September, and I needed a large number and an increased quantity of goods to cope with that — mostly sugar, salt, vinegar and spices, with Kilner jars to seal everything in. Several people in the district were buying goods from me. Owen and Wendy at the pub were my best customers, while Harold and Esme and many other farmers would buy my pickled red cabbage, pickled onions and beetroot, and chutneys in the form of gooseberry, apple and, my favourite, 'Norfolk' fruit chutney. I also made different kinds of vinegar, jellies, jams and sauces. I had a great time in the kitchen. But the necessity for additional essential cooking ingredients was now urgent.

My first call was to the grocers, H. S. Kingston, as it usually was. I gave the man my list. He spent time looking at the items and quantities.

'Which of these items would you like to take with you and which would you like us to deliver, sir?'

'I'll take the tea and the spices if you wouldn't mind delivering the remainder.'

'Not at all, sir. We'll have them to you on Tuesday afternoon. We have your address, I believe?'

'Yes, you do. It's a Salthouse address.'

'I'll try to bring the goods to you personally, sir. It's very nice to get out of the shop in weather like this, and I find your area very pretty.'

'Yes, it is. Thank you.'

I went to the hardware shop, Utting and Buckingham, to get some tools, a new pair of secateurs, a garden sieve, a ball of twine and some lubricating oil. The nursery shop had the plants I wanted, so I had them boxed, saying I would return for them. From there I rode to Gwen's mother's house on Commercial Road, parked the bike at the entrance to the recreation field and settled in the trees to observe.

She appeared almost at once with a basket of laundry to hang out, and my heart sang. She looked a little thinner, I thought, and there was not the spark of vivacity I remembered so vividly.

Suddenly, there was a huge 'BANG' in my chest, and I thought my heart had exploded. I saw a man following her! He walked over to her and hit her in the face, knocking her to the ground. An instant later, I heard her wail, and my blood turned to ice. Just then Christopher ran from the house, throwing himself over his mother to protect her. The man kicked him and laughed, and I heard Christopher's shriek, too. I turned to look at the man closely through my binoculars. I was utterly dismayed to find Mickey Foster, aka 'Piggy' from the dance hall, so long ago.

The memory of his challenge at the door – the lift of the chin and his, 'I'll have that girl of yours, in spite of you' – came back to me as if it were yesterday. The hair on my arms and the back of my neck was raised. I was soaked in sweat from the shock, and my heart sounded like jungle drums.

I knew that if I raced in there now, I'd blow my cover and all my planning, and I would not be able to adequately deal with the bastard. So I had to settle down and think.

Oh, God! What the hell had happened to my poor Gwen? How, in God's name had that bastard moved in? What the hell was going on?

I did some intense breathing and eventually regained control. My head was doing very well under the circumstances. I could have done some idiotic things just then, but sanity had finally prevailed over raw emotion.

That's a first, I thought, with a wry smile. But what I needed to do was to get myself away from there before somebody registered that I had been there longer than I should have been. I walked away, checking the treetops to maintain my cover. I needed more information, and there was only one way I could do that and keep my anonymity. It would be necessary to follow Mickey when he left the house. He would have to leave at some time, and I'd be there.

By chance, in Commercial Road I found an empty house that had been boarded up, nearly opposite Gwen's house. I loosened a couple of boards on the back door and wriggled inside, pulling the boards back after me. It would need close inspection to detect the breach. I went upstairs and had a good view of the front of Gwen's house.

Patiently waiting and watching had been one of my primary skills so long ago. I drank some water, sat on the floor and looked out of the bottom of the window. Slowly, I moved the folded curtain a little way across so that I could see through the gap between the curtain and the window frame. It would take very close observation by a well-trained sniper to have seen me, but I was still minimising the chance.

Darkness fell slowly, and still I watched. My groceries would be available to pick up tomorrow as would the things I had left at the garden shop. Nan would survive overnight. For now, my total focus was on 'Piggy'. I knew his real name was Mickey Foster and wondered where and how he fitted into society. He had a lot of self-confidence, even arrogance – yes, a better word – and from his approach to Gwen at the dance hall, it seemed as though he was collecting scalps, notches on his gun or numbers of conquests, not the girls themselves. That fitted. So he probably had a dominant male-oriented family, maybe a father or that big, older brother he had mentioned, but indeed he was both mean and spiteful. The more I thought about him, the less savoury he seemed.

Suddenly, a light showed at the front door. 'Piggy' came out, shrugging on his overcoat. He slammed the door and walked up the path to the road, turning left towards me. I ran down the stairs very quietly, eeled through the boards and waited in shadow at the side of the house for him to pass.

I let him get about a hundred yards ahead before quietly taking up my shadowing. He led me towards the railway station and turned into the bar of the Railway Inn. I moved to a place where I could see in through a window. It looked quite busy.

It was decision time. Should I go in and keep an eye and an ear on him? The chance of discovery was most unlikely, and I could undoubtedly bluff that one out. The chances of Mickey spotting me and remembering me as I used to be was also virtually nil. The memory of Gwen's wail came back with a shock. So what was I waiting for!

With my collar up and cap in place, and with my bearded face towards the bar, I walked into the warm, smoky room. I asked the barman for a small beer and took it to a corner table. The little mug covered most of my face as I sipped, looking around to take in the people there. Mickey was standing near the middle of the room, talking to a man and going through a slapping motion. So, he was bragging about what he had done, but who was this other man? He laughed with him, although not convincingly, I thought.

Mickey was drinking whisky, neat, and I got a picture of him arriving home drunk and taking to Gwen with his fists. Those pictures could drive me back to madness! I had to calm myself before I did anything rash. Wait, watch and listen. A sniper waited in his nest until all the conditions were in his favour. I was good at this, so I would follow these tried and tested sniping rules.

Mickey would greet men by name, with a great big smile, which I noticed was not reciprocated. So he was not popular but thought he was. He was so self-centred that he was unaware of his real standing.

'Mickey,' a man called out, 'going to give your old lady another work-out tonight?'

Mickey beamed widely, as though he were being complimented on his behaviour. He probably thought he was a top man, a big man, in control of his charges.

'You bet,' he said with a laugh.

The looks on the faces of the other men told of their disgust. It was apparent that they all knew about him and his 'way with women', while he was completely unaware of any criticism. It was equally obvious that there was no respect for this 'brave' man who used his fists on women and children.

At the end of the evening, the landlord called, 'Time, gentlemen, please.' I was in the last batch of customers to leave. Mickey had had ten whiskies by my count and was staggering a bit when he set off home. I kept back, as one by one the other drinkers went their own way, finally leaving Mickey to walk alone. I walked up beside him and said, with a smile on my face, 'Good evening. Did you have a good time tonight?'

'Yeah, I did, as a matter of fact. And who are you? I've never seen you before,' he said aggressively.

'Oh, yes, you have, Mickey,' I said, still smiling.

'No, I haven't,' he said, and stopped walking, 'and I've got a good memory for faces.'

'How's Gwen?' I asked, changing the subject, catching him off guard.

'How do you know about Gwen? She's mine, and the bitch will do whatever I want, see?'

'Is that why you hit her this afternoon?'

'Who the hell are you, and why are you spying on me?' he queried with a satisfying hint of panic coming into his voice.

'I am the ghost of dances past,' I intoned, still smiling.

'What the hell does that mean?'

Except for a half moon, there was no light where we were, near the railway yards.

'It means that you have no idea about love and kindness, only bullying and physical violence. You were once told that physical violence would come your way if you were seen in this town again, and that is going to happen to you, very shortly. If you harm Gwen or the boy in any way, I shall kill you. Do you understand that?'

'Who are you?'

'I am a ghost. I am already dead, so I will never have to pay for your death. Remember that. So leave Gwen and the boy alone.'

His face had gone deathly pale in the moonlight. He swallowed several times, his eyes dodging back and forth in a search for a way out. He tried to make a run for it, but I had anticipated what he'd do, the direction he'd take. I swept his legs out from under him. He crashed to the ground on his back, and I knelt astride him.

'You were warned,' I asserted, chopping down on his nose with the blade of my hand. 'Down' would only break his nose. 'Up' would kill him, and I didn't need that complication right now.

He blubbered and held both hands to his bloody nose. As a parting gesture, I dislocated the little finger on his right hand. If he thought long and hard, maybe he would remember that from a previous meeting we had had, in Gwen's front garden, but with the pain and the whisky it may take him quite a while.

For some reason, I laughed in his face and sent him into unconsciousness with a very satisfying blow to the jaw. Then I realised how clever that had been because when he woke up, he would not be able to untangle fact from fiction, fantasy from reality.

My own reality had been just that; reality, not fantasy. This was just something I had to do – protect my family.

Chapter 30

Making contact

Returning to the empty house opposite Gwen's, I slept soundly until a milk cart woke me at dawn. Finishing the water and food in my panniers, I lay back and reviewed the past twenty-four hours. There was nothing that could lead back to me. My cover was intact. I would have to pick up my purchases and go home to feed Nan, which meant getting out of here before people started moving about.

What of Gwen? She would be wondering where 'Piggy' was. How relieved would she be? Would she report him missing? I doubted it.

Ideally, I should leave now and have nothing whatsoever to do with Dereham ever again. That would be sensible – but my love for Gwen and my feelings of tenderness at seeing her in such a vulnerable state had captured me in an iron grip. I couldn't escape because, in truth, I didn't want to, which made for the most effective prison in the world.

My bicycle was still where I'd left it, so I slung the panniers over and rode to collect my groceries and garden things. When asked, my explanation to the grocer was that I had been detained last night by a relative of mine who had a sick child, and I had had to spend the night.

As my loaded-down bicycle cruised the roads and lanes away from Dereham, my thoughts were about the cause and effects of my actions. Gwen would be so relieved at not having that sadist around. How had that happened in the first place? I would guess that he had heard of my death overseas by chance, or from the Longham War Memorial, and moved in by force, threatening to harm Christopher if she didn't do what he wanted. Maybe he wanted a place to hide from the consequences of something he had done elsewhere. He knew Dereham and felt safe enough to go out in the evenings, but not during the day. He must have known where Gwen lived from having stalked her before and had reasoned that threatening Christopher would guarantee her silence.

How did she feel about that? Probably abused. Maybe she felt a shattered self-image, a hopeless future and in danger at all times from this bully.

How did I feel about her? Very protective, naturally, but not fazed by his intrusion, strangely. I wondered why that was. I thought that our love could transcend most of what the world could throw at us. What I had done in France, to change my identity, and my actions last night, told me that my love for her was as strong as ever. Or was I still just an unpredictably violent old madman?

How many husbands would kill – for their wives?

How many husbands would lie to the army and risk being shot for that crime – for their wives?

How many husbands would desert their wives to protect them from their own madness, knowing that they would suffer at least as much as their wives did?

Now I had to work out what to do next. Gwen would accept Mickey's absence as providential and thank her God for that, making herself and Christopher safe again. Once that happened she would return to a sheltered life, in which she could bring up Christopher as she saw fit.

Should I disturb that equanimity? Should I try for a chance to see her? Should I try to make her understand? What in the world was I going to do? If I got this wrong, we would be finished, forever, and I didn't think that I could stand that.

We used to have such a strong, sexy and mutually loving feeling between us, which was the envy of all. We could communicate on a level that was not usual between a man and a woman. And we were friends – excellent friends – sharing and laughing together. I remembered saying to her that I would give my life for a relationship as rewarding as my mum and dad's, and I'd bloody nearly done that, twice!

So how did I contact her in such a way as to make the best chance for us to work? I decided to sleep on it and let my head do some positive thinking now that it had had some quiet and healing time.

When I finally returned to my cottage, Nan was so pleased to see me that she nearly turned herself inside out. She danced and pranced, and smiled and smiled, licked and danced some more, but got very serious when the food arrived, and I was ignored for 'the duration'.

The following morning was bright and clear, with a beautiful blue sky, as I sat on the old garden seat outside the cottage with my first mug of tea. This was what I had dreamt about in the trenches: peace and quiet, with nature going about her business, giving me some beautiful sights, available only to those with the eyes to appreciate them, like that dewdrop in the morning sun.

The idea of chocolate swam into my thoughts. Where had that come from, and why? I tried to ignore the concept and concern myself with what I had to do today, but it persisted. Suddenly, just like putting the last piece into a jigsaw, the whole plan fell into place. I decided to leave it for a week or more so that any ripples left in Dereham from what happened to Mickey would have settled down, and I would have a chance to make sure that my strategy was right.

Chris Shaw

I cycled over to the Dun Cow with Nan running beside me without a lead. Her fitness level was excellent as we had been out in the fields for training – obedience, direction and retrieval, mostly – and she was doing very well. I had begun her training in the area of silent commands, and she was learning quite quickly.

She seemed to understand when I left her outside. Owen told me he had no objection to Nan coming in, on the understanding that if she did misbehave, she would have to stay outside the pub. I brought her in and did a mass introduction. She sat, looked around at everyone and then checked with me as to where I wanted her. I blinked at a spot on the floor under the table where Peter was sitting. She walked over, lay down and went straight to sleep.

'You've got a really nice dog there,' said Peter. 'She's doing well with her training?'

'Yes, I no longer need a lead for her, and it's getting to the point where she can anticipate my commands. In truth, it's a bit scary. She'll retrieve on command but sits and waits for my sign, then brings the prey, drops it at my feet and sits down beside me again. It's textbook and great to watch.'

'She's all right on her own then – at home, I mean – when you go to Dereham?'

'Yes, fine, but she's really pleased to see me when I get back. Here's a question for you, Peter. If for any reason I had to go away for more than one night, how would you and Pat feel about looking after Nan? I would give you her food, or money in lieu, of course.'

'She'd be very welcome to stay with us for however long you needed to be away. Pat and I love her, and she seems to enjoy our company, too. Mind you, you'd have to get Nan's permission too, I expect,' he laughed.

'Yes. As silly as it sounds I would tell Nan about it and about how long I would be away. She would need some exercise too, Peter.'

'True, and so do I. So she'll get a run in the fields. You'll have to teach me what to do to give her the maximum running around, and me the minimum!' he laughed again. So that was settled, and it would give me more freedom in the future if I needed it.

The door opened and the face of 'Faith,' the main bully, looked around the edge and spotted me.

'May I come in?' he asked. I looked at him using my old sergeant's trick. I gave him a stare for ten counted seconds with my face expressionless, while he fidgeted and sweated.

Finally, I said, 'All right, as long as you behave yourself.' He nodded, and I said, 'Peter?'

'Sure, but behave.'

He nodded again.

'Check with Owen,' I told him. Apparently, he had Owen's blessing too. He ordered a drink and started talking, and the bar went back to its normal, relaxed, conversational tone.

Chapter 31

A NEW LIFE DAWNS

The sky was overcast and threatening rain when I set out to Dereham just after noon on July 2nd, 1920. A jeweller provided me with a small box of good quality, but unembellished. I had written a note, which said, 'FRANK IS DEAD, BUT KEN LIVES.'

I had written it the previous evening on a piece of ordinary exercise book paper that I hadn't touched, using a ruler to make the letters. There was no possibility that it could be traced back to me. The chocolate I bought had a soft toffee centre, Gwen's favourite, and it was included in the box, which I tied with a small piece of white ribbon.

After doing some household shopping, I waited until it was dark and the road was clear then crept up to her front door and, with my heart in my mouth, silently slipped my little gift through the letterbox. The front room was used as an entertaining area only on infrequent occasions as nearly all the living was done in the living room and kitchen at the back. She would not hear my parcel fall, so would have no timescale for when it was delivered or who had delivered it.

My journey home in the dark was accompanied by some very poor singing at high volume and, lacking the real words to most songs, except for the army versions, I was glad to be alone.

Two weeks later, using the same technique and timing, I put another message through Gwen's letterbox to say that I wished to meet her at St Nicholas' Church at half-past two on Saturday, July 31st, alone. I told her I had news of Frank. She was to sit in the second-last row at the back of the church and was not to look around, whatever happened, but that she would be safe.

I was there half an hour early, hiding near St Withburga's Well. It was a pleasant afternoon, and the summer flowers in the churchyard were blooming, warming the place with their vibrant colours. There was sweat on my skin because this was such an essential turning point in my life. If I made a mess of things, or she rejected me, I didn't think I wanted to go on living.

Waiting for her with such great anticipation and in such peaceful surroundings, I let my mind wander into her life and what it must be like. Since I had dealt with Mickey Foster, his absence may have seemed temporary at least, and she may have lived in dread of the footstep on the path. However, there must have been some gossip, some rumour or conjecture that allowed her to know he had left town. Perhaps he had gone back to his family. With such a sense of security returning to her life, she would have felt freer to have a meeting – mysterious as it was.

A sudden shock electrified my whole body as I saw her approach. She didn't look about her as she walked down the path and into the church. She was wearing the lovely little hat that I had surprised her with soon after we were married, and her favourite matching olive-coloured coat.

I gave her five minutes to get settled and start to focus with a sense of anticipation. I silently entered, sitting behind her.

'Gwen Matthews, you are perfectly safe, but under no circumstances must you turn round. Do you understand? Nod if you do.'

She nodded. I could see her lovely red hair and slender neck, and I could smell her scent. It made me giddy.

'What is the name of your son?'

'Christopher,' she whispered.

'He, too, is perfectly safe. I say this because of recent events. Tell me, please, about Mickey Foster,' I prompted, gently.

'Why do you want to know about him?'

'Please, just answer my question.'

'He was a perfect beast. He threatened to beat Christopher if I told anyone or went to the police. I hated him,' she revealed, vehemently.

'Tell me about your husband, Frank.'

'Who are you to be asking questions like these?'

'Please, just answer the question, and be comfortable with what you are telling me.'

'He was as lovely a man as I shall ever meet. We had a wonderful relationship, and I really miss him!' Her voice broke, and her head dropped as she tried to suppress a sob. She reached into her handbag, fumbling for a handkerchief.

'What would you give, or give up, to have that type of relationship again?'

'I would do anything and go anywhere. The only exception is that I would not do anything that involved harming or stressing Christopher in any way. He is the most important thing in my life these days, bar none.'

'I repeat to you that both of you are perfectly safe. I have one piece of information for you: Frank is dead, but Ken lives.'

'Who's Ken?' she asked, searching for meaning.

'The next time we talk, I may explain that. We'll meet again in one week, same instructions. Wait five minutes before leaving and do not look round.'

I got out of there fast but quietly, went back to my little hiding place near the well, and watched her walk out of the church, making her way home. What must she be thinking? Her mind must be in a whirl. I wondered if she had found the chocolate I'd left on the seat beside her.

The journey home settled my nerves a bit. The conversation had gone well, I thought. I had controlled it and got precisely the information I wanted. The Mickey Foster thing had been one of those brutal incidents that could shake a lesser woman to the core, but my Gwen was made of sterner stuff. Anyway, that was over now, and I sensed that her equilibrium was returning.

The question that I really wanted her to answer was about the level of commitment she would be prepared to make, to be 'together' again. That was the eye-opener. But there was hope! By God, there was hope. I did quite a bit of 'jumping for joy' when I got home, much to Nan's confusion, but she joined in the celebration anyway, catching my mood.

The next job was to work out how I was going to move our conversation forward, how to approach my identity and how to provide her with some options without telling her the whole story. She might not be quite ready for that yet.

The following day I rode over to Harold and Esme's farm intending to do some shooting. Some rabbits and pigeons would not go astray. They welcomed me with tea, hot scones and jam. Harold fetched his gun. Nan came in for a lot of attention, and they congratulated me on her training. She was very good with the rest of her litter, having a little run around with them. However, she became serious and focused once I had her attention.

We walked about half a mile to a small wood. Harold said we would walk around the perimeter where we would find plenty of both pigeons and rabbits. Sure enough, about fifty yards from the patch of woodland the air came alive with pigeons swooping out of the confines of the trees, and the ground seemed alive with rabbits running in confusion.

'Take the pigeons!' he yelled. 'I'll go for the rabbits.'

It took no more than three minutes for it to be all over. I had a large pile of cartridge cases at my feet, about thirty I thought, and Harold had almost as big a heap.

'Well, Ken, that got a bit frantic. You've had a bit of practice at shooting, I reckon. I didn't see you miss one. That was one hell of a display, my friend.'

'A bit of wartime practice. These don't shoot back, and trust me, that's a lot more relaxing,' I said with a laugh.

I sent Nan after the kill to deflect any more wartime questions. She worked for quite a while, and we had a heap to carry. Luckily, Harold had thought to bring string and a knife. He cut a couple of stout hazel poles, and we tied the rabbits' hind legs together and threaded them on, then tied the pigeons on the other pole by their necks. We balanced the poles on our shoulders and walked back to the farmhouse. Esme met us at the back door. She congratulated us on the speed and quantity of the kill but grumbled about the amount of work she had to do.

'I'd like to take a couple of rabbits for Peter and Pat if that's all right,' I said.

'Now, Ken,' said Harold, 'for the record into the future, you can take out of our shoots anything you want, for anybody. We've got such a lot that they won't be missed, and it will ease Esme's chores. In fact, take some for Owen and his wife, Wendy, too, from both of us, and we'll throw in a couple of each for Owen to raffle, with the proceeds to go to the Church Roof Fund or something for the village that doesn't go straight into Owen's pocket!'

'Yes, I'll do that, and I'll make sure that they know it comes from your farm. Fair's fair.'

'That was bloody good shooting, Ken.'

'"Efficient food gathering and pest control", I think are the terms you are looking for,' I responded, grinning.

'We'll do it again soon,' Harold stated.

The handlebars were none too stable on the way home because of the weight of rabbits and pigeons, but Nan had done very well with her retrieving and got an extra treat that night. She smiled as

Chris Shaw

though she knew what it was for, but I think she was just happy to get a little something extra to eat. Well, that's Labradors for you.

That evening I went to the pub and gave the rabbits to Peter and Pat, and to Owen and Wendy. They were delighted. The raffle was set up at speed since there was almost a full house. The tickets were purchased thick and fast, some punters coming back to buy two or three times. Owen decided that to be fair, he would raffle the animals singly so that more people would win a prize. It was a very happy evening, with four lucky people going home with surprises for their wives. I won twice but donated my prizes back for other people to win, and I didn't buy a drink all night.

Nan and I got home about a quarter past ten. I locked the doors and topped up her water bowl, cleaned my teeth and read for a few minutes before blowing out the candle. Sleep came easily now. The nightmares had gone, and the black, insubstantial shapes had stopped descending from the night sky with their claws out, ready to tear the flesh from my body. They had been replaced with country scenes of woodland and marshes, and of farmers ploughing the fertile soil. There were flocks of seagulls like clouds behind the plough, and many rooks and jackdaws searching for worms, maggots, and beetle larvae buried in the soil. It was all very pastoral and calm, but still with a slight hint of a death/burial theme that my mind hadn't yet entirely purged.

Nan woke me with a very low growl. I put my hand on her head to silence her. It was still pitch-black as I went silently down the stairs and out the front door, grabbing a walking stick from the hat-stand as I passed. Nan was with me, staying close and quiet.

I made a half-circle around the cottage on the lawn and squatted at the base of the apple tree at the back. I listened, wide-awake, with my blood singing in my veins because the hunt was on, and this was my territory and my specialty.

There was a feeble imitation of an owl's call from my left, which was repeated to my right. There were at least two. A step falling on the gravel path near my back door gave away the third, confirming my thoughts that these were the three bullyboys from the pub, coming to take their revenge. What could I do to them that didn't have to include the law? They would have to be marked, somehow, bearing the signs of a beating, which, of course, I would deny with a smile.

Light flared, and a kerosene-soaked rag burst into flame on the end of a stick, outlining the man and throwing his shadow onto the cottage wall. My signal to 'go' sent Nan flying silently after the leader. She jumped on his back and bit his neck. He was so shocked and unbalanced that he fell on to the flaming torch, screaming that he was being burned.

The other two moved in to help – just what I wanted!

My curved stick went around the ankle of the first one, toppling him onto his back and exposing his nose to high-speed contact with my walking stick. He started screaming and blubbering that his nose was broken.

The one on the right came quickly to his aid, and the walking stick just happened to go between his running legs. He crashed down heavily, mashing his face into the gravel. He started screaming, too, about the pain. It became a high-pitched squeal when I took one arm up behind him and dislocated his shoulder.

'Torch-burn' was utterly terrified of Nan, who was making a great impression of a wolf trying to eat his face off. I let that go on.

'Broken-nose' had gotten to his feet, spread wide enough for my high-speed walking stick to provide severe doubts about his future as a successful parent. His scream, possibly heard in the village, became a soft moaning, like a mother mourning the death of her child.

I called off Nan. I could just make out the starlight reflected in her eyes as, next to me, she looked expectantly from one bully to the other for a chance to savage someone else should they threaten me. None of the three boys had seen me, but were down and just about out.

'Gravel-face' got to his feet first, trying to locate individual pebbles embedded in his face with the dirty fingers of his one working hand, still blubbering and snuffling about the pain, but hadn't, as yet, given a thought to disfigurement. That would come later.

'Torch-burn' also got to his feet, looking fearfully around for the 'Hound from Hell,' while 'Broken-nose' still lay like an unborn child, keening in his enveloping agony. They got him to his feet somehow, since he was very reluctant to unwind, and staggered off up my driveway. They were as wretched a group of no-hopers as one was ever likely to see in a month of Sundays.

They had seen Nan, but only as an enormous looming shadow thrown onto the cottage wall by the light from the torch, leaping at the leader/arsonist and giving her the appearance of being ten to twelve feet long – a very savage beast indeed – a creature of legend. That was just before the arsonist's body extinguished the torch and all hell broke loose. It probably hadn't taken any more than a minute for all that to happen. They would never know what had taken place because it was pitch-dark. I was particularly pleased about that since I was as naked as the day of my birth.

Thinking back, I pondered about any wartime influences in that exchange. My ears seemed to have picked up sounds of active artillery shelling, but a long way away. This told me of further improvement in my mental condition. I had felt particularly alive, and my speed had been quite adequate, so all in all a good result.

Before I went back to bed, I had a celebratory drink of crystal-clear cold water from the tap. I gave Nan a cuddle and told her, 'Good girl.' Now that I had had some fun, I fell into a dreamless sleep.

In the morning, I found a little tin with some kerosene still in it, a stick with some rag, which looked like part of a little girl's dress, and a spilled box of matches near the back door. That was an evil act – a seriously nasty thing to think about – burning a man and his dog in their own home in the dead of night. Still, a lesson learned, for them, and I didn't think there would ever be a return bout.

Chapter 32

FULCRUM

My thinking about the next meeting with Gwen was getting muddled. The more I tried to prepare a list of questions, the more confused I became. Again, I had to think sideways, like the idea about the chocolate.

Early on Saturday morning, August 7th, 1920, I started for Dereham with dread in my heart in case my plan didn't work. If the worst happened, I would be left with my rented cottage, my dog and my vegetable garden on the one hand, and on the other, a shattered, shocked and disillusioned woman who had had her love for me turned into pure hatred for getting the style, the substance and the timing of my re-entry into her life all wrong. She could be totally outraged by my thinking and my asinine, arrogant assumptions. That would leave a solitude that would remain with me for the rest of my life.

However, 'Carpe diem', the Romans might have said, and gamblers, adventurers, risk-takers and lovers the world over had grabbed that as their war cry. Now it was going to be my turn.

I had a supernatural awareness of my surroundings as I approached the church. The gusting wind drove the clouds racing across the sky giving a slow, arrhythmic light-and-shade effect as I checked the environment before walking into Dereham's Church of St Nicholas, twenty minutes before our appointment. I hid inside, behind a pillar.

The vast enclosed space was tomb-quiet, with sunlight stream-ing intermittently through the south windows. There was the aroma of incense and wood, floor polish and candles, with just a hint of chrysanthemums. Apart from the light show from outside, nothing moved. There was a powerful sense of peace, solemnity and silence.

Gwen arrived on time and sat one row forward of the empty back pew. I waited, letting the outside influences disappear from her mind.

Everything I would ever do, or ever be, hung in the balance right now. It was all down to what happened in the next two minutes. Putting my collar down, I unbuttoned my coat, took three slow, deep breaths and walked slowly out from behind the pillar towards Gwen.

As I approached, I looked into her eyes. As I reached her, I said, very softly, 'Hello, my love.' Her eyes flitted all over my face, and her hands flew to her mouth, her eyes enormous. She must have thought she was looking at a ghost.

'Frank?' she mouthed silently; then so softly, 'Is it really you?' I nodded and tried to smile, but my throat was too tight to answer her. She flew into my arms and held me in such a grip as to never let go. Tears were streaming down my face, and hers.

All the duplicity of the last few years, all the interminable hor-rors on the battlefields and the hiding and the scheming, fell away. I began to sob, uncontrollably, like a lost child. The terror, the nightmares, the screaming, the blood and the gore, all that death, the thunderous noise and horror were being washed away in a rain of our tears, in the safe and loving arms of my beloved Gwen.

For Gwen, her loss, her loneliness and her desolation had also been suppressed, but now there was hope of love, of safety, and of sharing once more. It was almost too good to be true. We hugged, we cried, we both sobbed in each other's arms, and we kissed. The love we two had for each other coalesced once more, and we were almost complete again.

After what seemed like hours, I sat her down in the pew beside me. She wouldn't let go of me, in case I slipped away in some ethereal fashion. We looked at each other with wet eyes, trembling smiles and smeared mouths, and tried to get things into focus. We kept touching each other, holding a hand to the other's cheek, kissing softly and stroking hair.

At last, I put my finger to her lips and said, 'Gwen, darling, we have weeks of talking before we can explore all our time apart. I am so, so sorry that things turned out this way, but I had to go away from you and come back as someone else. Understand please, my darling, that I'm now Ken, and I will tell you the full story as soon as there is time.'

'But where have you been? Are you wanted for a crime? Where have you been living? What do you do?'

'Whoa!' I said, holding up my hands. 'One thing at a time. The short version is that my name is now Ken Bullen. I have been invalided out of the army and live in the village of Salthouse where I rent a comfortable little cottage, grow vegetables and train my dog, Nan.'

'But why couldn't you come back to me? Why ever did you leave me thinking that you were dead, with your name on the War Memorial? Why? I can't understand why you would leave me. Me, who loves you more than anyone else in the whole world! Why?'

'The "why," my darling, is going to take a little while for you to understand and accept. I have been very sick. I was blown up by an explosive shell, which did quite a bit of damage to my body. But up here in my head, where no one can see, I was so stressed and shell-shocked as to be quite mad. Whenever I tried to sleep, I would wake myself, and everyone around me, with my screaming because of terrible nightmares. I was cut off from my comrades by my madness. I couldn't talk to anyone; I wasn't hungry, couldn't concentrate and kept getting into fights. I could only do my job, which was to kill. And I killed ... let's just say I was very efficient, but I was beyond saving. It was imperative to see if I could get myself better by being alone in my beloved countryside.'

'But why not come to me? I would have nursed you, darling.'

'Yes, of course, you would have, but please, Gwen, think very hard about this. You would have killed yourself, and probably our relationship too, by trying too hard. Think of Christopher being in those circumstances. I chose this way because if I hadn't healed, you would never have to know about me, and not be racked with guilt for failing! It was 'being cruel to be kind'. I just had to do it this way. Please try to understand, my lovely, lovely Gwen.'

'My poor love. You've suffered, too. What on earth do we do now? This is such a strange situation we're in.'

See that? I thought to myself. *Gwen has already accepted what took me months to appreciate. She's a clever woman with great survival skills, and this reunion of ours could not have gone better. You are a lucky, lucky man, Ken Bullen.*

'The reality, as I see it, is that you are a widow lady whose husband was killed in the war; Christopher is your legitimate son, and you have documents to prove all that. I am ex-Private Kenneth Bullen, honourably discharged and invalided from the army with papers to prove that. So, ex-army Ken Bullen would like to visit the lovely widow, Gwen Matthews, with a view to marriage, which would mean spending a lot of legitimate time with the aforesaid beautiful widow in that pursuit.'

'Yes, I see that.'

'Ex-army Ken would also like to spend time getting to know her son, playing with him and telling him about the fearless and wise father he had. We will be able to talk freely much of the time to fill in all the spaces. Will that suit my beautiful Gwen?' I said, trying to put a light touch to my delivery.

'Oh, yes sir, please sir, if you don't mind, sir,' she said, instantly picking up on my play. 'Of course! The chocolates! How silly of me. You are one very sexy man, Ken Bullen, and I love you!'

It was then that she smiled that most loving smile of hers. The one that had haunted me every day for the five years we had been apart; the smile that captured my heart; the smile that showed strength, vulnerability, and trust, all at once. A snippet of memory came back, 'A man could almost enjoy going to war with some sleep and breakfast like that'. Her smile was my sleep, my breakfast and now, my salvation.

'Now, my love, there are some hard decisions for us to make. For our plan to work, no one else in the whole world can know about me and my old identity. Not a single soul! Not even my family, and that's been very hard for me, but it has to stay that way. Not your family, your friends or colleagues at work, and most of all not Christopher. Remember, I am Ken now. Ken will be a very good stepfather for him if I am awarded that opportunity. Can you do that, my Gwen? My life and our future depend on my remaining Ken Bullen of Salthouse.'

'If it means getting you back into my life, I will fight the Devil himself! Yes, my love, I see how it has to be. But there is so much more to talk about. I have a million questions. When can we meet again?' she asked, with a certain yearning in her voice. I looked at her eyes, and the lids were slightly closed.

'Oh, my goodness. Not here, and not yet!' I paused. 'But soon, my love, I hope. If I came to call on you, on my bike, with a bunch of flowers to court the widow lady, Gwen Matthews, would that be acceptable, do you think? And will you be able to tell Christopher about me without alarming him?'

'Yes, we have good, honest communications, and I will explain our new friendship. Christopher will accept you once he sees that there is kindness and no anger in you. Would you be able to come on Saturday? We could have a picnic lunch in the field behind us if the weather is fine.'

'I will definitely look forward to that, and I'll bring the food, which may surprise you! I will also have to buy some new tyres if I'm to do so much travelling. One day soon I will bring Nan, my dog, and introduce her to Christopher. They will become the best of friends.'

There was a moment of quiet between us as we realised that we had formulated a plan to get back to near-normal lives. Amazing! It's true what the old women say about the 'woman of the house' being the 'mood-maker'.

Two little lines appeared above her nose as she frowned.

'You asked me the other time about Mickey? How much do you know about that?'

'When I came to Dereham, I would always look out for you from the field behind your house, to check that you and Christopher were well and happy. It was the one way I could keep in touch with you in the hope that one day in the future, today may happen.

'I saw him there once. My heart sank, thinking you had taken up with someone else. You called him a beast. Why was that?' I asked, adding another lie and changing tack to cover it.

'One day, he was just there and forced his way into my house. He threatened to hurt Christopher if I didn't do what he wanted. So I cooked, cleaned and fed him for a few weeks. He went out to the same pub every evening and came home stinking every night, but he didn't take advantage, except for his bullying. I'm glad he's gone. I would have been glad if you had dealt with him yourself!'

I didn't fall for it. Gwen certainly didn't need to know about any of that – ever!

We both stood up together as though there had been a signal. We hugged and cried some more. I dried Gwen's eyes with my thumbs, and she dried mine with her handkerchief, which smelled of perfume and powder – the smell of her handbag. We walked

hand-in-hand to the church door and into the rest of our life together.

As it would not be proper for us to be seen together holding
hands, I gave hers a squeeze and let it go. Gwen suddenly turned
towards me, with a stricken look on her face, almost fear.

'Whatever is wrong?' I asked.

'Margaret, your sister, is coming to see me this afternoon. What
shall I tell her?'

'Gwen, nothing in your life has changed,' I said calmly. 'You
have met a nice man called Ken who lives somewhere in North
Norfolk, you don't know where. If you are unhappy with that story,
then nothing has changed in your life, but if we are to be together
again, we have to play this very carefully. From a distance, my disguise may stand up, but up close, never. So my family and I must
never meet. That will be part of your responsibility. Go home now
and think really hard about what you want to do, and what you are
prepared to do because, above all, I must remain as Ken.'

'"Ken" will take some getting used to,' she said, 'but I do see
your point. I've come this far and endured so much that I will do
anything that's needed never to be apart from you again. I remember when you first put my engagement ring on my finger, I told
you, "I will always love you, whatever the situation", and while I
couldn't possibly have foreseen this situation, my statement still
stands.'

'Gwen, I'll visit you next Saturday at about one o'clock, with a
bunch of flowers. I'll come calling on you, and we'll have a picnic.
Whether I meet Christopher then, or later, I'll leave up to you,' I
added gently.

I knew she had a huge amount to think about during the next
week and wondered about the outcome. She looked around fur-
tively and then pulled my head down for a somewhat frantic kiss.
Well! She was still really, really good at that. She went to the church
door and, without a backwards glance, stepped out and walked up

the road towards her home. Her gesture of not looking back impressed me. That took some discipline and an excellent grasp of the situation.

Fortune had favoured me in not being seen by any of my family in Dereham. If this were to continue, I must never again visit on Fridays, which were Market Days, and their special shopping days.

Chapter 33

Minor transition

As I cycled home, thoughts of my family and friends came back to me strongly. I knew how much they had missed me and how much they would have cried over my death. That they had kept in touch with Gwen had been a tribute to that bond, but it must now be broken.

If we were to be together, instead of my visiting on a weekly basis, she would have to break her ties with Dereham and come to live with me in Salthouse. This would mean giving up her job at the post office, selling her house and getting Christopher into a new school. These were enormous decisions for a woman to make. If she were to give up her security and take her child into an unknown environment, she had to have total faith and trust in the man asking that of her. If she made those decisions, then the responsibility would come straight back onto me, and I would welcome it with open arms and do everything in my power to make it all right.

People in the village would deem it right and proper that I take a wife. If she were a war widow, as the child would imply, and we were married at a small ceremony somewhere, I could bring her to my cottage as my wife, and no one would be any the wiser. First, Gwen had to make some decisions, and then I could start to sow the seeds of a romance to the villagers.

Nan was delighted to see me. I fed her, and we sat outside in the evening sun, me with a glass of beer, which was something I didn't do very often. What a day! I had my love back and if that meant having a clandestine affair with her for the rest of my life, then so be it. I would love her, and care for her and Christopher, no matter what she decided.

It was August, and I had been back in Norfolk for three years. There were just three months of growing and harvesting to do before the weather closed down the sunlight and warmth. I took stock and worked out what my needs would be for the winter months: large quantities of tea to drink, sugar to make jams and preserves, and wheat flour and yeast to make bread and cakes. Milk and meat I could get at any time, but I might need to get some spices and lots of rock salt to make the brine to preserve the pork and brisket. There would be a glut of plums, damsons, and green-gages around Salthouse in about a month or six weeks, so I would get H. S. Kingston to send me twelve-dozen Kilner jars and half a hundredweight of sugar. They could also deliver the same in salt, two gallons of malt vinegar for the onions and pickles.

My seed merchant could supply rosemary, oregano, marjoram, thyme, basil and the like. They would proliferate, their leaves could be dried and the seeds separated for future use. I could also get some dried fruit that would keep until it was needed for fruitcake and mince pies for Christmas.

Then a sudden thought struck me. If my plans all worked out, I could have two more mouths to feed, and in winter too, with little or no income to speak of! I'd better plant more potatoes, onions and other root crops that would keep for the winter.

That would keep me very busy until I saw Gwen on Saturday. I thought I'd better take some flowers, which I could pick up along the hedgerows, and a present for Christopher. Now, what would he like? It took most of one day before the answer came in a flash of inspiration.

His own penknife, of course! Gwen would be horrified, but that should do the trick. Men and boys' stuff. It would have to be a good one, not one that would fall apart as soon as he started to use it. I would go to the sports store on Saturday morning or even that second-hand shop where I bought my gun. There was just a chance he had something of quality that would not cost me as much as a new one.

The gardening took pride of place in my work during the week, apart from a shoot with Harold on Wednesday. The gun was a joy to use, and Nan had mastered the task of collecting the dead birds and rabbits, and – something that I'd neither seen nor heard of before – sorting them into two separate piles!

I even shot a young hare, called a leveret. It was running flat out from right to left in front of me, in a field of wheat that had been harvested. He ran behind a set of sheaves on the right. I fired a shot at the other end, and the two met, to his detriment.

'I saw that,' said Harold. 'That was unbelievable. Never in my life have I ever seen or heard of anyone shooting at something they couldn't see! I'm very impressed.'

'Well, thank you,' I said, 'but I took the chance that he'd not change his direction or speed. He didn't. So we win.'

'That's a nice gun you have there. May I see it?'

'Of course.' I broke it and handed it over, open. 'I bought it from the second-hand shop in Dereham, but I don't think he understood the quality of the piece.'

'May I ask how much you paid for it?'

'Forty-five pounds, and that included the tooled leather case,' I said with a grin.

'My word, you did do well. Not that I know all that much about guns, but my estimate would be closer to ten times that, and maybe more. Well done! I think you won on that one. Let's go back now and have a beer and get these carcasses sorted.'

Nan had had a wonderful collection time and walked beside me in a very disciplined way.

By Saturday, all the gardening and the preparation for my Saturday visit had been done, and I cycled to Dereham with my shopping list and had the picnic food in my panniers. My need for a bunch of flowers was met, mostly, by wildflowers growing along the way. However, as I approached Dereham, I saw a 'For Sale' notice outside a nice, neat detached suburban house. There were no obvious occupants, but the front garden had a riot of blooms. There were gladioli, foxgloves, roses, snapdragons and night-scented stock. Some delicate asparagus fern was growing close by and added a nice touch to my 'floral arrangement'.

The grocers, H. S. Kingston, were outstanding as always, supplying my order and making arrangements to have the bulk goods delivered. Next, I went to the second-hand shop. The doorbell rang as before when I went in. The man, from whom I had bought the gun, was there and recognised me.

'Welcome back, sir. I trust the gun was satisfactory?'

'Yes, it was, thank you. It's been a thorn in the side of the rabbit and pigeon populations ever since.'

'Quite so, sir. What can I do for you today?'

'I'm looking for a penknife for a young man.'

'Very good, sir.' He opened a drawer, which contained a wooden box with an assortment of knives, from leather-handled sheath knives to pearl-handled fish knives. 'See if there is something in there that takes your fancy, sir.'

I carefully went through this selection as a lot was riding on the lasting quality and appearance of this boy's knife and would reflect, I hoped, the initial quality of my relationship with him. These were all pretty mediocre. Some had good blades of Sheffield 'eye-witness' steel, but the construction was either weak or loose.

'No, I'm afraid there's nothing here that gets my attention. Do you have any others?'

'Indeed I do, sir. One moment, please.' He went through a door behind the counter that had a curtain across it and returned with another box. I could see at once that these were of far better quality.

I looked at him and said, 'Ah.'

'Quite so, sir,' he said again, with a slightly conspiratorial smile. These were superb knives, some American, some European, and some better examples of Sheffield steel. I selected one with a carbon steel blade and a bone handle. The edge needed sharpening, which Christopher and I could do together, but the mechanism was very sound, and the knife was attractive to look at. It was the right size for a pocket without taking up too much room. The bone handle was the colour of a good cigar, but with a patina. Even I would feel pleased to own it.

I put it back in the box and looked at others, just to muddy the waters. It took about ten minutes, but I had the time. Finally, I picked it up again and asked the price.

'Four shillings, sir,' he said.

I sighed and said, 'I'd be prepared to give you three shillings.'

Straight away he replied, 'Three and sixpence, and it's yours, sir,' he said.

'Done!' I exclaimed. 'Provided you can let me have a presentation box as well.' We shook hands and smiled. He'd earned some profit for his employer; I had saved sixpence and got a box to put the present in.

'Any time we can help you with anything else, do please call on us, sir,' he said by way of a parting sales promotion. I nodded and smiled as the doorbell rang my farewell.

Now I had flowers for Gwen and a present for Christopher. There was just one thing more. I went into the sweet shop, where they had hand-made chocolates and boiled sweets, and bought three superb chocolates. Each looked like a pile of exquisite, brown silk. These were packaged beautifully and cost me sixpence. A very extravagant gift but it did, after all, represent the re-joining of two lovers who needed to spend the rest of their lives together; so let's just call it a romantic gesture.

There was too much to carry to trust myself on my bike with the flowers and chocolates, so I hauled the panniers over my shoulder and walked the short distance to Commercial Road. I knocked at the front door as etiquette dictated. I was not sufficiently well known to use the more familiar back door as yet. The bolts were pulled back. My face was hidden behind the flowers. When Gwen opened the door, all she could see was a bunch of flowers and a pair of legs. I pulled the flowers to one side, revealing my face with a huge smile on it.

'Good afternoon, Mrs Matthews,' I declared. 'I have come to give you a large posy of flowers and, if it pleases you, to share some tea and conversation.' I smiled all the way through my delivery and noticed that her shoulders dropped about an inch. She had been stressed a little; Christopher must be there.

'Do come in, Ken,' she offered. I gave her the flowers and looked deeply into her eyes as I passed her. I closed my eyes for a second and nodded in a silent message to say that all would be well.

'Look, Christopher. Look what Ken has brought.'

He came in from the kitchen and looked at me with a quiet stillness. He searched my face, which had a relaxed half-smile on it. He considered me for maybe ten seconds. Then I saw temporary acceptance. I held out my hand. He looked at it, hesitated, and then shook it.

'Hello, Christopher. I'm happy to meet you. My name is Ken Bullen,' I said and left it at that. He certainly did not need a whole string of words that may, or may not, be sincere. I then turned to Gwen.

'Hello, Gwen. You are looking very lovely today.'

'Thank you, Ken,' she said, practising the "Ken",' I thought.

'I have another present, this time for both of you.' A spark of interest came into Christopher's eyes for just a moment. I watched him shut it down – in case it had strings attached, I supposed. I thought to myself, *Mickey, you bastard, I'm delighted I got rid of you because you have changed my boy, and I now have to work very hard to get him back. So go and rot in hell!*

Outwardly though, I brought the paper bag of chocolates from behind my back and gave it to Christopher to open. He literally jumped for joy when he saw what was inside, quickly sharing the revelation with his mother, who blinked and smiled her approval.

'Let's have a cup of tea, and then we can spoil ourselves with the chocolates, too,' said Gwen, her eyes twinkling.

'Just one more thing before our sumptuous feast,' I said. 'How old are you, Christopher?'

'I'm more than five,' he answered thoughtfully.

'Well, Christopher, I have a present for you, provided your mother allows it,' I said and handed him the box. His eyes got big, and he checked me out again to make sure I was serious. Then he looked at his mother who, I saw out of the corner of my eye, nodded. He smoothly undid the string I'd put around the box, and slowly lifted the lid.

His cry of delight was almost worth all that terrible time at war, which faded even further in the presence of my Gwen and my boy. I found that I was absolutely delighted with the moment, this moment that contained the actual birth of our relationship and its happy overtones.

It was at that precise point when I recognised how much I had healed. My head had finally caught up to this point, from which I could start moving on instead of just standing still and hoping. Maybe now there could be a change in my reclusive ways, perhaps by joining the human race once more.

Meanwhile, Christopher had taken the knife out of the box and was playing about with it.

'Christopher?' I asked gently.

'Yes,' he replied, slightly distracted.

'While your mother gets the tea, I'd like to talk to you about knives and the responsibility of owning one. Is that all right with you? Would you like to learn about knives?' What small boy wouldn't want to learn about knives?

So I explained to him about the responsibility of knives and guns, and that keeping them in good condition was part of that responsibility. People should only have knives with them when they may need to use them, such as in the country, on picnics or walks; otherwise, knives should be left in the house.

While I was giving him this talk in a very gentle tone, I watched him get closer to me. He had no idea he was doing it, but it accurately reflected the safety he had begun to feel. I gave a silent 'Thank you' to any Gods that might be passing, just as Gwen came in with the tea tray.

While we drank the tea and consumed the beautiful chocolates, I said, 'Christopher, if you like, the next time I come, I'll bring you some oil and stone to keep the knife sharpened, and I'll show you how to do that safely. Would that be all right?'

'Yes, please. I would like that. Please, what do I call you?' he asked plaintively.

'Well now, that's an excellent question, Christopher. On the one hand I have brought you a present, which you seem to enjoy, but on the other hand, you have only just met me. So perhaps, for the moment, Mr Bullen should be my name, but when you feel comfortable with me, you can call me Ken. Frankly, I'd be pleased for that to happen sooner rather than later, but I'll leave that up to you.'

'Thanks, Mr Bullen, for the knife, and everything. I look forward to seeing you next time and learning how to sharpen it properly,' he admitted, hiding behind formality. 'Mum, can I go and show my knife to David?'

'Yes, darling, but be back before dark. That gives you two hours to play. Say "Hello" to David's mum from me.'

Christopher scampered off to show his new toy to his best friend who lived down the street. Gwen moved towards me with her tell-tale heavy eyelids.

'Oh, God! I've waited for this for too long!' She came into my arms with great urgency. Her tongue worked wonders as she pressed her whole body against mine.

'Quick!' she said, leading me upstairs and falling back on her bed. I pushed up her skirt and saw she was naked underneath it. I fell on her, hungry for her touch and needing her immediately. It was strong, it was so good, but it didn't last long for either of us. She wriggled from under and sat astride me.

'We have a lot of time to make up for, my new man, Ken. I need you near me at all times. Now, again!' She closed her eyes and used all her senses to enjoy this moment to its fullest. Her mouth opened and I thought she was going to yell, but it came out as a gentle, extended, 'Ohhhh!' Her face softened and she smiled in repose.

'Now that is what I call a reward for so much waiting. Oh! Ken, what is to become of us? I'll never give you up; not now, not ever again.'

'I think, my lovely Gwen, that we had better get ourselves downstairs for another cup of tea and some talk.'

'You're right. Christopher may be the full time away, but if David isn't home, he could be back quite soon. A pity, because I'm feeling quite hungry for you again!'

'You shameless hussy, Gwen Matthews!' I paused, and then said, 'So am I.'

We laughed and kissed. 'Get your new man another cup of tea and let's talk.'

She walked into the kitchen with more sway than was strictly necessary, I thought, and returned with a fresh pot of tea.

'Tell me your thoughts since we met in the church last Saturday,' I begged.

'Well, you've made a place for yourself in Salthouse with your dog, Nan, and your garden. You are known in the village as Ken Bullen and have established a life there. I'm here, living in my mother's house, now that she has passed away. I have Christopher, and his care and stability must be of the highest importance.

'You and I need one another like we need food and water, but I don't see how that can be achieved. I can't just arrive in the village with Christopher, and you can't live here because people might find out about you, whatever that means. I think we're stuck. Can you tell me what your change of identity means?'

'Gwen, I'd been on the battlefield for almost two years, and I was nearly insane. I couldn't talk to anyone, but I could function as a sniper and kill other snipers very efficiently. My failing health and my inability to think clearly told me that it was only a matter of weeks, or even days until my luck would run out and my turn for the worms would come. Sorry. That was a little too close to the mark.' I apologised.

'My observer got his face shot off by a German sniper, and we were in the wrong place when a German shell exploded. When I awoke in the hospital, I exchanged identities with him. Frank was killed off, and I returned home as Ken Bullen. I had to do that to give me a chance to heal without inflicting my insanity on you and Christopher, which would have completely ruined our ability to be together. If anyone ever found out, I would probably be shot for desertion. I would be dishonourably discharged, and there would be no pension for you. In fact, I could be charged with falsely getting you a War Widow's Pension, and certainly imprisoned. That would be the end of Gwen and Ken, forever.'

'How awful. You poor man!' she exclaimed with horror.

'I've been very circumspect about appearing anywhere other than Salthouse, in mortal fear that I would meet someone who used to know me or – worse still – a member of my own family. That would be the end of my life, and our life, together.

'First, I had to get myself well, because if that didn't work out, then the rest wouldn't have worked out either. If you've given any thought to this, you will have realised that I was right. It's been very hard on both of us, but it had to be this way. Can you see that?'

'Yes, my love, I now get more of the picture. You poor soul. And you, so lonely, too. So, Ken, how do we solve this problem?'

'Here's a possible solution, which, again, you need to think deeply about, understand and accept before we start to put any of it into practice. While the plan is just a plan, our life at present is simple, and there's little danger. But as soon as it starts to become a reality, the danger increases. Maybe this is not the only way, but it's the only way I can see right now.' I let this sink in.

'In essence, we get married. You sell or rent your house here, and both of you come to live with me in Salthouse. There will need to be some lead-up time to let people know about our romance, both here and in the village, then we can get married quietly here or there so that you have the piece of paper that makes it all legal. I haven't thought about schools for Christopher or work for you, but you have some thinking to do before we start to move in that direction. How does that feel to you, as a plan?' I asked.

'Well, you have been the busy one. I'm going to sit on your lap while we talk!' She did, and it was fine. 'Getting married again, to the same man, is not bigamy since one of them officially died before the second marriage. There's nothing basically wrong with the plan, but you're right, I have some thinking to do. You have some exploring of schooling and jobs to look into. Incidentally, Ken, isn't it about time I saw your circumstances – the cottage, Nan, the garden and how you live?'

'Gwen, darling, it would be an absolute pleasure to show off my cottage to you. Let's arrange for that. If I ride to Dereham next weekend and hire a pony and trap to take you and Christopher to Salthouse, it would be too much to go and return the same day. You could stay in the local hotel with Owen and Wendy on Saturday night. They're good friends of mine and would look after you very well. Of course, you could always sleep with me at the cottage!'

'If only that were possible, it would be wonderful. And please continue doing what you were doing, yes, just there. That's nice. What? Where were we? Oh, yes! I'm sure we could do that, and you would have time to clear out all those floozies you keep around to satisfy your needs!' Gwen said, coquettishly.

'I would, wouldn't I? Anyway, we could have a picnic lunch and a candle-lit dinner at the cottage. I could take you to the hotel after that. All the priorities will be observed, and the start of the public romance will be launched. Let me know if you want this to happen next weekend because you've got to be happy with the very rough outline of the plan I suggested, Gwen.'

'I've been doing that while you've been doing what you've been doing, and it's delicious! And the plan is pretty good, too! I can see that it could work. Certainly, the house could be rented out, and if we ever needed money, it could be sold. So, set up this little visit to Salthouse for next weekend, and we will see what you've been up to. Now give me a last kiss and a feel of your gorgeous body and be off with you. Otherwise, I shall just have to take you upstairs and repeat your treatment.'

We cuddled for quite a while, until there was a voice outside, saying, 'Mum!' Christopher burst in, to report on his visit to David. He looked at me and said, 'David said that he thinks you must be wealthy to buy me such a good penknife, Ken.'

There it was! 'Ken!' Acceptance; from a 'more-than-five-year-old' boy, and it felt as if I'd just been given a free pass through the 'pearly gates!' My boy had just shown his acceptance of me as a part of his life. Of course, I had no idea what I would have done if he had wanted no part of me. I looked at Gwen. She had her special smile and the very special twinkle in her eyes. She'd spotted it, too.

As I started to cycle the twenty plus miles home to my cottage, I thought of the incredible change in my life in just two weekends. I was reacquainted with my lovely Gwen and had been accepted as part of the family by my unknowing son. Close to three years' planning and just two weekends to cash it in. But I had to be very careful as I was not out of the woods yet.

The owner of the stables in Dereham was just leaving as I arrived to book a pony and trap for the next weekend. I paid him some money, as he didn't know me, and told him I would pick it up at about eleven o'clock on Saturday, and keep it until about four o'clock on Sunday afternoon.

Did I know horses? Had I used a pony and trap before? Would I stop to give the pony a rest and some water? I told him that I looked after horses like he looked after horses, with a smile, and the deal was done.

Arriving home was always a pleasure, partly because of my welcome from Nan, and partly for the peace and serenity the cottage gave me. Now it needed to be seen through Gwen's eyes, and I could see some things that shouted 'Man!' There was no tablecloth, and there were dripping candles and mucky windows – not dirty, but not clean either. Things around the cottage that had to work, like hinges and catches and locks, all worked perfectly, but the window-dressing could do with a woman's touch.

Chapter 34

THE PICNIC

Saturday dawned, and I was on the road early. The day promised to be hot and bright, with just a slight breeze. The sky was cloudless, and it was great to be alive. There were many pheasants on the road, flaunting their freedom before October 1st when the open season started and Harold and I could start shooting them. There was good money in pheasants, and my little account could be significantly swelled during this season if I applied myself.

The blackthorn hedges and the young, hundred-plus-year-old oaks passed by quickly as I pedalled the lanes of Norfolk, getting great pleasure from the bird life, the flowers and the lovely views from the tops of the hills.

It was nearly eleven o'clock when I drew up at the stables. George, or 'Oold Garge', in the Norfolk way, was busy with the harness on the trap, which was polished, painted and looked a treat. The little pony looked docile yet disciplined and nuzzled my hand when I came close as I had found a little pile of carrots. I fed her one and asked 'Oold Garge' her name.

'She be Millicent,' he said with a smile. 'The wife named her, so don't blame me. I calls 'er Millie, and she do seem to understand.'

'Fine,' I said. 'Then Millie she is. I must say the trap looks splendid and will quite impress the lady who is the subject of my affection.'

'Well,' said 'Oold Garge', 'that's what counts, sometimes. Good luck with all o' that.' He gave a wry smile, meaning 'rather you than me'.

'I'll leave my bike here and pick it up when I bring her back on Sunday if that's all right. Here's the balance of the money I owe you, too.'

I checked the harness buckles, the tightness and lengths of the leatherwork so that Millie would be comfortable and we would be safe. I got up into the driving seat, settled myself and took her out of the yard under the beady-eyed supervision of 'Oold Garge'.

I felt very vulnerable, sitting up there for all of Dereham to see, so turned up my collar and settled my cap further down on my head, which, with my full, dark beard meant that I looked like a pale splotch in a dark, hairy, unidentifiable blob, or so I hoped.

Gwen and Christopher were ready when I pulled up outside their house. Score another one for the lady as I would not have to wait around while she dithered about with what 'might' or 'might not' be needed – something that men are not, in general, very patient about.

Gwen's suitcase, made of leather-covered wicker that she had brought for both of them, was smaller than I had imagined and as I loaded it in the back, I told her about the change of plan; that we would be having dinner at the hotel, and did she need any extra clothes? She said she had it covered.

Christopher leaped up, sprawling out on the back seat. I helped Gwen up into her seat, as much for the contact as for balance. She twinkled her eyes at me, so I knew she felt the same way. We took off along the side roads. Soon Millie got into the rhythm, and she almost danced along. Christopher sat on a folded rug, and Gwen put up a pink parasol. We must have looked like something out of a stage show.

The day was perfect. The sun made white highlights on the glossy curved blades of the lush, green meadow grass. The multitude of greens from various trees, bushes and grasses intermixed with the bursting golden browns of sagely waving wheat and barley as far as the summer haze allowed us to see. This was pure Norfolk. Red Jersey cows, the colour of Devon's soil, grazed peacefully in that milk-warm summer sun, and the trees of the woodland swayed and talked lazily amongst themselves. A chuckling stream split the sunshine into scintillating shards, reflected onto the undersides of overhead leaves as we drove through a ford. A lark trebled and trilled its theme of love to its nesting ground-based mate. The pigeons and cattle filled in the score of this full orchestral suite. In truth, it was a constable-style, East Anglian summer pastoral landscape – idyllic, even to non-romantics.

With a couple of stops to spell Millie by letting her drink at two fords along the way, we pulled into the driveway of my cottage. Gwen was looking around with the intensity of 'one who would be examined on the subject, later'. Nan had come around, making a lot of noise in her excitement. I got down, settled her, and then helped Gwen down. My introduction must have looked very formal and sounded quite silly to an outsider, but such was Nan's loyalty that she would kill to protect those close to me. So the sniffing went on, then a lick of acceptance for both Gwen and Christopher.

We went inside my cottage, and I could see that Gwen was impressed with the cleanliness and tidiness. She had no idea how much work that had taken – then again, of course she did!

'Look around,' I laughed. 'See, I managed to get all the floozies out before you got here. Would you like a cup of tea or a glass of cold lemonade?'

'A cold lemonade would be just wonderful as a thirst quencher. Thank you.'

Christopher had a glass, too. We excused ourselves from Gwen so that I could show Christopher how to sharpen his knife, which, naturally, he had brought with him.

We went into the shed where I kept all my tools. I got out a can of oil, put a few drops on the sharpening stone and demonstrated the correct way to stroke the blade, at what angle to hold it and how to maintain that angle. It was important not to push down, I told him, but to softly glide the blade over, first on the rough side of the stone, and then how to finish it off gently on the smooth side. He tried it, testing the sharpness by softly passing his thumb sideways across the blade, not along it.

That all went very well. I could feel the intensity of Christopher's concentration in learning something new. I talked to him about the other tools, what they did and how they were used. He soaked up the information like a sponge. We re-joined Gwen, now that she had had a good look through the cottage.

'Ken, it's lovely,' she enthused, 'and you've got all sorts of foods and preserves. You are a very resourceful man. Now, another lemonade if you please, and then you can show me your garden.'

We walked down the path between the rows as I pointed out what I had planted, when it would be ripe and what I was going to do with it. Arm-in-arm around the garden, we admired the plants all busily growing, with the bees pollinating and the birds singing. Then we sat on the garden seat.

'I could be quite content here,' sighed Gwen, squeezing my arm. 'There is a calmness, a serenity here that is very rare. It has something to do with the balance. I can feel it, but I don't understand it. Nan is part of it, the garden is part of it, the cottage is part of it and you are part of it. That makes a nice square, with equal sides. Perhaps that's the balance. If Christopher and I were to come here, I hope we wouldn't disturb that balance.'

'I think you would add two more sides to form a hexagon and we could all live in a beehive!'

'Oh, the honeycomb shape. Yes, that too is balanced. Thank you, Ken, you are a soft, gentle and very loving man. I really am a fortunate woman.'

'I hope you didn't find any panties upstairs, left behind by the floozies,' I interjected, breaking the spell purposely. 'We have a picnic to go to, remember?'

She touched my arm in a gentle caress, smiling into my eyes. 'I didn't forget,' she said. 'I was just waiting until you got round to it.'

'Christopher!' I called. There was a muffled reply some distance away. Soon he came running, his socks down, his jacket off and a huge smile on his face. 'You've been enjoying yourself. What did you see?'

'I saw rabbits and a woodpecker – a green one – and rooks nesting, and lots and lots of pigeons,' he answered, all out of breath.

'– and what were you doing wrong?' I added. He looked horrified.

'Sorry, Ken. I was running with my knife open in my hand. If I had tripped, the knife could have stabbed me. You did say. I forgot. I'm sorry!'

'I'm just trying to keep you safe, Christopher. Now that you've thought of it yourself, you won't do it again. Would you get some water in a pail and give it to Millie for me while I get the picnic things ready?'

'Yes. Where is the pail, and where is the water?'

'There's a pail in the shed, and the water you can get from the pump over there.'

He scampered off, having something constructive to do. The box with all the food from the egg room was put in the back of the trap. I helped up Gwen, and again she twinkled and smiled. I called to Nan who ran beside us. What a happy sight that was. We all had grins on our faces, probably for different reasons. It felt good to be alive in the company of my loving family – something I only dreamed could actually happen. In the not-too-distant past, that would have brought about a gush of tears; now it translated into a warm fuzzy feeling.

Gwen was happy to be with me. Christopher, in turn, was delighted with all things new, accompanied by his wonderfully sharp penknife, and Nan. Nan – well, Nan was a dog, and to have her humans around her with new places to go and things to do and lots of new smells to interpret just had to be a great time in a dog's life.

We headed for this place I knew, not far from the cottage. I unpacked the rug and spread it under a weeping willow tree. Millie was happily grazing, Christopher and Nan were already exploring. I set things up under the trailing branches of the willow with their little pointed leaves on long tendrils, all swaying in the breeze. We lay back and watched the dappling effect of the sunlight. It was very peaceful.

'Food!' said Gwen. 'Now! I'm starving!'

'Goodness, I got so carried away with it being such a perfect day that I forgot the reason we're all here.'

'Christopher!' I called, and he came scrambling up the riverbank, closely followed by Nan. They both sat, Nan with her ears in the position she uses for her 'begging' face.

'Lie down!' She got down but didn't believe I was going to block her from doing her canine version of Oliver Twist.

We served out the bread slices, the ham, pickles and mustard. I poured a glass of my special lemonade for everyone. There was silence as the flavours were tasted and savoured. The tartness of the lemonade countered the sweetness of the ham perfectly, as did the gooseberries in the tart with cream.

'Have you ever thought of becoming a chef?' mused Gwen. 'This is seriously good food. Are you telling me you prepared all this yourself?'

'Well, yes. Doesn't everyone?'

'Can I go and explore some more?' piped up Christopher, eager to be off.

'Yes,' said Gwen, 'but don't go too far.'

It's the sort of thing that mothers everywhere in the world say – no qualification of how far is too far, or why, or even when to be back. It can drive men crazy, but these are the things we must let go, understanding that they – all mothers – are just trying to be responsible, maintain control and keep everyone safe.

We lay back on the rug in this most idyllic of places, looking at the patterns of the sunlight through the leaves and holding hands.

'Now that I've seen your cottage, the way you live and the things you do, I would be happy to give up my life in Dereham to come here to live with you – if you will have me,' she added with a low chuckle.

'Gwen, nothing in this world would make me happier, but why, in God's name, does there always have to be a "but?" Christopher has to have a school to go to, and either you, me or both of us have to have some income. Your training gives you skills with money and figures, with people, their management and with general organisation and clerking. There has to be someone around here wanting at least one of your skills.'

I continued. 'Me, I'm just a farm labourer who actually knows quite a lot about farming. However, because of the way that I live, I have actually saved money out of my miserly little pension, which, with some trading in this and that, has grown into quite a respectable sum. I think that if I continue to do what I am doing now, but more of it, and get in some day-old chicks and turkeys to fatten, then I shall be doing exactly what my mother used to do to supplement the farm income. She used to take her produce to the Dereham markets.' I paused for a moment, thinking carefully how to word this next part.

'BUT! And it's a big BUT! If I can join with other people around here, we could have a market of our own, say, each Saturday or even once a month. Everyone could bring their own produce and sell it for a retail price. My mother used to sell for wholesale, so she got very little money for all her effort. If I went around the locality a day or two before, to check on other people's prices, we could be quite competitive. Half a dozen windfall apples may get an elderly man or woman a couple of pennies they didn't have before. We'll call it a Farmer's Market, and anyone can bring anything to sell — farmers and villagers.'

'Oh, dear! Gwen, are you still awake?'

'Darling, I'm awake and awestruck with the way you just stormed through to build a moneymaking venture from nothing; a venture that will also improve the lot of everyone in the village. It will bring them together in an enterprise that will enthuse and motivate them, but I can see the trap!'

'What trap?' I asked. 'It's perfect.'

'It's a question of size,' said Gwen, warming to her subject. 'It will be perfect for one year or maybe two. Then you'll get the carpetbaggers coming in, who'll want some of the money we will be generating, for one service or another. Or else they will use blackmail by threatening to set up a bigger one somewhere close. They will try to steal our trade away.'

'Carpetbaggers? What are carpetbaggers?'

'They were North Americans who went to the conquered south after the Civil War in America to gain financial and/or political advantage while there was still some disarray in those areas. They tended to carry all their belongings in cheap bags made of carpet. They were entrepreneurs, but with neither conscience nor integrity, so they should be referred to as criminals. They are here, now, in Norfolk. They're everywhere in the world, in fact.'

'Gwen Matthews, your knowledge of things outside my knowledge is a constant surprise to me. Did they teach you that in the post office?'

'No, Ken Bullen, they taught me how to learn. That reminds me, where is Christopher?'

'Let's walk down to the stream to look for him. He won't be far away, and he can't be in any danger. So relax, Mum!'

'You are a thoughtful man, Ken Bullen. Do you think that if he is a long way away, we might just have time for a little loving in a meadow?'

'You are insatiable, but, yes, of course. Look, he's with Nan at the other end of the wood. So we have a little time. Come!'

We ran back to the blanket under the tree and indulged our senses in each other. A loving time, a time for loving, no time at all but all the love in the world. She tasted so good, gave so much and made sure that all our desires were satisfied.

We again walked down to the water and spotted Christopher running towards us with Nan dancing around him. They both appeared to have smiles on their faces; both were entirely in their element.

It was time to pack up and go back to the cottage. Millie seemed to have had her fill of grass. She seemed glad to be on the road once more.

Once back at the cottage, Christopher went into my shed to touch and wonder at the various implements I had in there. I had to do some watering with my watering can while Gwen cleared up the picnic things in the kitchen.

I reflected on what a perfect time this had been; nothing at all had detracted from it. This was how we were meant to be, almost a law of nature in its balance. That was the word Gwen had used, and it was good. Balance? Yes. Completeness? Yes, indeed. That too.

Chapter 35

BREAKTHROUGH WITH CHRISTOPHER

G ardening was such a contemplative pastime, and I hadn't finished reviewing all the lovely things that had happened that day when Gwen's call came for a cup of tea. It was quite the domestic scene, reflecting some sort of Victorian paradise, which should not have been possible in real life, but it was – just for today maybe – but I would take it!

With the tea finished and Christopher playing outside, I thought the time was right.

'I realise, my darling, that our time together as a threesome has been so short, but I'd like to talk to Christopher about some sort of permanent arrangement. Our time together is incredibly precious, and I don't want to waste any, but my timing has to be right, otherwise it may actually damage our planning. You know him better than anyone on earth, so what do you think, Gwen?'

'Is that a proposal, Mr Bullen?' She arched her eyebrows and looked at me with that sexy, half-smile of hers that was half-challenge.

'It will be when we have Christopher's needs taken care of. There'll be no ring this time, but you have the one I gave you the first time around. Do you realise what a priceless situation this is? It should be re-created as a play in the Drury Lane Theatre! But, what about Christopher? I know this is really important to all three of us.'

'Darling, he's a lot more grown-up than his age would suggest, which is why I was happy with your present of the penknife. I think that if you asked him now, he would give you an answer that would reflect his true feelings about you, and about the three of us being together. This is very fragile, I understand, but both of us have to be prepared to accept his answers to the questions that we ask as part of the responsibility that I've taught him. It may delay our arrangements for a while, but it may not, too. Just ask the right questions, and I do think now would be a good time.'

'Very well, wish me luck,' I said, getting up and going to look for Christopher. All I really had to do was to look for Nan and there was Christopher.

I called him over. He came at a run.

'Christopher, come and sit down with me, please. I'd like to talk to you.' We got settled on the garden seat. This was going to be difficult.

'I have a few questions to ask you, just to see where we stand. Is that all right with you?'

'Yes,' he said, not embellishing it.

'The first one is fairly big, and it's this. Do you trust me? Do you trust me never to harm you or your mother?' Then I shut up.

'Yes,' he said. No qualification.

'I do enjoy both your company and your mother's company. If I wanted to think about asking your mother to marry me, how would you feel about that?'

He thought for the longest ten seconds of my life. Then he looked up at me and smiled. I could see her smile in him. My heart skipped a beat.

'I think that would be an excellent thing.'

'Why do you think it would be an excellent thing?'

'She's lonely, and she likes you.'

'How do you know that, Christopher?'

'Well, she sort of "lights up" when you're around. She smiles a lot,' he confessed.

'And you? Do you like me, too?'

'Yes, and not just because of the penknife. You are patient with me and don't make me feel guilty or bad. I feel safe with you, not like that other man who came to the house. I think Mum feels safe with you, too.'

'I think, young man, that you are very, very shrewd, and honest. I believe that you and I could become excellent friends. I can't replace your dad, but I will do my very best for you, and that's a promise. You don't mind your mum and me getting married, and I promise to do my best for you. Shall we shake hands on that?' We shook, and I gave him the first hug. He clung! Just for a moment, he clung to me! There went my heart, thumping around in its cage again, but thank God for no tears.

'There will be hugs on demand in my house. What do you think of that?'

'That sounds more than good.' He laughed and said, 'Let's go and give the good news to Mum. It'll make her very happy. You'll see!'

We had our first three-way hug, and I kissed her in front of him, and he didn't mind. This, of course, was remarkably different behaviour to that of every other family in the land, but it felt right for us.

'So, let's get ready for our celebratory dinner, shall we? You have fifteen minutes. Let's go! Tidy time!' I enthused, clapping my hands in mock authority.

There seemed no point in taking things too far. I let Gwen have the first turn at the bathroom and the bedroom mirror while I stayed downstairs.

Chapter 36

A ROMANTIC DINNER

It was still well before twilight when the three of us set off, looking smart, happy and gay. Gwen wore a single-piece, green linen dress that nearly came up to her knees. It also bared her arms and neck, which was a considerable change from the pre-war fashions. The dress would have fallen straight down, had she no bust, but she wasn't built straight, so neither did the dress behave that way. It curved and moved in exciting ways. It had bright yellow embroidered flowers on the front, which I guessed she had sewn herself, and a complementing bright yellow sash around her hips, which also tended to accentuate her movements. To me, she looked up-to-date, unfettered and entirely desirable. She also had a matching yellow scarf draped around her shoulders and would undoubtedly turn some heads tonight.

The bar was open when we got to the hotel. I ushered Gwen and Christopher into the saloon, the room where women were allowed to have a drink. The public bar was about a quarter full, and I saw Peter sitting by himself. The drinks came, and I excused myself to invite Peter to join us. He was delighted, and after being introduced, he made some charming comments about Gwen's beauty and Christopher's handsomeness. They accepted the compliments gracefully. Then Peter mentioned my ability to look after myself but announced it to the rest of the bar as well.

He regaled them with a none-too-truthful version of the fight I'd had with the three big boys who had troubled Peter. There was much one-armed gesticulation. Two little worry wrinkles appeared above Gwen's nose, while Christopher beamed at me as if I were Jack Dempsey, the reigning World Heavyweight Boxing Champion.

Fortunately, our presence was soon required in the restaurant. We took our leave of Peter with a promise to meet Pat on Gwen's next visit.

Our table was beautifully laid out with a candle and a bunch of flowers. The glassware and cutlery gleamed; the tablecloth and napkins were heavily starched and very white, contrasting magnificently with the dark oak beams and furniture. Wendy was at my side with a wine menu.

'Wendy, can we have our wine by the glass, please?'

'You, Mr Ken Bullen, and your fine party, can have exactly what you want, when you want it, tonight,' she said with a grin.

'Do you trust me with the drinks?' I asked Gwen.

'As with everything,' she replied, with her dazzling smile.

'Can we have a crisp white with the pheasant pâté, a full-bodied red with the lamb, and I think, unconventionally, a return to the crisp white with the crêpes, to counteract their sweetness. It will also be perfect, too, with the cheese board.'

'Perfect, Ken,' said Wendy and Gwen in unison. I got the distinct impression that the ladies had communicated a lot more information than just spoken words. I had learned not to get in the way of this, which at times was known to give advanced warning of something we men had entirely missed.

When the first glass of white wine came for Gwen and me, with a glass of lemonade for Christopher, I proposed a toast: 'May this wonderful and happy day be repeated as often as possible, throughout all our lives.'

Christopher lifted his glass, and Gwen twinkled again, raised her drink and sipped, with her eyes still on me.

'So, who's the big hero?' asked Gwen, wanting more information.

'They were just bumbling farm boys who were trying their hand at bullying. They just had to be put in their place, that's all.'

'Did you really run the biggest one into the wall, head first?' asked Christopher, with a degree of awe.

'I tried very hard not to fight him, because nothing is achieved by fighting, except perhaps self-preservation. Fighting is a last resort, not a first. They just couldn't be trusted not to hurt Peter, so I brought it to a swift end. Do you understand that, Christopher? It's essential in life that you use negotiation first.'

'Yes, I do,' he said. 'I have problems in the playground sometimes because I don't have a father.'

'How on earth do you cope with that, Christopher?' asked Gwen, apparently appalled at knowing nothing of this before.

'I usually say, "And your point is?" and they have to think about that. It seems to sort it out,' replied Christopher with a smile.

'Well done, well done, Christopher! I'm mightily impressed!' I declared, clapping my hands and patting him on the back. 'You are indeed wise beyond your years.'

Just then the pheasant pâté arrived, and we started to sample some of Wendy's excellent cooking. With the crisp white wine as a complement, it was perfect. The lamb shanks came with their slightly tart, red currant jus, accompanied by the full-bodied red wine, both of which were exceptional. We left a gap before dessert with another glass of red, talking about this and that, which segued into the fiery crêpes, much to Christopher's alarm.

'Can you eat food that's on fire? Why would you burn it at the table?'

'It's the way the French cook these pancakes. They do it to burn off most of the alcohol from the brandy, just leaving the brandy taste. Do you like it?' I asked.

'Not bad,' he said, condescendingly. I think he was covering up for not liking it, but being polite. That was good discipline plus excellent social skills. Gwen had done a first-class job raising him.

'Christopher, would you like some cheese?'

'No, thank you. I don't think I can eat anymore. Mum, can I go up to my room? I brought a book, and I'd like to have a read before I go to sleep.'

'Of course, you can, darling. Don't forget to clean your teeth first, and I'll be up a little later to tuck you in and say good night. Have you got your key?'

'Yes, Mum. Good night, Ken. Thank you for a wonderful day with Nan and the knife and the picnic. It was grand!'

'You're very welcome, and I liked our talk together.'

He waved and walked up the stairs, out of sight, carrying his key.

'That is one excellent gentleman in the making, Gwen Matthews. You've done a really excellent job of bringing him up.'

'I tell him the truth, always, and I don't condescend to his age. I show him examples of behaviour around us, and we talk them through. It's not hard, but you have to start early, I've found.'

'He didn't like the crêpe, though, did he?' I asked with a smile.

'No, but he covered well, don't you think?'

'Beautifully. And what am I going to do, to complete this most perfect day on this earth, to be remembered for the rest of my life?' I asked.

'In about a quarter of an hour, I'll go up and tuck Christopher in, if he's still awake, which I doubt. Then we can round off the day quite satisfactorily, I believe, as long as you are out of here by midnight!'

Gwen went on, 'Thank you, my wonderful Ken, for a perfect day from my point of view, too. Clearing our marriage with Christopher was a great coup. I didn't know whether he was ready, but obviously, he'd given some thought to it. I thought Mickey might have made him shy about having another man around, but I think it has taught him a lot about people and trust. What did he say when you asked him?'

'He said he thought you were lonely, and that you "lit up" when I was around. That's pretty good for a more-than-five-year-old.'

'The penknife was inspired,' said Gwen.

'But not as much as my patience with the follow-up lessons, apparently.'

'I'll just go up to make sure he's asleep and comfortable. I'll see you in a little,' said Gwen, with her eyelids heavy and her mouth soft.

'Count to two,' I said.

Wendy came to clear the table. I complimented her lavishly on the quality of her food.

'That meal was the perfect end to a perfect day,' I told her.

'I'm glad you liked it. I enjoyed cooking it, and Gwen and her boy are just lovely. Pull the back door shut when you leave,' she said as she walked away.

You girls! I thought. *You are so fast and bright. We men have no way of keeping up with your subtle-information exchange system.* I discreetly checked whether anyone was paying me attention, left the table and walked up the stairs to Gwen's room. I tapped on the door.

'Come in if your name is Ken,' was the reply.

I opened the door and went in. Gwen was under the covers. Somehow I knew she had nothing on. Very slowly, I took off my clothes in the candlelight while she watched. To prolong the play, I folded them carefully, and when I took off my underpants, she gasped and beckoned me in urgent invitation.

We wound around each other, kissed deeply, and there was a great urgency in her. She guided me, and it was just the sweetest feeling in the whole world. There was a lot of energy between us, and she was soon making little mewing noises until a final deep-throated sigh.

Chris Shaw

After a little while, she kissed me again and wriggled out from under me, straddling my waist. Again, I looked at her perfection through a lover's eyes. She was lost in the rapture of the moment. Her eyes were closed, her mouth soft, lips slightly open and moist, her beautiful red hair in disarray, and her breasts, with their pink aureoles and tumescent pink nipples, danced to her movements. I could feel her trying to slow the whole process to get the maximum pleasure, and I stopped my movements to help her achieve that. There was a sheen of sweat on both our bodies, and in the candle-light, she was absolutely stunning. Eventually, her need was too great, and her rhythm increased. I was afraid she would cry out, but a series of soft exhalations was her response.

She lay on top of me, sated and exhausted.

After a while, I said, 'Mrs Gwen Matthews, you are so beautiful. Will you marry me?'

'What, now?' she said immediately, and because of the ridiculousness of the situation, we both started to laugh. The more we laughed, the more noise we made, and the more important it was that the noise needed to be kept down. This in turn made for greater tension that increased the need to laugh. We stuffed quantities of blanket in our mouths to minimise the sound, and looked totally ridiculous, kneeling and bouncing there on the bed and dancing around naked with tears in our eyes. This lead, of course, to more laughter. Finally, after several false finishes, we did quiet down. She just said, 'Tomorrow.'

I stroked her back, first with the pads of my fingers, and then with my nails, circling slowly.

'Oh, mmm!' she said, turning herself to fondle me. The wine had increased my staying power no end. I turned too, feeling the heat of her – her honey flow. With tongues and fingers, we caressed each other, taking our time in the pleasure of our bodies, but again, she increased her rhythm, and we climaxed together, clinging hard to each other, getting the echoes and ripples of pleasure, lasting, and lasting.

Neither of us wanted to move. We both wanted more, but we kissed deeply and slowly, tasting the sweet scents of love – of each other. We fell asleep, caressing and murmuring sweet nothings, gentle things, with no language but love and caring.

I awoke in the dark, dressed and let myself out, making sure the back door clicked behind me. I found Millie grazing quietly in the field nearby. She whickered as I approached, so I stroked her neck and muzzle. She got me home in no time. I let her out of the traces, putting her in the fenced meadow next door. Nan had known it was me returning and didn't bark. We took ourselves to bed.

Almost immediately, it seemed, Nan gave a single bark meaning someone was coming. I opened my eyes to blinding sunlight. The angle told me it was after nine o'clock in the morning. I washed my face and cleaned my teeth, did something with my hair and ran downstairs. Gwen and Christopher were sitting on the garden seat, enjoying the morning sunshine.

'Good morning,' I said. 'Have you had breakfast?'

'Yes, we've had breakfast, packed, said our "Thanks" and our "Goodbyes" and walked over here. What have you been doing?'

'Can I get you a cup of tea?' I asked, avoiding answering a direct question.

'That would be lovely,' said Gwen. 'I'll give you a hand.'

She came into the kitchen behind me as I turned to look at her. Her face and eyes were as fresh as a young girl's. Her smile was so wide and warm, it melted my heart.

'You're extra beautiful this morning. How come?'

'I had a lot of beauty treatment last night from a stranger who understands those sorts of things. It's no wonder I look my best.'

'So, tell me, why doesn't it work for me?'

'Obviously, not nearly enough practice, darling,' she said, with one of her alluring smiles.

Oh, God! Please never, ever let me do anything to dampen that beautiful smile. I would die rather than allow that to happen.

'Christopher, a cup of tea for you?'

'No thanks, Ken. I want to take Nan down to the wood and see if we can find a hedgehog or a weasel or a badger. Is that all right, Mum?'

'Yes, dear. Try not to get too dirty and come back when the sun's high. We have to leave for Dereham at about one o'clock.'

'Yes, Mum.'

I continued making the tea when I was spun around and kissed, thoroughly.

'What was that for?' I asked.

'For being the greatest husband this girl ever had, once and soon-to-be twice.'

We took our tea out to the seat, drinking in silence. Then she asked, 'What do we do now, my love?'

'See if this makes sense. We collect as much paperwork as we can: birth and marriage certificates for you, Christopher's birth certificate, your mother's death certificate, her Will too, and, of course, Frank's death certificate. I will use my army discharge papers to get a birth certificate, but it may take a while. I know about Ken, his parents' names and where they lived, but it will still take time.

'When we have all these, we will then apply for passports, not for any particular reason, but once we have our passports, with Christopher included on yours, of course, it means that all the other bits of paper have been verified and validated. We can then leave at a moment's notice if anything particularly nasty happens.' I stopped to take a breath and then continued.

'Before the passports become a reality, we can call the banns of marriage for the three weeks needed, and get married in the Church of St Nicholas here in Salthouse. The vicar here is the Reverend James Bowden, and I know he will be delighted to do the honours. I've met him, and he's a nice man. Tell me what you think about that.'

Gwen was thoughtful, pondering all that I had outlined. She said, 'I have a special box at home where I keep all my paperwork things, which I call "A Safe Place". I'm ready when you are. Talk to the vicar and see what you'll need in the way of paperwork. It may be that your army discharge papers will do. I'll need someone to give me away, and you'll need a Best Man. I don't really want a big wedding – we've been there – just a small local village wedding. A few drinks and a bite at the pub afterward will be sufficient for me.'

I asked, 'How do you feel about Owen giving you away? Wendy can be your Matron of Honour or glorified bridesmaid, and Pat can be your support team. I'll ask Peter to be my Best Man. I suggest we ask Christopher to be our usher so that he's involved. He won't have to ask whether guests belong to the bride or groom's family. He can just accompany guests to their seats, filling them from the front to the back. We'll invite all the village folk; it wouldn't do to leave anyone out. Do you want anyone else?'

'No. It would be tempting the fates to have anyone who could bridge the link between Dereham and here. So, word-of-mouth invitations only.'

I put my fingers on the back of her neck and ran them up into her hair. She groaned and came into my arms, kissing with a lot of enthusiasm. We stood up and walked inside. It was just the lack of time that meant it was not quite as satisfying as last night, but it was still closer to heaven than most people ever get, I would think.

Christopher returned with a very excited Nan, who was quite put out when I told her to stay. I caught Millie, who was having a great time in the meadow next door where the grass was high above her fetlocks and harnessed her to the trap.

The 'Observations and Excitements of Christopher and Nan in the Wood' were related in great detail during our journey to Dereham, with dreams of having a gun and being able to shoot the 'bad' things in nature – foxes, weasels, pigeons and the like – in order to protect the good creatures – basically, everything else. These were creatures that were helpful and productive to the farmers.

We had a couple of rousing choruses of 'Frère Jacques' and tried, unsuccessfully to sing it as a 'round,' dissolving into peals of laughter at the comedy of failure. It was a perfect time, a proper family time together, and if it weren't for my wartime experiences there would not have been a cloud on the horizon. Maybe there was just a trace of my background depression remaining. Perhaps, too, it was a sense that when things are this good, don't expect them to last too long. Maybe there were still some shadows of paranoia that needed to be illuminated and dissipated. But I managed to enjoy the moment, and made sure that Gwen and Christopher did, too.

We arrived at Commercial Road as a chorus, loud but in tune. I unloaded the trap, made sure that they were settled in and then made my move to get the trap back to the stables by four o'clock. I gently kissed Gwen goodbye in front of Christopher. He was slightly embarrassed but not unduly so. Another hurdle jumped. They both thanked me profusely, Gwen with a look of great happiness on her lovely face, and Christopher with another hug.

I took my leave, confirming my visit next weekend. I returned Millie and the trap to 'Oold Garge.' He gave Millie a good look-over and said he thought she had gained weight.

'She did have some tall and lush grass to graze on,' I told him, 'and she seemed to enjoy the trip. I weighted the luggage in the trap so that she didn't have much weight to carry through the shafts.'

'You, sir, can take her out again any time you like. My horses don't always get treated as well as this.'

'Fair thee well,' I said, jumping on my trusty bike and pedalling home with a broad smile on my face.

Chapter 37

ANOTHER WEDDING TO PREPARE

The sunshine was pouring in through my bedroom window when I awoke the following morning. I lay there thinking of the past weekend and how busy I was going to be during the coming week. There was the visit to the vicar to see what paperwork would be needed. I had to also get the information from him about acquiring a birth certificate. And I needed to talk to Owen about having the reception at the hotel. There was some lead-time for this, and I wanted Gwen to be part of it. If we could do that next weekend, it also meant that she could meet Pat, Peter's wife.

I decided to visit Harold and Esme to find out about our shooting during the pheasant season. They welcomed Nan, and Esme gave me a cup of tea and a scone, hot from the oven, with jam and cream.

The fact that Harold knew a couple of spots where there were pheasants in profusion that were outside privately owned estates sounded like excellent news. We only had to make a few changes from last year, which had been highly successful.

Meanwhile, we agreed that another rabbit and pigeon shoot was overdue, especially after I told him about the deal I had with Owen.

'Let's have a shoot this week.' Thursday was agreed upon.

Chris Shaw

Next, I made my way over to see the Reverend James Bowden who was fussing with a candlestick when I entered the church. He greeted me, and we shook hands. He was middle-aged, late forties maybe, with a round, pink face and a tonsure of greying hair. He would not have been at all out of place in a Dickensian novel with a pair of small, gold wire-framed glasses. He had a ready smile, and a relaxed attitude.

'Hello, Ken Bullen. I do believe I owe you a large vote of thanks. Was it not you who organised some raffles of rabbits and pigeons at the pub, with proceeds going to the Church Roof Fund?'

'Well, yes, actually. Those animals were excess to requirements, you might say, and it seemed a good opportunity to contribute to the community. It was only a little, but I hope it helped. It was, in truth, rather selfish on my part, as hunting and shooting those creatures is very enjoyable for me. Owen ran the raffle and transferred the funds, so I really wasn't that involved.'

'Too modest by half, Ken, but thank you anyway. My message to you would be, "Go out and enjoy yourself some more!" ' He gave a great laugh at this, but I noted he had a good business head.

I asked for his advice about my marriage and the paperwork necessary to fulfil both the secular and pastoral requirements.

'My approach tends to take a fairly simplistic attitude to these things,' he said. 'If you have proof of identity, your intended wife has proof of identity, you both tell me that you want to marry each other and in the three weeks that the banns are announced no one has come forward to say anything valid against either of you, then I go ahead and marry you.'

'Vicar, would you accept my army discharge papers as proof of identity? All my other papers were lost in the turmoil of war,' I asked him.

'Of course, dear boy. These have been such dreadful times that certain allowances have to be made. Ideally, a birth certificate would be the document I would prefer, but I will be happy to bend the rules for a soldier who has been overseas and has probably seen and done things that my mind can only have nightmares about. Has your intended lady got a birth certificate?'

'Yes, she does. She also has a six-year-old son from a previous marriage, but she has all the paperwork regarding that too. How can I proceed?'

'Well, let's see. I need to see your documents and theirs. I would like to meet this lady and her son, too, and have her confirm that she intends to marry you. Once all that is done, I shall publish the banns locally. If there are no objections from anyone, we'll set a date, and I shall marry you,' he said, making the whole thing sound so simple.

'Thank you, Vicar. I shall get all that organised for next weekend. I will fetch Gwen and her son, Christopher, in a pony and trap. What would be the best time for you? No doubt you'll be very busy on Sunday. Would Saturday be more convenient?'

'Yes,' he said. 'I will have services on Sunday, of course, but any time that's convenient to you, Ken, I'll be happy to see you.'

'Thank you again, Vicar. You have been most informative and kind. I will see you next Sunday, with my lady and Christopher in tow!'

Walking out of the church into the sunshine, I breathed a huge sigh of relief. Now, Gwen needed to know about this and we needed to hire the pony and trap again. Then we could get the whole thing underway. I would write her a letter, which she would receive probably tomorrow – Tuesday, or Wednesday at the latest – asking her to get all her paperwork together and bring it this coming weekend. I would also ask her to see 'Oold Garge' and book the pony and trap for Saturday as the stables were on her way to work. It would also save me writing another letter and probably forgetting to post it.

She would be ready for me on Saturday morning and, while not doing a total repeat of last weekend, she could stay at the hotel again with Christopher. I felt a little worm of excitement and anticipation in my lower belly.

I needed to alert Owen to Gwen's stay, and Peter and Pat about a meeting. If we treated Peter and Pat to dinner in the hotel on Saturday, we could discuss the wedding and their roles in our plans, with Owen and Wendy, too. Yes, it was getting complicated. It was probably about time I resorted to making lists, my preferred organisational technique.

Drinks and dinner that night in the hotel would allow me to set up the meetings with Gwen at the weekend. The rest of the week included shooting with Harold on Thursday, gardening, training Nan, cycling to Dereham on Saturday and finding out where to get a copy of my birth certificate – well, Ken's, anyway.

Thursday came with one of those fine drizzles that cut visibility, making everything wet and uncomfortable. I cycled over to Harold's farm with Nan.

'I'm getting married in a month or so,' I said to Harold and his wife, conversationally. 'Naturally, you're both invited, as is the whole village, although it's going to be a low-key affair.'

'You old dog! When did you get time to court a woman?' Harold laughed.

'In between training Nan and planting seedlings, of course. Why?'

He thought that was really funny, slapping his thigh several times in his mirth.

'– and I suppose you'll go to the wedding between picking your strawberry crop and hoeing the weeds! You're something again, Ken Bullen. Tell me, who is this fortunate lady?'

'Her name is Gwen. She lives in Dereham and works at the post office. She has red hair and an almost six-year-old boy called Christopher. It's been a bit of a whirlwind romance, but we are well-suited.'

'Do you mean to tell me that you have ridden your bike backwards and forwards to Dereham to court this lady on a regular basis?'

'Well, yes, of course. How else would I get there?'

'You must be really fit, then. That must be all of fifty miles as a round trip! What do they say? "Love knows no bounds." I'm very impressed, Ken. Was she the one who dined at the hotel last weekend? Everyone's talking about her and how lovely she was. You dog! You "hider of lights under bushels!" We would be honoured to come to your wedding. If Esme can help with the catering, let us know, please,' said Harold, still slapping his thigh occasionally.

'Wendy will be looking after the food for the reception,' I said. 'Perhaps Esme would like to talk to her. Intruding into the conversation between two or more women is, perhaps, not the wisest thing a man can do.'

'Lot of sense in that,' said Harold.

After the shoot, I left with my share of the pigeons and rabbits, which I dropped off to Owen at the hotel.

'Part one,' I grinned.

'Promptly paid,' he declared. 'And I look forward to Saturday when we can have a sit-down talk with you and Gwen about the wedding plans. Wendy is getting quite excited about the prospect of feeding the whole village. "Putting on a fine spread," she called it.'

'Owen, we don't want her to stress about providing a Garden Party at Buckingham Palace, you know. We'd just like some nice bite-sized food to go with a few drinks to accompany some good conversation after the wedding.'

'I totally understand you, Ken, but I think you would know some things about women. They'll do what they want to do, irrespective of what you have in mind!'

'True,' I agreed, 'and Harold's volunteered Esme's services to help Wendy. I don't want to get in the middle of that, so maybe you can tell Wendy what I said and then leave it to the girls to organise it in their own way?'

'Ken, you've got a very tricky little mind inside that hard head of yours. I'll bet there's some other stuff in there we don't know about. You certainly surprised the village by suddenly turning up with a stunning red-head with a view to marriage, in a surprisingly short time! No prying, though.'

I left him with the words, 'If only you knew', accompanied by my little smile.

Chapter 38

CLOSER TO 'W' DAY

Saturday was a better day for the weather. The trees were just beginning to change into their autumn colours with their greens slowly turning to yellows before going to reds and browns a little later. They were beautiful earth colours of nature that foretold the death of the year. It was the end of this cycle, slowly descending into isolation from the sun and its warmth. The colours, which I call my autumn rainbow, were soothing yet stimulating at the same time. In my mind, to miss witnessing this natural phenomenon would be a terrible waste.

My bike was eating the miles as my legs and lungs were good. I parked it, carrying my panniers to Gwen's back door, which opened suddenly. I was almost flattened by a flying woman who wrapped her arms around my neck in her attempt to throttle me. There were strange squeaks followed by a kiss, which drove everything else out of my mind. Finally, she let go and stood back, her lovely eyes dancing and shining. If the eyes were the windows to the soul, she must be one very happy girl, and I delighted in it!

'That, young lady, was some welcome! Thank you.'

'Come in. Come in,' said Gwen in a rush. 'There's so much to talk about.'

'How about a cup of tea while a poor old man tries to get his breath back?'

'Of course. Silly me, you've just come halfway across the world on a dilapidated velocipede, and here I am, totally uncaring of your aged and frail condition!' she remarked, with the back of her hand to her forehead.

'Shh!' I said. 'She might hear you and "fail to proceed"!'

'She? She? Competition is she?'

'Not at all! I rely on her to bring me to you, which she does with monotonous regularity!'

We dissolved into laughter at the game, and she hugged me again. She prepared the tea and told me she had found out how to get a copy of Ken's birth certificate. Apparently, the post office had the forms to request one, and Gwen had taken a copy. It had to be filled out then brought back to accompany an interview. That shouldn't be too hard since it was being done by an acquaintance of Gwen's.

'Does anyone at the post office know of your plans?' I asked her.

'Oh no, not at all. I took all your thoughts and suggestions very much to heart, darling. It would be a betrayal to tell anyone of them.'

'Are you ready to leave for the weekend away?'

'We're packed and ready. I'm just waiting for Christopher to come home. He's playing football on the field behind us and is due any moment, which is why just the hug!'

'I see,' I said seriously. We were off again, creating another role-playing game.

Christopher arrived out of breath, ran up to me and gave me a hug.

'Hello, Ken,' he said. 'When can we go? I'm so looking forward to being in Salthouse and seeing Nan again.'

'When you've washed and changed, and I've fetched Millie and the trap, we'll take off. So don't panic. I'll go to get her now, and we'll all be ready at the same time.'

He dashed upstairs, and I kissed Gwen goodbye. I very nearly didn't get out of there! 'Oold Garge' was waiting for me with his hand on Millie's bridle and a smile on his face.

'Hello, Ken,' he said. 'I'm going to have to give you a discount if you become a regular,' he added with a grin.

'I would have thought that two weekends on the trot would have me qualified for that already,' I countered.

'I like that,' he said. '"On the trot!" That's funny, that is. And that girl of yours is quite a looker. If I was a bit – well, quite a bit younger, I might have given you a run for your money, there. Nowadays, just looking, with no actual involvement, seems to be the best I can do. Mind you, my wife might have had something to say about that,' he revealed, with a slightly guilty smile.

My bike went into the stable. I jumped up on the trap, took the reins and bade him farewell.

'Same time on Sunday. Four o'clock,' I shouted back over my shoulder and saw him nod.

The journey was fine. I pointed out to Gwen and Christopher all the beautiful colours of the trees that I'd seen on the way, and we talked endlessly about arrangements that had to be made. I told her that weddings tended to revolve around the women, as I'd heard somewhere, so she should save all her wisdom for Wendy and Pat. By the time we arrived at the cottage, we were pretty well up to date on everything.

'You do talk a lot,' commented Christopher.

'I agree with you, Christopher, but it's a way of communicating with another person, getting into their head and sharing the same information to make the right decisions. If it's the right person, it's fun, too.'

He nodded and ran off with Nan, down towards the wood.

'He'll be gone a while,' said Gwen with a suggestive look in her eye. I knew that look very well by now. We kissed all the way up the stairs. She was panting when we reached the bed. She fell backwards on it and dragged me by the neck with her. I wrapped my arms around her hips and squeezed her close to me. She started to move against me. I raised her dress, and she unbuttoned me, still kissing, and we were together again, striving to give and take the most pleasure. She wrapped herself around me, both arms and legs, and we came together, slowed together, loved together.

Leisurely, she lay back, spread-eagled. She was just the most beautiful sight in the whole wide world. I hadn't stopped, entirely, but my movements were small and slow. It was some time before she picked up the rhythm. Her eyes opened in surprise and then became heavy-lidded as the heat built again. Her hands were strong and urgent, pulling me higher. This time, it wasn't as frenzied but more collaborative, looking into each other's eyes as the tension mounted. Her lips parted, her eyes closed and she climaxed until the energy drained out of her, relaxing once more. No words were necessary.

A little while later, we had a cup of tea and called to Christopher, who had some lemonade. I drove us to St Nicholas' Church. It was a large church for an area with such a small population but was very bright inside since, unusually, there were plain glass windows, not stained glass as in most churches. The ceiling was dark blue with orange stars. It was a moment before I realised that the stars were actually dried starfish, and I only discovered this because they were of different sizes and configurations.

The vicar was on hand and free, so I did the introductions. He took us into his vestry and sat us down around a small table.

'Ken tells me that you wish to get married to each other. Is that correct?' he asked Gwen.

'Yes, that's correct,' replied Gwen.

'And what do you think about that, Christopher?' he asked unexpectedly. Devious, I thought, very wily. Almost sneaky. I'll have to watch him.

'I've already told Ken and my mother that I'm happy about it,' Christopher answered, somewhat formally.

'Jolly good,' the vicar announced, beaming broadly. 'Now, if I can see some paperwork, I'll make some notes, which won't take long. Then we can all be out of here on such a beautiful day; it's truly one of God's special days.'

He fussed over the details for a while and then we were free to go. Just before we left the church, I said to him, 'Vicar, how do you distribute the wedding banns? Do you get greater coverage than this Parish, for example?'

'No, Ken, I don't. At each Sunday service, for three weeks, I make the same announcement. If someone comes forward, his or her comments are examined. I don't foresee any problems. Do you?'

'No. Gwen has been married before, but she has her late husband's death certificate.'

'Yes, and it is precisely because of those sorts of comments that I have made a note of all your documents. Have you been married before, Ken?' he asked.

'No.' I said. No embellishments, no body language to suggest otherwise by looking elsewhere or staring at him, just a flat statement. How did I do this? Preparation. I thought it might be one of the questions that would come my way, and it was true – Ken had never been married.

'Have you got a day in mind for the wedding?'

'Not yet, Vicar. That's another reason for the visit this weekend, to ask you about the dates you have free in about a month or six weeks. We can discuss dates this evening with the interested parties and not have to revisit you with more questions.'

'A grand idea. I will just get my diary. Excuse me for a moment.'

'I have a little worm of anticipation in my tummy about all this,' said Gwen, beaming at me.

'So do I. We'll get a range of dates to see what suits you, then Owen and Wendy with the hotel bookings, and finally Peter and Pat. That shouldn't take long.'

The Reverend James Bowden came back with his diary.

'Given the three weeks for the banns, I have both the 16th and the 23rd October free at the moment. Those are Saturdays. If either of those dates suits you, let me know, and I'll book it.'

'Thank you very much,' I said and shook his hand. 'Just a question. Vicar, could you possibly do a wedding on a Sunday?'

'Certainly,' he said. 'Would you prefer a Sunday rather than a Saturday?'

'I would, actually, yes. Would that be a bother?'

'Not at all. I have a service at eight in the morning, another at midday. If we were to aim for say, half-past ten, how would that be?'

'I'll discuss this with the others, of course, but I think Sunday the 24th will be the favoured date. Anyway, thanks for all your help in this matter. I'll confirm the date as soon as possible.'

'A great pleasure,' he said. 'I look forward to your happy day.'

We walked away from the church along the stone path between the gravestones, which acted as reminders of the finite and sometimes fickle nature of life, and then drove back to the cottage for a spot of lunch. Christopher wanted to be off exploring with Nan again, and Gwen told him to be back in no more than two hours as we had to get cleaned up to go to the hotel for talks about the wedding arrangements and to have dinner with Peter and Pat. He looked up at the sun's position, did a silent calculation, nodded to us and ran off with Nan dancing around him – a very happy sight – as they disappeared across the field towards the wood.

Gwen had her seductive eyes again, so we went slowly upstairs and lay on the bed.

'I can't believe all this has happened, and in such a short time,' she said. 'You have been very busy, my love, and are obviously enthusiastic about the outcome.'

'Well, yes, of course, I am. The chance to have you with me all the time, to talk and discuss our days and our plans as a family, to garden, cook, love and share, will be as close to heaven as I can imagine in my life. To have lost you once almost destroyed me, but to have you back is paradise.'

'Yes, darling, I do understand. My sorrow at your loss was almost the end for me, too. If it weren't for Christopher, I don't think I would be here now. But I am, and I'm alive and tingly and hungry again!'

She smiled down at me and whispered in my ear, 'Yes! Keep doing that. It feels so good that I feel like sunshine all over.'

The time for words was over, and we indulged ourselves very slowly, building the tension with endless kissing everywhere, exploring with fingers and tongues the textures of each other's skin, muscles, sinews and curves – a whole afternoon of personal indulgence, of making up for time lost and turning old sorrows into pure joy.

After a while, I made a pot of tea and said to Gwen, 'You realise the significance of the 24th October as our wedding date, don't you?'

'Of course! I did in the church, but dared not think about it then or I might have said something to give the game away. Six years to the day since we were married before! What a huge amount of living went into that time. I intend to make the next six years so happy that it will make up for all that lost time!' she beamed.

The tea had just been poured when Christopher came home with Nan, who went straight to her water bowl. She must have been running an awful lot to be so thirsty. Gwen got Christopher cleaned up while I locked up, and we drove to the hotel, where Peter and Pat were already sitting in the saloon bar.

The introductions made, we sat with a drink each. I excused myself and took Christopher to get their rooms and the luggage arranged. This let the others have time to get to know each other. Christopher opted to stay and read, as I thought he would, because all this boring grown-up talk was really more than a boy could stand. On the way back, I checked on Millie to make sure she was watered and had food, then returned to the party.

As I arrived, Peter excused himself for a moment. Pat leaned over to me and said, 'Ken, I don't think I ever thanked you enough for protecting Peter from those 'bully boys'. He hasn't said so, because he is a brave man, but I think he was terrified. If there is ever anything I can do to repay that kindness, you have only to ask!'

'Thank you for your vote of confidence, Pat. I'll tell you and everyone else that it was nothing, but in truth, it could have gone horribly wrong. It didn't, and if you would be kind enough to help my lovely Gwen on her wedding day, I will take that as an unnecessary "payment" in full measure.'

We smiled at each other. Peter returned, and we went back to discussing the forthcoming wedding, and who would do what, where and when. Owen and Wendy joined in, and we agreed that 24th October would be the best date, if for no other reason than to give us an extra week, should there be a hitch. They felt they could cope with the Sunday trade as well as the wedding, since most of the Sunday trade was composed of locals, anyway. There were also people they could call on to help out if needed.

More and more was discussed, and we were all left speechless at just listening to Owen's very concentrated description of the things that he saw needed to be done. It was brilliant. It was all there. I decided to get one more drink each before dinner. The conversation gradually got back to normal. Apparently, Owen was very bright and had an excellent grip on the hotel business in general, and weddings in particular.

The evening went very well. Peter and Pat accepted Gwen as a good friend. The meal, while not up to the gourmet standard of our last 'Wendy-meal,' was still tasty and substantial: roast beef and Yorkshire pudding with roast potatoes, fresh green peas, horseradish sauce and lashings of gravy made from the meat juices. The dessert was mixed berries – strawberries and raspberries – with clotted cream, fresh cream, and a wafer, crisp and golden. The peas and the berries had come from my garden as part of a new deal I had been working on with Owen and Wendy for some months.

'How was dessert?' I asked Peter and Pat, as part of my market research.

'Just delicious,' they both said, 'so fresh that the berries could have come from someone's garden today!'

'I thought so too.' I smiled.

We had a liqueur and called it a night. They thanked us for a beautiful meal and left.

'Peter and Pat are just lovely,' exclaimed Gwen. 'You are fortunate to have such good friends here, but then I think you are a charming man who would make friends easily, anywhere. How come none of the ladies of the village have approached you – or have they?' asked Gwen, half-seriously.

'I've kept very much to myself, watching my back like any good paranoid would. I would have appeared quite cold and detached, I think. Then again, I gave no one any encouragement.'

'Well, you can encourage me, right now, Mr Ken Bullen. I'll go up to see to Christopher. What's my room number?'

'Room 33.'

'As long as you remember!'

She walked up the stairs very slowly, with a swing of her hips that was quite startling. As before, Wendy came to take away the plates.

'You did very well with that door last time,' she said. 'I hope you will continue to be that efficient.'

'Peter and Pat both enjoyed the peas and the berries. They thought they had been picked today. Isn't that nice?' I countered.

'Seriously, Ken, Gwen is one gorgeous woman, both outside and on the inside. She will make you a wonderful wife. I can see the happiness you get from each other's company and wish you a long

Chris Shaw

and delightful life together. There, I've said my piece, and Owen and I will give you a good send-off.'

'Thank you, Wendy. Your meals and your warm hospitality have made my Gwen feel quite at home in the village. Please know and understand that I would take off my own arm before causing her, or Christopher, any unhappiness that could be avoided. You have my word, Fairy Godmother.'

We both smiled and understood.

'I love the way you say, "my Gwen," but then, I'm just an old romantic!'

She left, and I went upstairs. I quietly walked into Room 33, closing the door behind me. There was Gwen, standing in a black garter belt and fishnet stockings, with the totally frivolous covering of some see-through gauzy material, and only the candlelight behind her to tantalise me with a misty profile. Fishnet stockings!

'You brazen hussy!' I whispered. 'Come here and be spanked and loved to death.'

'Oh, yes, please,' she said breathlessly. And didn't we play some games that night! She had once before expressed a wish to explore, and while I had no real knowledge of anatomy, or where all the magic, secret places were, it was, perhaps, a mutual exploration of fun and pleasure, a little pain, but with love every time. The stockings were, maybe, a bit of a catalyst, and full trust led to further discovery and delight.

I left quite late, but not before I had put into her mouth the chocolate that I had stolen from the dining room.

I raced home, sorted out Nan and fell into bed. Before I knew it, bright sunlight was streaming through the bedroom window. Oh no, not again!

It looked to be about seven in the morning, but I felt rested. Face, teeth, hair, breakfast, tea and back to the hotel to see if I could be there before they were ready to leave.

They were in the lobby as I drove up.

'Good morning, my Gwen. Good morning, Christopher. How are you both this fine morning?' I chimed, trying to be awake and cheerful, hoping the tea would kick in very soon.

'We are both extra fine. Christopher had a long sleep, and I had a deep sleep. We are ready to go, but where?'

'Soon we shall have to see the vicar to confirm the date, but it's a tad early for that. Why don't I take you on a trip around the village? You haven't really seen much of it – not that it will take us very long. How would that be?'

'Yes, Ken, that will do very nicely, thank you.'

I gave Gwen and Christopher a running commentary on who lived where and did what. I explained to them that the flints used in making most of the buildings in this part of the world were fossilised sea sponges. They were found in many eastern areas, including most of Norfolk and much of Suffolk, mostly embedded in chalk. Also, that the chalk itself was composed of an almost infinite number of tiny sea creatures that had died and fallen to the seabed a very, very long time ago.

The farmyards that we passed were alive with animal noises as the morning feeding was underway. Esme, who was sorting out feed for her chickens and pigs, hailed us and approached the trap. I got down and made the introductions.

'I'm getting ready to go to church; otherwise, I would have invited you in for tea and scones,' she said, regretfully. 'However, I've had a word with Wendy, and I'll be happy to help with the wedding feast!'

'That's marvellous,' said Gwen. 'You are most kind. The next time we are in Salthouse, you and Harold and Paula are invited to have some lunch at Ken's cottage. I guess that you haven't been there yet. He's not the most sociable man in the world, but I'm going to try to change that, a bit at a time. I'll leave him to make arrangements with you and look forward to seeing you then. For now, thank you again, Esme.'

I wheeled the trap, and we drove to the beach, or as close to the beach as we could get. Leaving Gwen in the trap, well rugged and equipped with my binoculars, Christopher and I ran up the vast bank of shingle and over the top to the water's edge. What was it about men and boys everywhere in the world, that made them throw stones into stretches of water, whether a stream, a lake or into the sea? Some of us had a powerful urge to look into bodies of water to see if there are any fish or anything else that was interesting. I have always done it, and it can be just a small puddle on the road after a shower of rain, but I have to look down into it.

We satisfied that urge by throwing about a hundredweight of stones into the North Sea, which didn't seem to notice. It was too rough to play 'ducks and drakes'. We had a short walk looking at the different coloured pebbles, watching the waves and trying to identify the gulls, ducks, and geese in the vicinity. Exercise, instruction and fun were all included. Just a dad and his son having a fine time. How wonderful that was.

Gwen was getting chilly when we returned. Christopher was full of stories, some factual, others with some imagination built in, as in, 'There could have been a pirate ship passing this beach not long ago, Mum!'

We drove slowly around the lanes with both wild and cultivated flowers in profusion. Some of the cottage gardens showed a lot of work and creativity in their floral displays. We came to St Nicholas' Church, found the Reverend James and confirmed Sunday, October 24th, 1920 as the date for our wedding, and 10.30am as the time.

'Have you got all the information you need, Vicar?' I asked him.

'I have, yes, and I will keep in touch with you as the date gets closer. Good luck to all of you!' and he waved us away.

'Right,' I said, 'back to the cottage for some early lunch. Then I'll get you back to Dereham so that I'll be able to cycle home in the light. That would make a change!'

I was ready for a cup of tea by the time Dereham and Commercial Road came into view. We unloaded the trap and got Millie a bucket of water. Christopher went off to find David to tell him all about his adventures.

'A week is an awfully long time to be away from you, Ken,' Gwen said wistfully.

'You don't think I disagree with that, I hope.'

'No, darling. Soon we'll be married and living together under one roof. That will be my idea of heaven, too. It was so good before, and now with Christopher, it will be sensational. I'm so looking forward to that but I know we have lots of practical things to do before that can happen. I will talk to the antiques man in town about selling off some of the furniture and bric-a-brac. What I've got in this house from my mother would never fit in your cottage. I'll sell that and then rent the house, which will mean talking to an estate agent. I know Bill, who runs the biggest agency in Dereham, and he'll find someone reliable for us.'

'It looks to me like our 'Grand Plan' is coming together very well, soon-to-be Mrs Gwen Bullen.'

'Yes, my love, but we always did work well together. I've been wondering what it will be like to have a break from the post office, and spend time in the garden and the kitchen.'

'And the bedroom, don't forget that!' I said. We kissed, and I returned Millie to 'Oold Garge', cycling home with my head filled with more things to be done.

Chapter 39

EDUCATING CHRISTOPHER

The remaining weeks flew by. Every weekend I fetched Gwen and Christopher using Millie and the trap, enjoying the journeys except when it was wet. Gwen spent time with Pat, re-arranging the original wedding dress and talking about the million things that needed to be arranged, even for a small wedding!

Gwen also spent time with Wendy, organising the details of the reception, the menu and the refreshments. She told me that she had been able to modify the 'Banquet' that Wendy had in mind, to no less than a 'Sumptuous Feast!'

Christopher spent his time with me, after we had dropped Gwen at the Dun Cow for more discussions. We gardened, watered and picked fruit and vegetables. I started his cooking lessons. We started with basic weights and measures, progressed to the science of cooking and preserving, health, safety and, above all, cleanliness, and then some of the various methods that I used.

He learned to read and understand some of my favourite recipes, and also about the presentation of food. He soaked up all this information, and in a short time I could say to him, 'Christopher, get me four ounces of plain flour, sifted, please.' He'd be off like a shot, washing his hands first and then weighing the flour on the old spring-loaded Salter scale, tapping the sieve to sift the flour into a bowl.

All of this was interspersed with our walks with Nan and observations of all the activity that was going on around us. I would get him to stop and listen, identify the birds from the sounds that he heard and learn their nesting habits and preferred nest positions, the eggshell colours, hatching times, fledging times, migration and flight characteristics. I asked him to try to mimic the birdcalls. To my delight, he was pitch perfect, although not yet able to get the right note order, but that was a physical coordination problem with his mouth and lips. He showed great promise for musical potential.

I asked him which direction the wind was blowing from, and he learned to describe its nature. There was speed, direction, temperature and humidity, then the scents and odours perceived. Was there the smell of snow or ice? Was there warmth that brought with it the smell of the ocean? Finally, I got out a map and we linked the areas where the wind had come from with the prevailing weather conditions in those countries.

We discussed the identification of trees and bushes by their leaves, bark, flowers, and their pollination methods, and whether they were deciduous or evergreen. Sometimes, I would take a magnifying glass to show the boy lenticels on the branches, stomata under the leaves, and the exquisite detail of lichens, and of ferns with 'packets' of spores under their fronds. Then we talked about the nature of parasites that inhabit certain plants.

Later on, we transferred all this knowledge to the garden, where parasites were more in evidence and, commercially, much more significant. There were also considerations of soil types, organic versus inorganic materials, fertilisers, mulch, pollination, and how to pick and preserve each of the crops. We covered water quality, and the science of watering.

It sounded like a vast amount of information, but if the person on the receiving end was a young, dedicated 'sponge,' who retained information as it was given to him, it didn't take long. The 'Teacher', though, needed patience without any form of punishment for getting something wrong. 'Good judgement is based on experience,' I told him, 'and experience is based on bad judgement.'

I gave him a bat – a modified fence paling really – and threw stones to him, which he tried to hit a great distance. He started off connecting with about seven out of ten, but by the end of ten minutes was doing nineteen out of twenty. It must be remembered that he was still only 'more-than-five-years-old', and that told me he had excellent hand-to-eye coordination. It wasn't just a test he passed, it was also adding to my knowledge of him, and probably his knowledge of me, too. We spent some outstanding times together, and I made sure we laughed a lot to try to develop his sense of humour. He relaxed with me. What a bonus. He had his mother's smile and an honest directness that made him a handsome and attractive young man. He had come almost all the way out of the place that Mickey had driven him.

It was during one of these wonderful times with Christopher and Nan that we had a visit from little Paula. I heard Nan's single bark and wondered who could be calling. Paula wheeled her new bicycle around the corner of the cottage, with a big, happy smile that spread to her eyes until she spotted Christopher. She came to an abrupt stop and stared at him.

'Hello, Paula,' I said. 'Come and meet Christopher. Christopher, this is Paula, who was very kind and gave Nan to me.' I got them both a glass of lemonade to ease any social shyness.

After the children had been playing for a while, it came time for Christopher and me to get cleaned up and to join Gwen for dinner. Paula was a bit reluctant to go as they had been having such a pleasant time together.

'What did you think of Paula?' I asked a little later.

'She's really nice,' was all he would say.

We washed, tidied ourselves and drove to the pub. Gwen was having a drink in the saloon with Pat and Wendy when we walked in. Christopher excused himself to go to his room to read, to get away from all the 'grown-up' talk. I ordered another round for everyone.

'How's everything progressing?' I asked.

'Ken, leave it to the women, and it all gets done,' said Gwen, smiling at the game she had started.

'Great!' I said, starting to get up. 'I'll go and join Peter in the bar next door, then.'

'Don't you dare!' blazed Gwen.

I smiled my most disarming smile, leaned down close to her face and said, 'Gotcha!' They all laughed at the game, and Pat and Wendy made their escape.

'How are you getting along with Christopher?' asked Gwen.

'Well, he's very bright and soaks up information quickly and accurately. We've talked about natural history, biology, botany, animal behaviour and identification, plant identification, pollination, and plant diseases and their treatment, soil types, cooking and cricket so far. His hand-eye coordination is better than good, and his attitude is absolutely first class. If he were my boy, I couldn't be more pleased!'

'Silly man! Yes, Ken, our boy is beautiful and astute, but then he had a good start with his father.'

'Oh, yes, but he has his mother's smile, which I absolutely delight in.'

We walked hand-in-hand to the restaurant. Over dinner, Gwen informed me about the state of the wedding preparations.

'You know, I really think the whole village is using the excuse of our wedding to have some sort of mass celebration. Somehow, everyone wants to get together and become a closer-knit society but, apart from the pub, there is no one single umbrella to gather together. Our wedding, therefore, has become a perfect excuse.'

'That tells me that my idea of a Farmers' Market will go down well. I think we had better get the wedding over; you ensconced in the cottage and the honeymoon over before we start thinking about that. Otherwise, our lives will get far too complicated. Now, let's eat. I'm starving!'

The conversation continued throughout the meal. The date, the dress, the banquet and the reception were all 'taken out and looked at'. Christopher's role as an usher was discussed, and the thought came to mind that maybe Esme might like Paula to be a bridesmaid, thus giving Paula and Christopher something to do together. We decided the idea should be raised when they joined us for lunch at the cottage the next day, as we had promised Esme.

Gwen went up to see to Christopher. Wendy, right on cue, came to collect the dishes from the table.

'You've really got the hang of that door now, haven't you?' she said with a half-smile.

'I have no idea what you are talking about, my good woman!' I said, haughtily.

'Yes,' she said, 'I am a good woman. You could ask Owen, but he wouldn't tell you!'

'Enough of this. Away with you! I have places to be and things to do,' I said, enjoying the game, but not wanting to get too close. She left with a lilting laugh hanging on the air.

I knocked and went into Gwen's room. She was in bed and beckoned me over. I sat on the edge and held her hand. There was something she wanted to say. I waited.

'Ken, darling, would you mind awfully if we just cuddled this evening?'

'Not at all. You do remember me, don't you? A spare ex-husband, who understands you very well, and, in truth, would welcome one early night in six months! I'll pick you up after breakfast, and we'll prepare for Harold and Esme coming round for lunch.'

We kissed at length, and I left, narrowly missing Wendy who was still in the kitchen. I didn't feel like any more of her repartee.

I arrived home to my welcoming cottage and my very demanding Nan. She was fed, my teeth were cleaned and my candle was extinguished, all within ten minutes.

By nine in the morning I had eaten breakfast with Gwen and Christopher at the hotel, carted them back to the cottage, and we had sorted out the lunch menu for Harold and Esme's visit. Christopher and Nan had gone off to explore the woods, and we were alone. Talking seemed to be on Gwen's mind. We sat outside on the seat, drank tea and discussed the wedding and some wartime stuff, just to give her a little taste to make her feel part of it. We went back over the whole reunion thing, and I was congratulated on my handling of the situation, albeit slightly grudgingly because Gwen still felt that I should have been more trusting of her flexibility.

'So far the banns haven't brought about any nasty surprises,' I said.

'And what, pray, would we do if you were discovered?'

'We would pray, and we would leave – to where, I don't know. This was part of getting passports organised, for just such an occasion.'

'At least we have a plan. The wedding and all the arrangements are on track. Wendy has the menu, and Owen has the drinks in hand. Let's see what Harold and Esme think of Paula taking part.'

They arrived about half an hour later, and Christopher came charging in with Nan.

'How are you, Paula?' asked Christopher.

'Better for seeing you,' she replied.

After some apple pie and cream, and a lot of excited discussion about the upcoming nuptials, Harold, Esme and Paula left, with effusive comments to make about the food and the hospitality. Christopher and Paula both said 'See you again soon', and parted.

Chapter 40

AN OVERTURE TO FAMILY LIFE

Christopher ran off again with Nan to the wood, while we made our way upstairs to have a little sleep because of the wine. We were awakened by Christopher's shouting, 'Ken, Mum, come quick! It's Nan!'

I was down the stairs, without realising I had been upstairs and knelt down on one knee in front of Christopher.

'Tell me,' I said.

'Nan's got her head in some sort of noose! I couldn't get her out. I think she might be dead!' I ran into the shed, grabbed a pair of pliers, shouted to Gwen to boil some water and followed Christopher towards the wood. We both ran as fast as we could to where I could see Nan, quite still, on her side.

I knelt down beside her. It was obvious she had found a snare, and, like every other snared animal in the world, she thought she could pull her head out of it. There was a deep cut around her neck where the noose had cut in, and she didn't seem to be breathing.

The pliers cut through the wire tying the snare to a sapling, allowing me to pull her clear of the woodland and onto the meadow beside it. Next, I felt for the wire around her neck, got the pliers through it, cut it and peeled it out of her flesh.

She still wasn't breathing. I grasped her muzzle and blew into her nose, released it and kept repeating it. Finally, she tossed her head and snorted, got to her feet, fell over and then slowly and unsteadily got up again. She shook herself thoroughly and looked at me as if asking me what was going on. I held her and patted her, and Christopher cheered. I gave him the pliers to carry, picked up Nan and brought her to the cottage.

Gwen's worried face met me at the door. She beckoned me in, and I lay Nan on the towel that Gwen had placed on the kitchen floor. I mixed some of the boiled water back and forth between two jugs until it was cooler, added some iodine then started to bathe the area around Nan's neck. The concentration of iodine was not strong enough to sting but would lower the germ count to help the wound heal.

With the broken skin painted, I tore a piece of clean sheet with the aid of Christopher's knife, which I got him to open and hand to me handle first, and wrapped it around her neck. Eventually, she got to her feet, shook herself, looked at us, and smiled in her dog way.

Another crisis averted. I hadn't realised quite how close Nan and I had become. It came as quite a shock that I could have lost her.

'Well done, Christopher. That was both quick and smart thinking on your part. You have just saved Nan's life, and I'm very grateful to you. She's become very dear to me.'

'And you just have to be the best Dad in the whole world!' he said, coming into my arms.

I felt the prickle of tears behind my eyes but held them back.

'Thank you, Christopher. Your mother told me that she loves me, and you just called me "Dad," and those are the two most important things that have ever been said to me in the whole of my life.'

We embraced. I patted Christopher's back, and we stood back. I looked into his eyes and saw love and happiness, akin to hero-worship.

I told him, 'From now on, I will be content to spend the rest of my life making sure you are both safe and happy. I will make any sacrifice necessary to give us a great life. You are my loves and my darlings.' We had a group hug, and I broke the spell by calling for some tea to 'fortify against the spirits of dog snares!'

Chapter 41

More planning

It was quite early when I arrived at the Dereham Post Office the next Saturday morning. I had my papers as well as the form filled out to apply for my birth certificate. I was soon seated in a small room. The lady who Gwen knew came in, we introduced ourselves, and my papers were taken and scrutinised.

'Do you know where your birth certificate is?' she asked.

'No I don't. It was in my cottage in Hampshire, but it was lost, with everything else, in a fire soon after I had left for the war. The army sighted it for identification purposes at the recruiting office, then I put it away safely. The police seemed to think that squatters or Gypsies had broken in and had been living in my cottage while I was away. It burned down, but nothing was able to be proved.' Then I stopped talking.

'You have your parents' names and their address, but again you don't have their death certificates.'

'No I don't, and that's part of the same story. Both parents died, as you can see from this form, in a train accident before the war. I had all the paperwork, but it went the way of my birth certificate.'

'Why did you decide to live in Norfolk?'

'Well, I met a bloke from Norwich who was in the trenches at the same time as me, and he kept on and on about Norfolk and how beautiful it was. After the war, because I no longer had a cottage, I thought I would try it; so here I am.'

'How did you meet Gwen?' A killer question!

'Do you need that for my birth certificate?'

'Not at all. I was just curious, but that's private, I expect?'

'Well, yes, it is rather. It was slightly embarrassing, actually, and the last thing I would want to do is to embarrass Gwen. I'm sure you understand.'

'Oh, quite!' she said. 'It's a pleasure to meet a gentleman for a change. Thank you, Mr Bullen, for your time, and for answering my questions. You will have your birth certificate in the mail within two weeks.'

'Thank you for all your help,' I said. 'Do you by any chance have anything to do with passports, too?'

'Yes, we do. When you have your birth certificate, we can use it with your army papers to apply for a passport through this office. Are you thinking of going overseas?'

'No, but if we were to go on holiday, it would be nice to have one on hand and not have any last-minute panic,' I answered smoothly.

'Lucky you!' she said, rising from her chair and smiling.

'Thank you, again,' I said, and got out of there before there were any other personal questions asked.

Gwen was full of talk when I reached Commercial Road in the trap.

'Let's leave it for the journey, shall we?' I was still a little spooked from the interview, in truth.

I drove out of Dereham, and we were near Gressenhall before I realised that we had been silent all the way.

I apologised to Gwen, telling her that I'd been disciplined to be quiet for long periods of time. I then asked her what she'd been up to during the week.

'Well, I've talked with Bill, the estate agent, who's found a nice, reliable couple to rent my place, with an option to buy when we are ready. The man who runs the second-hand shop, David, has offered to take everything I want to sell. He said that he would give me an itemised quote for all the pieces. If I don't think it is enough money, I'm free to take any of them back and not sell them.'

'Thank you, Gwen, for your report, but please draw a breath now and then, or you'll expire!' I joked, lightening the atmosphere.

'It did all come out at once, didn't it?' she said with a smile.

'That's excellent news indeed. An important question, my love: how do you feel about all this? Is it too fast for you? Have you and Christopher both settled it in your minds? Especially about the house.'

'I can't wait to join you in Salthouse. I already feel very much at home there with you and Nan at the cottage. Christopher, too, loves Nan and being around you. We've had a big talk about it, and that's what he said. Am I right, Christopher?'

'Yes, Mum. Dad, I love being there with Nan in the wood and helping out in the garden. It's much better than Dereham – well, except for David. I'll miss him.'

Gwen continued, 'Thanks are due to you, my love, for taking all the time and effort to cycle backwards and forwards to make arrangements for us. It really feels to me as though I should be living there right now. Let me just say that it feels – right.'

'Good. I was afraid that the time frame might be too fast for you. Now, my birth certificate will be through in about two weeks. The lass told me that she could handle the passports, too, which is good. However, she did ask some very personal questions, such as "How did we meet?" I thought that was a bit rude!'

'What?' cried Gwen. 'That's none of her business. She was being a busybody! I'll have a word or two with her when I get back!'

'You might like to think about that for a while before you start to burn your bridges, my love. There's no point in upsetting someone who could be in a position of power should you ever have to re-apply for a job there. It's not worth it in the short or the long term. No harm was done,' I said, placating her sudden anger.

'How did you meet Mum?' asked Christopher.

I didn't look at Gwen because it would have taken some of the apparent truth from the story I was about to tell.

'I met your mother at the post office, of course. I wondered if she was married even though she had a wedding ring on. When she told me that her husband had died in the war, I asked if I might call on her with a bunch of flowers, to have a cup of tea and a talk. She said, "Yes", and I turned up with a bunch of flowers, for a cup of tea and a talk. That's the story.'

Yes, my friend, a story indeed, but it fitted the facts as Christopher knew them, and Gwen would find the plot easy to assimilate.

'But you knew about me, didn't you?' asked Christopher, not wanting to let go.

'Yes. Gwen said that she had a fine son of nearly six, called Christopher. She didn't tell me that you didn't have a penknife. That was my own bright idea! Do you know why she told me about you?'

'No. Why?'

'Most men, who aren't married, want to have their own children, not someone else's. It was Gwen's way of seeing if I was one of those sorts of men. I'm not. I love you both, very much, and feel as happy as a man can be,' I finished in a flourish.

'What's going to happen to me when we move here? I want to move, but I don't know what's going to happen. Where will I go to school?'

'Christopher, I've discussed this with the Headmaster of Gresham's School near Holt. He thinks there will be a place for you there next year. Once the wedding is over, we'll all go over to see him to find out what he thinks of you and what you think of the school.

'Maybe you'll understand this, and maybe you won't, Christopher, but going to this school would be the biggest chance for you to make yourself the best person you can be. At an ordinary school, you would get to run around in the playground at breaks. At Gresham's, there would be cricket, football, rugby, maybe hockey, probably some shooting and athletics. There, you could learn about the best books to read, in English and perhaps in Latin and French, too. You can learn about the geography of the world – not just Norfolk, but India, Africa and Australia, too.'

Phew! Where had all that come from? I looked across at Gwen. She had a happy, satisfied smile on her face, holding herself as if she were about to wave to someone on the road in a regal manner, somehow. I'd love to be able to do that for her again if it made her happy, but I had no idea of what 'it' was. Status? Time alone? Giving her a break from twenty-four-hour responsibility? Who knows? Mine is male thinking: inherently selfish or self-centred, at least.

We arrived at the cottage to be met by a somewhat frantic Nan in her welcome. Christopher had a glass of water before he and Nan set off into the wood for another adventure. Paula arrived soon after and went to join them. I made a cup of tea for Gwen, and we sat outside.

'You were very ready with a story for Christopher.'

'I worked it out ages ago as a simple cover story to use where appropriate. All the facts are there; there's just a lot of the beginning left out!'

'What else upset you about the post office interview?'

'She asked me why I had settled in Norfolk when I had lived in Hampshire. It could have been much trickier if she'd picked my Norfolk accent, rather than a Hampshire one. I told her I had been in the trenches with a Norwich man, who was always extolling the virtues of Norfolk, so I had decided to give it a try. It's a reasonable story if you have no suspicions. She bought my stories, but I wasn't at all comfortable there for a while.'

'I can imagine. The story you gave Christopher of our meeting was jolly good. Well done! Are you all right now?'

'Yes, love, and we'll have a lovely meal with Peter and Pat this evening. I didn't tell you, but they gave me lunch yesterday after I had been shooting with Harold.'

'I remember that you were going to go. How did you get on?'

'We had a bumper harvest – over a hundred birds!'

'What on earth do you do with a hundred pheasants?' she said in shocked surprise.

'You pay off your debts, give some to close friends and send the remainder to a man in Norwich who pays cash for them. Harold took the birds to him the same day and will give me my share when I see him next. It should be a tidy sum of money. We'll need that for the wedding. I can always go shooting to pay off the hotel bill, as well.'

I followed Gwen indoors to start lunch and got thoroughly kissed for my trouble. Lunch was very nearly delayed, but unpredictable children do not a romantic life make. They walked indoors to wash their hands just as the final item was put on the table.

Nan had her begging face on, so I gave the children my talk about feeding dogs at the table – that is, you don't. If you do, they get a variable amount of food, designed for human use, and you also get to lose some control to the detriment of both the dog and its owner.

After lunch, Christopher and Paula asked permission to go to the wood again, leaving us to do what we do best.

Chapter 42

TO THE VICTOR GO THE SPOILS

The meal at the hotel of roast chicken with sage and onion stuffing, roast potatoes and broccoli, with gooseberry pie and custard for dessert, was as usual, quite delicious. As usual, too, good conversation was a delightful accompaniment to our meal.

There was a massive crash as the head of an axe suddenly appeared through splintering wood from the front door of the pub. It was pulled clear with visible effort, and I knew in my bones that it was 'Faith', the bully, who had come to try his luck again. This time, he seemed to be intent on killing me because demolishing Owen's front door was not the act of a rational man. He must have known, somehow, that his target was inside. He could have just opened the door and walked in, but he wanted to intimidate me as well as everyone else.

So, he was wound up about something, and I was about to find out how tightly wound he was. I had to protect the other patrons, whose reactions would be relatively slow and confused. I would plan to slow down the action so they could follow what was going on and get out of harm's way, if necessary.

Eventually, 'Faith' got the shattered door out of his way, kicking away the last pieces. He walked menacingly into the bar, a giant of a man with his axe over his shoulder. He obviously didn't need any backup, but I checked behind him just to see what the odds were really going to be – and there was Mickey Foster. A sudden recall of our first meeting reminded me that he had mentioned a brother – a 'really big brother', and I now saw the family resemblance in the little blue 'piggy' eyes. So, 'Faith' was he, and I realised too, that there was great danger in Mickey working out both my identities.

I motioned to Owen to keep out of it and slowly got to my feet. The sudden silence built the tension as I walked towards Mickey's brother, leaving Gwen, Peter and Pat at the table.

There was confusion in 'Faith's' eyes for a moment because I should have backed off. He hadn't learned anything from our first fight.

His face was very red. His eyes were suffused with blood vessels and his 'blood was up'. I guessed that he had drunk a full measure of 'Dutch courage', and someone had wound him up like a tensioned mainspring – Mickey! This man was enormous, about six feet four inches tall with bulging muscles that were hard in outline because of the tension and the anger in him. The silly thought came to me that he was missing a horned helmet.

'I thought I told you to ask permission to come in here,' I said, slowly but loudly.

He slowly scanned the patrons, located me and ROARED! No words, just an animal sound of intimidation and bloodlust. He tore his shirt from his hairless upper body, which was covered with burn scars from the night he had tried to set my house on fire with Nan and me still inside. He watched as I ambled over towards him, my hands loosely in my pockets. He licked his lips, smiled and hefted the axe over his head, his piggy-blue eyes narrowed as if looking for a trick.

'No guns, Owen!' I shouted, relaxing my stance, pointing at Owen and looking away to my left, his right. An old, old trick but he fell for it. His eyes flickered right, his attention and concentration momentarily diverted. I hit him as hard as I was able, right on the 'button', that spot one inch up from the point of the chin towards the ear. I gave it everything I had, starting from my toes, calf and thigh muscles, the twist of the back, then the whole of my upper body strength, going through the line as far as possible. He was here to kill me but had given me this one chance. The bones in a hand are tiny and delicate, so I used the pad at the base of the hand, not my fist.

It shook him badly, but somehow he managed to stay conscious and upright. He raised the axe over his head once more.

'Kill him!' shouted Mickey, pointing at me from behind.

I waited.

I slowed down time by concentrating very hard on the head of the axe, particularly at a splinter sticking out from the haft. I got into that floating sensation that splits seconds into smaller and smaller pieces as I watched the axe head start to descend. I worked out exactly where its journey and momentum would take it. My move of only six inches put me outside the arc, which he didn't have the power to change once he'd started. The axe buried itself into the parquet floor with tremendous force, about an inch and a half from my toes. It was not going to be easy to remove.

He was bent over, straining with all his might to get his weapon back. That was silly because he could easily have beaten me to death with his fists. Too much reliance on a weapon; I'd seen that so many times before. Amateurs! He was doubled over, straining, and completely at my mercy.

I danced around behind him and kicked him between his spread legs as hard as if I was trying to score from the halfway line for the 'Gunners' against 'Spurs', right on full time. He screeched and folded but still scrabbled for my ankles. If he caught one, he could have pulled me to him, crushing me to death in his arms. I danced away, coming back with my heels onto his fingers – once, twice, three times.

There was a deep, deep hatred in those little piggy eyes, so like Mickey's, and I knew at that precise moment that he was mad –

totally out of control, and that he wouldn't stop until he, or I, were dead.

'Owen,' I surmised, without looking at him, 'this one's not going to stay down. He's insane, and I don't want to have to kill him or hurt him any further, but he needs to be restrained until the constabulary arrives.'

Just then, "Faith" made one wild sweep at my legs with one of his. I saw it coming but was an inch too low as I jumped. I went down with a thump onto my back and rolled to get away from him.

Before I could get up, he was standing over me with a chair raised over his head. I noted his red eyes, the sweat pouring off him, his little smile of impending triumph and a rope of bloody spittle dripping from his open mouth. He knew he had me exactly where he wanted me. His whole body strained to bring the chair down as hard as possible, but my time frame was still slowing the action and, to me, he moved as if he were in syrup. I got on to all fours, scampered between his legs, rolled, and then kicked his knee sideways. There was a distinct 'snap' as a ligament gave way, followed by a wild, inhuman bellow from deep within him. It was part rage from the excruciating pain and part utter frustration for his failure. He went down on one knee just as the chair splintered with massive force on to the open floor.

His mouth opened in a grimace, and his eyes closed in agony. I noted a tiny pimple on the exact spot on his jaw as I hit it. The zone I was in allowed me to feel the full sensation of my individual muscles taking part in speeding that blow to his chin. Toes, ankles, calves and thighs all pushed. Back muscles twisted. Shoulder, upper and lower arm forced the heel of my hand at top speed towards and beyond the target of his chin. It felt very satisfying in both its coordination and its final force.

I felt his jawbone dislocate with a sickening crunch. This time, the energy must have shaken his brain enough for the 'curtains' to finally come down, rescuing him from further suffering. This enormous man subsided with a sigh, laying still on the floor – no longer a threat. His torso was at very odd angles, but not a drop of blood had been spilled, apart from his split lip. This was in spite of his murderous intent with axe and chair.

My world came slowly back into focus as I did some deep breathing and some slow, stretching exercises with my arms and legs.

I looked for Gwen to make sure she was all right. The three that I'd left at the table were still there, but they were all in shock at the violence and its proximity to them. People in Civvy Street didn't get much of a taste of this sort of thing – it upsets their equilibrium. They would have seen all this take place in no more than ten seconds or so, but to me, it felt like ten minutes, such is the effect of the zone.

'Owen!' I shouted, 'Drinks! On me! And someone grab him,' I yelled, pointing to Mickey who stood in the doorway with his mouth open.

I had no idea where my offer of drinks had come from, but it was inspired. All the fear generated in the crowd by the violent action was now allowed to escape, channelled into something they could well understand – a relaxing drink. Everyone was talking at once.

I walked across the floor with my eyes on Gwen. She was silently weeping. I took her in my arms, hugged her and stroked her back, told her it was all over, that I was safe and not hurt in any way, and that everything was okay. Finally, I coaxed her, 'What can I get you to drink?'

'A double Scotch, neat, now, before I collapse!'

I sat her down, fetched two Scotches and sat with her until the stress went out of her. I then stood up and addressed the room.

'Ladies and gentlemen, I really must apologise for upsetting your tranquil evening. However, the fault, I believe, was not mine. This large bully came into the bar on my very first visit here. He tried to intimidate Peter – with absolutely no effect, I assure you. I dealt with him then and got his two friends to carry him home.'

With all eyes on me, I continued. 'What none of you know is that he and his two companions came to my cottage in the dead of night, some two months ago. They tried to burn it down with me, and my dog Nan, asleep inside. I dealt with that situation, too, and all three of them left considerably worse for wear.' Everyone just stared at me with horrified looks on their faces.

'So, tonight, I believe he came here to kill me, because, as a large and powerful man, he could not handle the indignity of losing – twice. The scars you saw on his chest were the result of falling onto the burning torch he was about to throw onto my thatch. Nan jumped up on his back at a very appropriate moment, and he fell onto the flaming torch. I think the police will find that his companions, together with his brother, got him liquored up tonight, then wound him up and sent him here with revenge and killing on his mind.'

I continued, 'Again, ladies and gentlemen, my sincere apologies for causing you any fear or trepidation, but he had to be put out of action. Do have a lovely evening, or what's left of it.'

The round of applause came as a surprise as I walked over to my beloved. Gwen was soft around the mouth, with eyes that said, 'My hero!'

We walked out, hand-in-hand. I intended to wash my face and hands, but we were followed by the most ribald comments from the drinkers and diners that I had ever heard, outside the army. We smiled at each other and kept going.

'Oh, my love, I was so terribly afraid for you! I never thought you could win against someone so big and so angry! I'd said good-bye to you in my mind, and my heart broke!'

Her tears came again, and I did a lot of patting, hugging and kissing. At one point there was a subtle change and, let's say, we celebrated my victory in style.

When Gwen had re-applied her face and got rid of the tears, we went back to the saloon where we had left Peter and Pat.

'I still haven't got two hands, but I'd clap if I had!' said Peter, remembering the first event. 'And thank you for the vote of confidence.'

'I have no idea how you did that, but I'm really relieved you did,' said Pat.

'Where are the prisoners?'

'Owen and a couple of men tied them up and took them down to the cellar. They've called the police and the ambulance, but they'll be a while,' said Peter.

'I see they haven't got the axe out of the floor yet,' I said. 'Perhaps Owen will turn it into a King Arthur style competition: whoever removes it will be elected the next King of Salthouse, and maybe he'll make another donation to the Church Roof Fund!'

'That's you,' said Peter, 'King of Salthouse, and your lady, Queen Gwen-evere!'

'Not bloody likely! I just want to get married to this lovely lady here and live a quiet life.'

The constable arrived about half an hour later on his bicycle and took statements from us in his little notebook with an indelible pencil, which he had to keep licking. I led the way because I wanted this to go in a particular direction. I made it all very simple, with no mention of my previous contact with 'the bully in question' at all.

'This huge man, armed with an axe, broke through the front door with no warning and intimidated the patrons. I got in two lucky blows, which slowed him enough for Owen and a couple of other men to tie him up and put him in the cellar. The ambulance has been called in case he had any injury other than a headache.'

'He has been seen around here occasionally, sometimes with two others. We don't know who he is, where he lives or what set off this unprovoked attack. That other man shouted, 'Kill him' just be-

fore he attacked me. Thank you, officer. Good night.' The policeman nodded and indicated that I could go.

I believe every patron, at this point, filled his glass again and
had a little thinking time about this: *Here's Ken, saving us from this
giant "Viking," yet again! He doesn't talk much about himself, but apparently has had a lot of army training in shooting and unarmed combat that
we know about. He led that policeman through a very simplified version of
what happened, mentioning nothing about the two previous episodes. We
must support him, come what may. That means going along with the story
he told the policeman. It was nice of them both to invite us to the wedding.*

That's what I hoped was the general consensus. The last thing I
wanted was to get anywhere near the police, courtrooms or public-
ity.

Owen came over to our table.

'If you keep doing this, Ken, I'm going to have to pay you a
'Bodyguard Fee!' But thank you, my friend. That was a very nasty
man indeed, and there's no one else here who could have stood up
to him like that. I thought you were a goner when that axe was
coming down for you. How did you judge that so finely and move
so quickly?'

'Some day, I may tell you about that. I'm just pleased that my
luck held.'

'So am I,' said Owen. 'The police have taken them both away in
handcuffs in the ambulance with an armed guard. There was a
problem with the big man's jaw, and he's not walking all that well.
That constable has taken down all the statements, and it all looks
very straightforward if I'm any judge,' affirmed Owen.

I thanked Owen and said, 'In the meantime, I'm bushed. I need
sleep. So I'll bid you all goodnight.' I walked out with Gwen, divert-
ing up the stairs as naturally as going shopping, except for her low
chuckle.

There was no way I could sleep after all that action. I was very
stimulated, and Gwen took full advantage of it, full of participation

and cooperation. It seemed we couldn't stop – it was a need that couldn't be satisfied, until finally, exhaustion played its part, and we fell asleep in each other's arms. We only woke twice during the night; each time making love was much slower than before.

The light through the window woke me with a start. For the sake of appearances I had to be out of here, if for no other reason than to keep Christopher on track in the ways of the world as they had to be performed.

I dressed quietly, slipped out of the back door, locked it and rounded up Millie, walking her silently over the grass for a hundred yards or so. How stupid were these rules? Queen Victoria had a lot to answer for, but then again, she had been so severely depressed by the loss of her own beloved husband, Prince Albert, that strangely, I could identify with her.

Nan was a bit confused at my late arrival but begged breakfast anyway. I decided that we, as a family, should go to church that morning as the banns were to be read for the first time; in retrospect, it was a brave thing to do.

An hour and a half later found me back at the hotel, washed and changed, where Christopher and Gwen were just finishing their breakfast. I joined them for tea and told them I thought it would be a good idea for us to attend church.

St Nicholas' Church was a huge, well-lit space. Many of the faces there I knew from the pub, and there was quite a bit of 'nodding' recognition. The Reverend James told the congregation of the forthcoming marriage of Mr Ken Bullen and Mrs Gwen Matthews. He asked that if anyone had any reason to suppose that this should not take place, to please let the vicar know. There was a silence, which hung in the air forever, or so it seemed. Finally, he went to the last hymn to be sung, and I let my breath out, unaware until then I'd been holding it.

After church, we went back to the cottage for lunch.

'I just adore your light and healthy meals. Not only are they delicious but they keep my waist neat and trim as I hope you have noticed.'

'Remind me to give it a thorough kissing at the first opportunity, and I'll definitely notice it.'

'Do you realise that in the whole time we've been together we've never had a cross word?' I asked.

'Why should we? We love each other, we talk about everything and we're friends. If one of us needed to be dominant, it probably wouldn't work, but we tend to work to our strengths. Is there anything wrong with that?'

'Absolutely not, but I have a feeling it's quite unusual.'

'Not with us, my love, ever!'

We embraced. I packed up the trap, locked the door, said goodbye to Nan and called to Christopher.

Chapter 43

THE SUM OF ALL FEARS

We arrived in Dereham, unloaded the trap and had a cup of tea preparatory to my bike ride home.

I shook Christopher's hand and then gave him a hug, telling him we would talk more about Gresham's School and violin playing next weekend. I left Gwen with a big kiss and a big squeeze!

'Ken Bullen, you'd better watch out next weekend. You're in my sights!'

'Oh, good!' I said, with a grin from ear to ear, and climbed into the trap, waving as I went. I squared up the money with 'Garge', picked up my bike and wheeled it to the entrance.

I had one leg over the crossbar when a voice behind me said, 'Hello, Corporal. How are you, Frank?'

Oh, God! My worst fears in the world had just come true! Ice was pumping in my veins. I was in total shock. What should I do? *Don't panic! Don't panic! Don't panic!* My mind thought furiously.

I looked around, very slowly, into the eyes of my old sergeant. We stared at each other for what seemed a long, long time.

'Hello, Sergeant. I never did find out your 'civvy' name.' I was stalling for time. My blood was ice-cold, and the hair on my neck and arms was raised, but I couldn't go round killing everyone I saw as a potential threat. This was a desperate moment. The rest of my life, but more importantly Gwen's and Christopher's lives too, depended on what happened in the next few seconds.

Since I had swapped places with Ken Bullen, I had considered every contingency, working through alternatives, always looking for solutions to keep my identities separate. I'd covered all my tracks to eliminate any chance of feedback, stayed away from all my relatives and former friends and successfully set up an entirely new identity. In disposing of Mickey by associating him with his brother's attempted murder, I thought all the things I had done were successful and for a good cause. And they were, from my point of view. However, lying about my identity from the army point of view was a very different matter. My point of view would dissolve like salt in water should the army ever learn of my deception. I would be incarcerated in a military jail for quite some time.

I thought my arrangements were all wrapped up and proceeding according to plan – and now this! Totally out of the blue! My blood pressure was beginning to sink like a stone from the shock, and soon I might not be able to stand up.

My sergeant was here in Dereham! What were the odds? I never did manage to talk in depth with him about anything personal. By the time I had achieved some familiarity with him, I'd started going off the rails. Nobody could talk to me, at least not with any hope of getting any sense from the conversation.

I knew the sergeant as a fair man – hard, but fair. There might just be a chance of salvaging something from this disaster, but I would have to proceed with delicate care, one little step at a time. This was the second biggest gamble I would ever make, with just one throw of the dice.

'It's Jim, actually, Jim Hughes. What are you doing here, Frank?'

'I live near here. What about you?' I knew to always ask questions to control the conversation, but this was the sergeant. We knew each other. So what now?

'I live in Dereham. I thought you were dead. You were reported dead. What happened?'

'Sergeant. Jim. I would like to tell you my story, but it would totally depend on what you would do with that information.'

'All right Frank, just tell me this: did you hurt anyone on our side?'

'No, Jim, I didn't.'

'Did you break any rules that could lead to someone else getting into big trouble?'

'No.'

'I'd always known you as a truthful man, Frank. Do you feel like sharing this with me, on the basis that I won't tell another living soul or endanger whatever life you have here? That is unless you have crossed a line, which I know we both fully understand.'

'Jim, if you would do that for me, I would count you as the best friend a man ever had. On the other hand, if you harm me, or any member of my family, I will hunt you down and I'll kill you, and you know I can do that! But in truth, I would be very relieved to get this stuff off my chest, and if I were to tell it to anyone, I would have picked you as one of two people.'

'Let's go somewhere where we can sit down and talk, then.'

We found a pub in a side street off Market Square. I ordered drinks, and we sat in a corner. We touched glasses, which I thought was a good sign because this man could kill my little family and me with just one word into the right official ear. I was mortally afraid.

'Jim, first I will give you my word that I have not harmed anyone, in any way, on our side in the army. I have bent the rules of the army and have damaged a couple of civilians, but not in the line of duty, so they don't warrant your concern. Nobody has been hurt or disadvantaged. Will you accept that as my premise?'

'Yes, Frank. Tell me your story, and I give you my word that as long as you've not hurt any of our chaps, I will keep it to myself.'

We shook hands. I started pouring my heart out to my former sergeant. By the time I'd finished, we'd had a dozen glasses or more in front of us, but we were both still stone-cold sober. For some strange reason, we both sighed deeply at the same time. He looked me in the eyes, and a smile started around the corners of his mouth. It grew, and it grew until he let out a huge bellow of laughter.

'Well, I'm buggered. You dog! You clever corporal, you! The same girl! A second time! Well, if that doesn't beat everything. I now realise, Frank, sorry, "Ken", that I did indeed hold your family's lives in my hands. You must have been shitting yourself. Sorry about the suspense, but the moment I saw you I thought you must have killed Ken. I could not have let that pass. You do understand that, I hope?'

'Yes, of course, I do. I, too, would have been very cynical if the boot had been on the other foot.'

'So what are you going to do now?'

'I'm going to buy you another beer, Jim, and we'll drink to my happy family and to our friendship over the years to come. Then, I'm going back to Gwen's to sleep on the couch. I can't face a long journey on my bike tonight. I'm whacked!'

'I'll buy the beer to show good faith and ask you if I may come to your wedding.'

'My friend, you would be most welcome. Are you married, Jim?'

'Yes, her name's Barbara, and I love her more than the air I breathe. We've got a small rented cottage just outside Dereham, and have two very talented boys, Peter and Robert. They show great promise in the career department. They are really happy and well adjusted. They play well together but are a tad fixated on the glories of war at the moment. God forbid that any of us, ever again, has to go through that shit!

'Just so you know, Ken, Captains Stone and Youngman 'bought it' in the heavy artillery barrage that came in retaliation for Hill 60. Also Paul, your signaller, got shot by a Jerry sniper for not keeping his head down. So, I'm probably the last person who knew you as Frank – in the army, anyway.'

My old sergeant continued, 'Ken – see, I remembered – I have no idea how you survived as long as you did. You were totally burned out. I was expecting your corpse to turn up with a sniper's bullet in your head any day. How the hell did you get better after all the crap you went through? You were quite insane towards the end.'

I revealed, 'I put it down to the peace and tranquillity of my native Norfolk, Jim, doing some small-scale farming, which is in my soul, and the return and the love of my good lady. Add to that the acceptance and love of my boy, who, of course, can never know the truth.' Jim just nodded for me to continue.

'I am now Ken Bullen, small farmer, shooter of edible creatures, lover and provider for two people who rely on me to make a stable and happy family. You, Jim, were my worst nightmare, but now that too has been resolved. Thank you for your understanding. Write your address on this piece of paper, and I'll make sure you get an invitation.

We shook hands, and I weaved my way to Commercial Road, went around the back, parked the bike and knocked on the door. It was a very wide-eyed Gwen who opened it. The first thing she did was to check me for broken bones or leaking blood in great quantity.

'Gwen, love, I've had too much to drink, and I need to sleep on your couch,' I said, unsteadily.

'What happened?'

'I will tell you in the morning. Just know that it was the best news we could ever have. In the morning –' I said, as the couch came up and hit me.

I awoke with Christopher peering down at me. I blinked and tried to recall where I was and why this scene was so unfamiliar.

Chris Shaw

'Good morning, lazy-bones!' said Gwen, in a bright and breezy manner.

'What happened to Dad?' asked Christopher.

'It's all right, you two. I met someone I needed to talk to, and we went to the White Horse. I drank more than I should but wisely decided not to try to cycle to Salthouse. Any chance of a cup of tea, Gwen?'

'My hero can get a cup of tea any time. Christopher, get your things ready for school and be off with you.'

'Yes, Mum. I hope you're better soon,' he said, smiling at me, and ran out to join his friends, no doubt to tell the story of the latest chapter in his dad's saga.

The cup of tea came with an urgent request for information. Gwen sat on the side of the couch and listened while I told the story of meeting the sergeant and our subsequent conversation.

'So you see, while it was an occasion where my worst fears came true, we worked out that no one had been harmed by me. The army would have paid a pension anyway, and there was no conflict in our getting married twice – quirky, yes, but no harm would be done. I've invited my sergeant, whose real name is Jim, and his wife, Barbara, to the wedding. They will be the only people from outside Salthouse to be there.'

I went on, 'Gwen, I had to put all our cards on the table because Jim is a fair man, and he was much more inclined to accept our situation with the whole truth.'

Gwen responded, 'Darling, I'm sure you did what you had to do. I did know that there always was a fear in the back of your mind that our whole house of cards could come tumbling down. I can only guess at your feelings when you met Jim!'

'He's the last. Everyone else has gone. With Jim on our side, we'll be able to have a carefree life. My God, I've so looked forward to this moment.' We hugged, and one thing led to another, but she did get to work on time.

Chapter 44

New friends and old friends

Over the next two weeks, an enormous number of arrangements came to fruition. Gwen's excess furniture and ornaments went to the second-hand shop. Such was their quality that she got a generous price. The house itself was cleaned and readied for the new tenants.

On one trip, I took a small wagon instead of the trap, in which we transported all the things that Gwen and our son would need in their new home – all their clothes, some of her furniture, including Christopher's bed, and all the extraneous 'stuff' that we all carry around with us, forming an essential part of who we are as individuals. It included pictures, cutlery and crockery, a lamp and some jewellery, a writing desk with some mementos from childhood – scrapbooks, drawings and the like. I began to wish we had opted for the larger wagon!

'Oold Garge' did ask me if I wanted to buy his stables. I told him that:

a) I'd bought and paid for them already, and

b) That there was a woman involved, so all this frantic activity was only temporary, or so I sincerely hoped! This, too, would pass.

He said he got more entertainment value out of us than he got pleasure from the money I gave him. 'Better than Vaudeville,' he reckoned. I suggested a refund, but that fell on stony ground.

Eventually, all Gwen's belongings were in place in our little cottage, and the echoes in the rooms disappeared. She busied herself with arranging and re-arranging furniture, making lists of things to be done after the wedding, like new curtains all round, a fresh coat of whitewash for the outside of the cottage, green paint for the window frames, a new henhouse – and so it went on. There was a distinct sense of déjà vu. I called it nesting and left her to it. Otherwise, there would be two of us fretting and no work getting done.

A week before the wedding, Gwen left her work at the post office for good. She took a room in the Dun Cow. Gwen's new tenants told her they were delighted with her house. Their rent was also most welcome.

Christopher and Nan had been left to entertain themselves. Paula came over often on her bike to play with him.

We visited the Reverend James in that last week. The wedding banns had produced no activity from the parishioners, so Sunday the 24th of October, 1920 at 10.30 a.m. was booked, and all we had to do was to arrive on time. He would do the rest. We thanked him for his help and he, in turn, blessed us.

'The improvement in the finances of the Church Roof Fund since you arrived, Ken, has been most extraordinary. The church and the parishioners are most grateful.'

'I'm pleased to help, Vicar. I mean, we can't have Owen and Wendy making so much money that they retire and leave the pub, now, can we?'

'True! There is that. I'll see you lovely couple on Sunday. Good luck with all your arrangements.'

We went back to the cottage. As Christopher and Nan were not in sight, we went upstairs and lay on the new mattress.

'Is all this going all right for you, my love?' I asked.

'Yes. It's almost déjà vu, except that there are now Christopher and Nan, and of course, Paula.'

'That's just what I thought. Then we have some time for a little loving?'

I opened her top and nuzzled gently. Her little pink nipples hardened to meet my tongue. We met, and she used a lot of strength to get as close to me as possible. I rolled over, and she kept repeating, 'Yes! Yes! Yes!'

Her eyes closed, and her hair mussed, her motions gaining speed to a crescendo as she arched her back and took me as deeply as possible. I caressed her waist and ran my hands over her breasts, teasing the nipples. I massaged her neck and ran my fingers through her hair, which I grasped, pulling her mouth to mine. We kissed with depth, and she was off again. She took my hands and put them on her hips, and we made some truly remarkable loving. The ripples of pleasure continued for quite a while as her breathing slowed and she came back into focus.

When she finally had her breath back, she said, 'I'll give you this, Mr Ken Bullen, you are well-named and you definitely improve with age!'

'And, you, my love, are so beautiful that I never want to stop. I love you in every way there is, and I will make sure that we have a long and happy life together. That is my promise to you. No more wars. No more depressions. No more shell shock, and no more nightmares. From now on, it's farming and loving, cooking and loving, and marketing – and more loving!'

'Yes, please,' she said with her low chuckle. Just then there was a bark from Nan, and we made a frantic effort to be decent when Christopher came into view.

What we needed was lemonade all around and a family meeting.

Gwen asked, 'Christopher, this is Friday. What do you need to get ready for Sunday?'

'I've got my suit, a clean white shirt, my tie, a pair of grey socks and my black shoes, Mum.'

'How clean are your shoes?'

'Probably need a clean.'

'Right, get to it then and lay everything out on your bed. Once I've checked that it's clean and tidy, you can pack it in your suitcase, and we'll take it to the hotel. Harold and Esme have offered to have you over for a couple of days to stay with them after the wedding. Would you like to do that?'

'Yes, Mum, that would be nice.'

'Good. Ken, what about you?'

'I, too, have my suit, a white shirt, an appropriate tie, clean shoes, and socks, but, of course, Christopher and I are at a disadvantage here, because we can't ask you about your dress for the wedding day as yours is a secret!'

'True. You'll both have to wait and see.'

I'd returned the wagon, renting Millie and the trap for the week, and bringing my bike back with me for a semblance of last-minute independence but also with the ability to run errands. I took Gwen and Christopher to the hotel to get unpacked and comfortable, and went to see Peter. We discussed the arrangements over a beer. He had the ring, and he and Pat were well aware of all their duties.

Owen and Wendy, too, had everything in hand. Wendy was apparently well advanced with the food, with Esme's help. All the invitations had gone out, and replies had been counted. Of two hundred and thirty-two souls in the village, fifty-seven had accepted the invitation. The rest were children, the aged or infirm, who were confined to their homes or their beds, plus those who were away from the village for one reason or another. Peter and I discussed all this, and because we couldn't think of anything else to be done, we had another beer.

'I'm delighted we met, you know,' said Peter. 'You saved me from a beating, brought us food and have been a good friend to both of us.'

'Well, I saw the loss of your arm as probably slowing you down a little, socially, so I just thought I'd take up some slack. Besides, friendship is about sharing, and you are doing me a big favour by being my Best Man.

'Do you remember the first beer I bought you? "Don't worry about it. It'll work itself out over the years", I told you, and it has. People like us don't have to keep score, Peter.'

'True. I've enjoyed your company, and Pat really likes Gwen. We can see each other whenever we want and that's really nice. Pat and I have a close and loving relationship, and I can see that you and Gwen are besotted with each other. No questions, eh?' asked Peter.

'Rather not,' I said.

'Man of mystery! I'll tell you what I think, and you don't have to say a thing. I think you've known Gwen for a long time. I think the war came along and spoiled things for you both. I've had a good look at Christopher. He certainly has his Mum's smile, but there are aspects of his personality that come straight out of your mould. Harold tells me that your shooting is extraordinary, perhaps even sniper standard! He's never seen you miss a bird or a rabbit. So I don't think that you were just an observer.'

Peter continued, 'You've kept well away from people, in general, for nearly two years, and I've seen the nightmares, the depression and your general health improve out of sight in that time. So, I think you are not who we know you as, and this "someone else" had to have parted from his family because this "someone else" didn't come out of the army cleanly, or he would have been in the bosom of his family. Now, that can't be you, because you received an honourable discharge and a pension. So I wonder who it can be?'

'That's what I would call "a speculative waste of time", Peter. We could have had another beer while you were flapping your old gums about. Anyway, thanks for the entertaining story. You should write a book! I'll probably see you tomorrow. If not, I'll see you before going to the church on Sunday. Don't be late!'

He smiled the broadest smile I'd ever seen him smile. I winked at him as I went. No tattletale, that one. Clever though, bloody clever!

'Just one more thing before you go, Ken. You may not have caught up with a newspaper article in Thursday's Eastern Daily Press. It reported that the giant who tried to split you in two with his axe has been sent to jail for life. His name was Seth Foster, by the way. His brother, Mickey Foster, was charged with being an accessory to murder for his comment, egging on his brother to kill you. It seems that the bullying little brother slipped when going down some steps in the jail. He will be in a wheelchair for the rest of his life, caused by a broken spine. He'll be in the hands of others, some of whom may not be overly kind. Funny the way things turn out sometimes, don't you think?'

Another chapter closed with some added security for us.

That evening, my sergeant, Jim, and his wife, Barbara, were due to come and stay at the Dun Cow. Jim had said he wanted to have a look at this part of the world, intending to move from Dereham so that his two boys could go to Gresham's School near Holt. I was due to pick them up from the railway station and bring them to the hotel.

Checking on Gwen and Christopher, I got waved away as they were busy.

'Going to pick up the sergeant and his wife,' I said, mostly to myself.

'Right, we'll still be here,' came the reply.

I put a rug in the trap for Barbara as it was getting chilly. It was quite late in the year, and the sun was going down with all the fiery colours of a real East Anglian sunset – the red colours of fire and blood, intertwined with gold bands and the surly deep purple to black of a nasty bruise.

The journey was quite short, and Millie enjoyed stretching out. My timing was right as the train pulled in about five minutes after

I had arrived. I shook hands with Jim, and he introduced me to Barbara, a cheerful, stocky lady with a shock of bouncy blonde hair and a lovely smile.

'Delighted to meet you, Barbara. I'm very pleased you could come to our wedding, and I'm sure Gwen will be, too.'

'Thank you, Ken. Jim has told me you served together in that terrible war in such awful conditions. It's a miracle that you're both alive to tell the tale.'

'True, but personally, I've left all that far behind, and I'm trying to get on with my life here.'

'Good for you, Ken,' smiled Barbara. I helped them into the trap, gave Barbara the rug and stowed their luggage.

'It's beautiful around here. Do you enjoy the area?' asked Barbara.

'Yes I do, and if you enjoy the countryside, you'll find this North Norfolk coast very hard to beat. There are saltwater marshes with ducks, geese and lots of water birds – waders, gulls and the like. There's the beach on the other side of a great shingle bank, and woods, fields and streams. For me, there are lots of pigeons and rabbits to supplement my meals.'

We chatted on like this as Millie trotted through the autumn landscape of dusk in North Norfolk until we reached the hotel. I made sure that Jim had everything in hand and went to find Gwen. She had a mouthful of pins and both hands full of material. She squeaked when I told her that Jim and Barbara had arrived, discarded both pins and material, touched her hair in a mirror, squared her shoulders and looked at me. We held hands and walked into the saloon bar. Jim and Barbara were already seated with a drink. Jim got up as we walked over.

'Good Lord! Gwen Bell! How are you after all these years?'

What? I thought. What the hell is this? The sergeant knows my wife? When is this nightmare ever going to end? Is this some sort of crazy cha-

rade to perpetuate my demons, designed to drive me back into madness? Why have the Gods got it in for me?

'Well, well, Jim Hughes! I haven't seen you since we were in primary school. You were my husband's sergeant, weren't you? He's spoken of you a lot, and I think we both have cause to be very grateful to you. Thank you for coming to our wedding.'

'And this is my wife, Barbara. Barbara this is Gwen, Ken's wife-to-be on Sunday. We knew each other in primary school; back then, she had knock knees. Lovely hair, of course, but knock knees!'

'Hello, Gwen. I'm so pleased to meet you. "Miss Knock Knees" no longer, I would guess!'

'No longer, Barbara, thank goodness. It all sorted itself out naturally in the fullness of time. Ken, would you get me a dry sherry please?'

We chatted for an hour or so about the wedding, about the village, and about the people. I had a little information about Gresham's School that I had gleaned from various sources, including the school itself. Jim and Barbara mentioned that one of the reasons for coming to Salthouse was to send their two boys to school there.

Apparently, it was ancient, built in Elizabethan times. It was very well thought of as far as the quality of its students was concerned. The students I had seen on my one visit seemed relaxed and happy, were smartly dressed and showed above-average attitude, self-discipline and manners.

'If we can afford it, we'd like to send Christopher there,' I said.

'Christopher?' queried Barbara.

'He's my son by a previous marriage. My husband died in the war,' said Gwen, looking at her.

'Oh, my dear, I'm so sorry. I didn't know. I'm so pleased that you've got a second chance, so to speak. Ken seems very nice.'

'Yes, we get on very well, and Christopher loves him, too.'

Together with Peter and Pat, we all had dinner together on that Friday night, and the company turned out to be just splendid. There was a lot of laughter, shared reminiscences, jokes, stories and tall tales. Peter had to tell about my fight, again! Jim gave me a nod and a smile. He had now seen what I had by way of family, friends and the potential for a happy life. I knew he'd keep his word.

Jim and Barbara borrowed the trap for a couple of hours on Saturday morning and again in the afternoon to have a look at the area for themselves. For the rest of the time, the trap was put to good use transporting people and goods for wedding arrangements.

That Saturday was definitely Ladies' Day, and there was a huge amount of 'goings on', but I had no idea what they were. I put myself on duty to do errands and to lift anything heavy. I talked to Jim and Barbara, who seemed quite taken with Salthouse village in all its moods.

Barbara told me she did some painting and was inspired by the marshes, the beach, the church and the village. They had seen the road to Holt when they arrived and had driven along the coast road to Kelling and Weybourne. They delighted in the whole area and said that it seemed a perfect place to live, provided, that is, a person didn't want lots of shops and all the dubious advantages that cities could give. Since I could cycle to Dereham, I wondered what advantages cities actually had. But that's an old argument, and it's all according to one's taste. Gwen didn't seem to miss Dereham, although I suspected she missed my sister Margaret's company. Margaret had married a handsome sailor and had moved to Felixstowe in Suffolk.

Our party of six were joined by Owen and Wendy, and Harold and Esme that evening, and we had a grand time. There were more stories and jokes, monologues from Owen, and singing from Wendy who, it turned out, had a beautiful contralto voice.

Gwen took me to one side.

'My darling Ken, we have had some very close calls in the last few hours, but we've managed it well. I'm going up to bed soon, and I will see you tomorrow, my love.'

'Darling, I totally understand. This is your time; you are making the rules you want, and I will, naturally, abide by your wishes. Your wishes tomorrow night, however, may be slightly different, but I'll be happy to abide by those, too!'

'You are a darling man. I knew you'd understand. Kiss me goodnight, and I'll see you in the church tomorrow.'

We kissed, very gently and with understanding. Gwen looked me in the eyes, winked, and went up the stairs to her room, not without a certain amount of provocation, you understand. That woman 'does' stairs really well.

I took Millie home and got her safely sequestered in the fenced meadow next door. I fed Nan, cleaned my teeth and went to bed.

Sleep did not come quickly. I thought about Peter working out most of my secrets, of Jim knowing Gwen at an early age, and of Harold's knowledge of my shooting prowess.

There was no doubt that we were known and loved in the village, and that my acts of 'heroism' had been told and retold. The question, of course, had always been: would somebody find out my real identity, and more importantly, do something about it? The revelation had been certainly closer today than at any other time. Once the wedding was over, I thought, we could keep a low profile until I felt safer and our passports had arrived.

Christopher would go to Gresham's School with Jim and Barbara's boys, and that would be a good thing as they could look after each other. Gwen and I would, maybe, see if we could make the Farmers' Market a viable moneymaking concern.

Chapter 45

TOGETHER AGAIN

I awoke on October 24th 1920, remembering the last time I'd been in this position at our farm in Longham with my beautiful family around me. Now, it was just me – with some friends of course – but mainly just me. There was an emptiness, a loneliness, in the silence of the cottage. For a moment, I felt a twinge of bleakness; was it a shadow of my wartime depression? This was not something that I'd expected. I took a good look at what was causing it. My conclusion was that it was a temporary aloneness being experienced, hopefully for the last time – ever. I knew Gwen would be by my side for the rest of my life. A ray of sunshine lit my inner being. I saw life stretching on, with Gwen walking beside me, laughing, sharing and loving.

My body was scrubbed, hair brushed, beard and nails trimmed, shoes cleaned and a white handkerchief was in my top pocket with a spare. I had money and my tie, centred with a Windsor knot, so, yes, all was present and correct. A careful look in the mirror revealed sanity with a slightly fatuous look, undoubtedly happy, but self-assured too.

I still needed to catch Millie, drive to Peter's to pick up the two of them, plus Jim from the hotel, who had offered to drive people to and from the church. We needed to get to the church by half-past ten. The time, by Gwen's Westminster chiming clock, was ten o'clock. Perfect!

Peter and Pat were ready and smart. I let Peter hand Pat up into the trap and climb up himself. He had to make two attempts at it, which we ignored. He sat beside me, and Jim moved us out of the hotel yard to the church.

I looked around at the lovely day we had been given and listened to the church bells. It was all so emotive. There was an area buried deep inside some people that responded to church bells. Bells were not musical in a classical orchestral sense, but they did resonate, especially in the English countryside. Conceivably, this was because there had been centuries during which church bells called people to the fellowship of religion. They also represented bad news or, indeed, even imminent danger like war or invasion.

The dry autumn leaves made a red, brown and yellow noisy carpet as we drove over them. The black, bony fingers of bare twigs outlined against the scudding white clouds pointed to approaching winter. The wind was light and refreshing, but there was still some warmth in the occasional sunshine.

We arrived at the church and sat for a moment in the trap.

'How do you feel?' Peter asked, touching my arm.

'In truth, a bit bleak. I woke up with it this morning, and this depression won't seem to leave.'

'I'll guarantee it's not first-night nerves!' he said. Little joke there. 'I'll also guarantee that in no more than ten minutes it will be gone, and you will be all smiles, with your spirit soaring. I'll bet you a rabbit on that!'

'First class, Peter, my Best Man. You're on with the rabbit. But right now I've got a date with the woman I love more than life itself, who is my right arm – sorry – and my eternal love.'

'She always has been, Ken.'

I looked at him sharply. He smiled his happy, benign little smile. 'It's so obvious to me since I'm also still in love.'

It was a temptation to ask him what he meant, but I thought it was better left unsaid. He helped Pat from the trap, and Jim wheeled it around to transport more guests. I led the way into the church, and we went directly to the front, right-hand pew. Pat went to the front, left-hand pew as a show of support for Gwen. I thought that was lovely of her and smiled across at her. She nodded her understanding.

The church filled up to some background organ music. At last, the organist began playing Richard Wagner's 'Wedding March', and I thought, *Here we go again.*

I turned to look as Gwen approached. She was breathtaking. Stunning. Beautiful. And she had her special dazzling smile, too, which I had literally gone through hell to see again. *Oh, God! How lucky could a man get?* I thought to myself. *I love you, Gwen Bell, Gwen Matthews and soon-to-be Gwen Bullen. Thank you, Ken, for lending me your name. I'll carry it with pride.*

Owen brushed up very well, I noticed, as he escorted Gwen down the aisle.

We stood side by side, and that wonderful mental link that we had started to work.

'You look absolutely beautiful.'

'Well, thank you. I'm so glad to finally be here.'

'I'll bet. Enjoy it. It's the last one!'

'I hope!'

I turned to smile at Wendy, who had Christopher and Paula in tow, and I nodded at both of them. Then I turned back, and the vicar began. As before, it all happened as if in a dream. Peter presented the ring with a flourish, bringing a smile to everyone.

I could almost hear the "click" as the circle closed, when the vicar finally said, 'I now pronounce you Man and Wife'. My depression lifted in that instant, and I knew that I was no longer an imposter. Now I was surrounded by the love of my wife and son, good friends and the chance for a wonderful new beginning.

Afterword

This story has been woven to include some people I knew in Norfolk, many of whom were also part of my family. However, in this story, some are out of context in time and relationships while others are entirely a figment of my imagination. That imagination has also allowed me to change the roles of the main characters, in both time and history, and how they played them.

My uncle, Cyril Frank Matthews, and aunt, Gwen Bell, were married in 1938 but had no surviving children. Cyril was shot down over the North Sea as the RAF pilot of a Blenheim Bomber in 1941, and Gwen did work at the post office in East Dereham for many years.

I have tried to weave a new tapestry from what was a real-life tragedy and turn it into a story with a happy ending. I can't change actual history, but I can attempt to make things more fulfilling for my lovely Auntie Gwen and for Uncle Cyril (Frank), the love of her life. Auntie Gwen also loved me for the whole of her life, and, as the boy she had so wished for, I fervently hope that I was able to be a part of fulfilling the family life she had so dearly wanted.

Gwen Matthews, née Bell was, in real life, a generous and loving person with gorgeous red hair. I wish I had met my uncle, Cyril Frank Matthews, but I only knew about him through my mother, Margaret Shaw, née Matthews. I would like to say that I have based the character of Frank on myself, but I was never that strong, wise or accomplished.

Chris Shaw

However, I have been blessed with the love and friendship of my Rebecca – a relationship closely akin to that which Frank and Gwen were so fortunate to achieve in this novel.

In absentia, I wish these lovely people, their families and their descendants, well. This would have been the life they would have had, if I been in charge of things.

Chris Shaw

Cyril Frank Matthews and Gwen Matthews on their wedding day

ABOUT THE AUTHOR

Chris Shaw was born in 1939 in Felixstowe, Suffolk, UK. He lived there with his mother during the war years, with occasional periods of respite from the bombs and doodlebugs on his grandparents' farm in Longham village in central Norfolk. He is a prize-winning writer, and his stories have also been featured in The Weekend Australian.

Chris was educated at Framlingham College, qualified as a pharmacist and spent three years in London, then seven years in the Caribbean, travelling as a medical representative through the British-based islands.

With his family, he emigrated to Cairns, Far North Queensland, Australia, in 1973, working as a retail pharmacist until he retired in 2009. He owned two pharmacies.

In 1991, he married his beloved Rebecca at Trinity Beach, and they have never had a cross word.

If you enjoyed *The Imposter*, read on for a snippet from Chris Shaw's next novel about a world-title boxing champion in *Hammer & Tongs*.

'Shug!' was the sound of a boxing-gloved fist hitting a jaw. His jaw. Hah.

So begins the story of Sam Smith, an amateur welterweight boxer from Whitechapel in London. Sam has a secret that allows him to keep winning matches against all-comers at his weight.

Eventually, his success sees him turning professional, and this novel charts his journey up the ranks to becoming a contender for the World Champion.

Sam is married to Mavis, and they have two daughters, which sounds routine until his life is beset by the police, SAS and the FBI – all have to be involved in the ensuing crimes of fight-fixing, murder, American gangsters, kidnapping and blackmail.

You can follow Sam's journey in *Hammer & Tongs*. Anyone with the slightest competitive sporting spirit will be enthralled by his story.